Rebellion

Raena Rood

One Foundation Publishing

Rebellion

Raena Rood

"Have I not commanded you? Be strong and courageous. Do not be afraid; do not be discouraged, for the Lord your God will be with you wherever you go."

—Joshua 1:9 (NIV)

For Ben:
My mapmaker, political genius, and ethical inner voice. Being
your mom has been the greatest honor of my life. I can't wait to
see all the places you'll go.

Chapter One

I can't do this. I don't belong here.

Kira stood in the cramped kitchen of the abandoned house she shared with Aunt Reeva. Her fingers nervously picked at the chipped gray polish on her short nails. The meager glow of a battery-powered lamp cast shadows over the room, barely illuminating the overstuffed rucksack slumped against the worn cabinets, its frayed canvas and rusted zippers evidence of countless journeys.

For ten long minutes, Kira had been staring at the rucksack, her thoughts spiraling, anxiety gnawing at her insides. Desperately trying to think of a reason to stay behind in Emmitsburg.

No.

Not just stay behind.

To return.

To Vita Nova.

To the life she'd left. And to her father.

She chewed on the inside of her lip, one finger twirling a loose thread from the sleeve of her frayed sweater.

Life in the Unregulated Zone wasn't easy, but Kira had

learned to see and appreciate its wild beauty. The vibrant wild-flowers that defiantly bloomed through cracked sidewalks, painting the abandoned streets in vivid colors. The wild animals that roamed through the town, unbothered by the humans in their midst, despite being hunted by them for years.

But when night fell, and the darkness swallowed all of that rich beauty, Kira's childhood fears of the Unregulated Zone would resurface, clawing their way to the forefront of her mind.

I don't belong here.

I want to go home.

A week ago, the thought of returning to Vita Nova would have been inconceivable to Kira. She had been eager, even excited, to leave it all behind.

Her job as a volunteer advocate in the government center, where she scheduled appointments for people to die and then granted almost any wish they had for their Final Week.

The Compulsory Clinic, that awful place where her mother and so many others had drawn their final breaths, their deaths mandated by the city.

The Reverence Ceremonies on City Island, where the entire city gathered every Sunday evening to meet the newest Volunteers and revere the ones who had most recently given their lives for the good of all.

She had yearned to be free from Vita Nova once and for all.

But as their departure date grew closer, something inside of her had shifted.

This was it. She was leaving Vita Nova, possibly forever. The fear of returning to the city after all she had done was suffocating. But the thought of never going back terrified her even more.

Most of the other people who had hidden in Emmitsburg for years had already fled, terrified by the mayor's looming search-and-destroy mission in response to the bombing of the

Tenements. While Kira was still recovering in the infirmary from her plunge into the Susquehanna River, they had abandoned the town, desperate to put distance between themselves and the city, unwilling to wait for the rest of the group. With so few left behind, there weren't enough people left to serve as Watchers, let alone defend the town against the Patrols.

Staying in Emmitsburg was no longer an option.

In just a few hours, Kira, Will, Aunt Reeva, Teddy, and Brack, along with his wife, Grace, would abandon the town to the animals. They would venture deeper into the Unregulated Zone than any of them had gone since the days before the Job virus swept through the world. Away from their crumbling relic of a town, with its dwindling resources and dwindling people.

And away from the walled city across the river, where death was worshipped above all else.

They would search for something better.

She drew in a deep breath, wincing as pain flared in her chest from her fractured sternum—a constant reminder of how close she had come to drowning in the river.

And how hard Will—sweet, kind Will—had fought to save her. He had leapt from the broken span of the Walnut Street Bridge, injuring one of his own ribs in the process. Aunt Reeva often joked that they were like an old couple, hobbling around, clutching their chests, and grimacing.

Will had risked everything for her.

Kira had done the same for him.

She loved him, even if she couldn't yet say the words aloud. Will was more than just a boyfriend. He was her anchor, her tether to something solid in a world that was unraveling. Even when the words escaped her, her body knew the truth—she felt incomplete without him, uneasy when he wasn't by her side.

When Will wasn't with her, Kira's chest ached for a different reason.

She couldn't go back to the city.

Will needed her. So did Teddy.

And she needed them, too.

She leaned against the battered kitchen table, stuffing her hands into the pockets of the worn jeans she had scavenged from a box in her attic room earlier that day. They fit her perfectly, though she tried not to think about their previous owner—whether she had died of the virus, been robbed and killed by looters, or met her end at the hands of Patrol soldiers.

Kira shoved the thought aside, banishing it the way her father had banished the sick from Vita Nova. Her gaze drifted back to the rucksack on the floor. Everything she owned, her entire life, was packed into that bag—just a few clothes and basic toiletries. There were no personal items, nothing that spoke of who she had been before. She had left Vita Nova with nothing, and now, with her sprained ankle and fractured sternum, she couldn't afford to carry any excess weight.

A distant grumble of thunder broke the silence, pulling her from her thoughts.

Kira looked up at the kitchen window. "I'm never going back there," she whispered, her voice resolute. "No matter what."

A flash of lightning lit up the sky outside, burning its afterimage into her vision. She blinked, and for a moment, she saw her father's eyes staring back at her.

Those same gunmetal-gray eyes that mirrored her own.

Chapter Two

Rain battered the attic window, the storm outside accompanied by a symphony of thunder and wind. The loudest claps of thunder seemed to shake the very bones of the house, making Kira fear that the entire structure might collapse around her. The attic felt like it was closing in, the shadows thickening, the air growing heavier, almost suffocating her.

Amidst it all, a quiet voice whispered in her ear.

He's coming.

Kira jolted upright, heart pounding, her breath catching as she scanned the pitch-black attic for the source of the voice. Huddled in the corner beneath threadbare, multicolored blankets, she squinted into the darkness, straining to see anything beyond the oppressive blackness that surrounded her on all sides.

"Will?" she whispered, her voice barely audible over the storm. "Aunt Reeva?"

No response.

But someone had woken her up. Someone had whispered

those words—*He's coming*—loud enough for her sleep-addled brain to register them over the cacophony of rain, wind, and thunder. Even now, the words lingered in the air around her, almost electric, like a current running through her body.

Outside, the storm raged on, lashing the metal roof with a fury that seemed determined to tear the house apart. It had begun before she'd gone to bed, a deluge of biblical proportions that only grew more intense as the night wore on.

Kira wiped the sheen of sweat from her brow. The air was thick with humidity, making it difficult to breathe. She longed to crack open a window and let in a bit of fresh air, but she didn't want to let the rain in.

She climbed to her feet, forgetting her proximity to the attic's sloped ceiling. Her head collided with a rotten support beam, sending a sharp pain shooting through her skull. Flecks of wood crumbled onto her pile of blankets.

"Ouch!" She pressed her fingers to the tender spot on her head, already knowing a bump would soon form. Just another injury to add to her growing collection.

When Aunt Reeva had explained that Kira would spend her nights in the attic until they left Emmitsburg, Kira had asked if Will could stay with her. The request had been inno-cent enough, but Aunt Reeva's reaction was anything but. The old woman's face had flushed with anger, and she had peered at Kira with narrowed eyes, as if suddenly questioning the kind of person she had invited into her home.

"No, he cannot, young lady," Aunt Reeva had said, her voice firm. "Not under my roof. Not until you're married. The little boy, Teddy, can stay with Will across town. You'll sleep by yourself, and I expect you'll manage just fine."

Kira had opened her mouth to explain, to clarify that she hadn't meant it the way it had come out, but one look at Aunt

Reeva's face had silenced her. She'd nodded, muttered a quick "Yes, ma'am," and dropped the subject.

Kneeling, she ran her hand along the floor, feeling the rough wood, the grit of dirt, and the tattered edge of her quilt. Then her fingers closed around something cold and heavy—a flashlight. Not one of the cheap plastic ones her mother had kept under their kitchen sink in Vita Nova for power outages. This one was solid, twelve inches long, and as heavy as a hatchet—more weapon than tool.

Aunt Reeva had given her the flashlight on her first night in the attic, a gift meant to trick her into feeling safe. But Kira knew better; the flashlight was more for show than anything else.

Aunt Reeva had made one thing clear: never use it at night.

Not unless it was an emergency.

Well, if someone's inside the house, hiding in the dark, waiting to kill me, that qualifies as an emergency.

Even though she wasn't sure Aunt Reeva would agree, Kira hovered her thumb over the rubber button on the side of the flashlight. She hesitated, thinking about the windows on either end of the attic. If she turned on the light, someone might see it.

She had to be careful.

Aunt Reeva was smart. Her group had evaded the Patrols for years by staying in small, scattered groups across Emmitsburg, living in musty basements and cramped attics, and practicing strict light discipline at night.

Kira pulled on her boots, ignoring the loose laces, and made her way out of her little corner, walking hunched over to avoid another painful collision with the beams. She headed for the center aisle, gripping the flashlight tightly, her thumb still resting on the power button.

She crept through the attic, carefully navigating the labyrinth of rotting cardboard boxes. Aunt Reeva's group had already sifted through the attic's contents, leaving behind a jumble of useless items. Old photo albums, moth-eaten clothing, and forgotten trinkets littered the floor, barely visible in the darkness. Kira strained to hear anything unusual over the relentless storm, but there was nothing.

Still, she kept her grip on the flashlight, ready to wield it as a weapon.

As the wind howled louder, Kira tilted her head and squinted at the peaked roof, evaluating its ability to hold back the storm. Only a few inches of rotting wood and a thin sheet of galvanized steel separated her from the onslaught outside. The relentless pounding on the roof intensified, like a thousand fists hammering away, desperate to break through and drown her.

Hoping to succeed where the river had failed.

Kira resisted the urge to check her watch, knowing that the light from the screen would destroy her night vision. How long until dawn? She'd been lying in the attic, half-awake, for hours.

Suddenly, a burst of lightning illuminated the attic. But before Kira could get a clear view, the light vanished, leaving her blinking away spots in her vision. She squeezed her eyes shut and counted, bracing for the thunder that followed. Two seconds later, the sky exploded with sound, rattling the attic windows in their frames.

Still, the voice lingered, a soft whisper in the back of her mind.

He's coming.

Kira weaved through the overturned boxes, reaching the narrow aisle in the center of the attic—a strip of clear space between piles of discarded junk. Because of the slant of the roof, it was also the only place where Kira could stand without knocking her head on the beams. She moved slowly, mindful of the rusty nails that jutted from the overhead supports at random places, serving no purpose other than to infect her with tetanus.

After countless nights spent tossing and turning in the cramped space, she knew the layout of the attic by heart. The stairwell was ten paces from her sleeping spot, and from there, two short flights of stairs would take her down to the second floor, with its three empty bedrooms and unused bathroom.

Another flight of stairs led to the main level. A left turn at the base of those stairs would take her into a living room filled with dusty furniture and rodent-chewed rugs. A right turn would take her through the kitchen to the back door, which opened into an overgrown backyard. The short hallway off the kitchen led to a first-floor bathroom and the staircase to the basement, where Aunt Reeva slept.

Her only option was to go downstairs, check the house, and make sure Aunt Reeva was safe. If she was lucky, the storm would pass before she finished her sweep of the house, and she could relax enough to catch a few hours of sleep before dawn.

Another flash of lightning spurred Kira into the stairwell, and she descended with one hand on the wall, the other clutching the flashlight. The wooden stairs creaked under her weight, their groans loud enough to set her on edge. She froze, listening for any sounds in response to her movement, but there was nothing—just the pounding of her own heart and the storm's endless roar.

I could turn on the flashlight, she thought. *There are no windows in the stairwell.*

But she wanted to protect whatever night vision she had left for when she reached the main part of the house. So she moved slowly, cautiously. The last thing she needed was to fall and re-injure her ankle, which was feeling almost normal after a week of rest.

Five steps to the landing. Another five to the door at the base of the stairs.

The noise of the rain faded as Kira left the attic behind. But the sudden quiet was unnerving, as if the house were holding its breath, waiting for something to happen.

When she reached the bottom step, she transferred the flashlight to her left hand and wrapped her fingers around the cold marble doorknob. It refused to budge, sending a jolt of panic through her. A horrible certainty prodded at the edges of her mind: *You're trapped in here. Someone locked you in.* But finally, with a groan of old hinges, the knob twisted, and the door creaked open.

On the other side of the hall, she could just make out the faint outline of a bedroom door hanging ajar on the other side of the hall. It had once been a child's room, the chipped pastel blue paint and faded train stencils on the walls remnants of a happier time. Though she couldn't see inside, Kira knew that if she aimed her flashlight into the room, she would reveal a moldy twin-sized mattress clinging to a metal bed frame. Mouse-chewed holes littered the mattress, each sprouting yellowed foam like flowers in a decaying garden.

With a shiver, she turned away from the bedroom and headed for the stairs, instinctively trailing her fingers along the wall in search of a light switch. It would take more than a week to break that habit. Over here, there were no lights. No electricity. No running water.

Pausing at the base of the stairs, Kira cautiously poked her head around the corner and peered into the kitchen. Shapes emerged from the darkness—the sharp angles of a battered kitchen table and chairs, her rucksack waiting on the floor, the broken refrigerator with its door hanging open.

On the far wall, a pale rectangle of light marked a twopaned window above a stainless steel sink that had been dry for more than a decade.

She stepped out of the stairwell and headed for the short hallway that led to the basement door. All that was left to do was confirm that Aunt Reeva was safe and asleep. Then she would retreat to the attic to wrestle a few hours of rest out of this endless night.

But when she turned the corner, she froze.

A dark figure stood halfway down the hallway, blocking the door to the basement.

It's Will, her mind insisted. *It has to be. He said he'd be here before dawn.*

"You scared me," she said. "What time is it?"

A low, muffled chuckle echoed from the darkness, a sound that was vaguely familiar.

A cold realization swept over her.

That isn't Will.

The silhouette was all wrong—too tall, too lanky, nothing like Will's frame. And Will would never just stand there in the dark, staring at her, trying to freak her out. He would say her name, step forward, wrap his arms around her, and tell her she was safe.

But the figure in the hallway did none of those things.

A terrible thought sliced through her mind: *It's the Lawless man. The one from your nightmares. He's real.*

He's always been real.

Terror gripped her, twisting her insides into knots. She stumbled back, pressing herself against the wall, her breath coming in short, panicked gasps. She clapped a hand over her mouth, stifling the scream that threatened to burst free.

The dark figure remained motionless, towering over her, broad shoulders rising and falling with each breath. It was eerily still, almost like a statue, until it slowly tilted its head to one side, as if studying her. She could smell the musty stench of rain-drenched clothing, stale cigarettes, and, faintly, the vaguest hint of copper.

Blood.

Kira's mind fired off a series of commands to her limbs— *turn around, run for the front door, get out of the house*—but her body refused to obey. Her limbs didn't seem to receive the messages from her brain. Either that, or they were choosing to ignore them.

A flash of lightning lit up the sky outside the window, its light searing through the kitchen and giving the terrible shape a face.

The face of a Patrol soldier.

One she recognized.

Her eyes drifted to his hand, and she saw the glint of a pistol aimed directly at her chest.

"Scream, and you're dead," Alaric Render muttered.

Chapter Three

The lightning died, plunging the interior of the house into complete darkness. Kira strained to see the Patrol soldier, her eyes searching the shadows, but the blackness was impenetrable. She couldn't tell if he was advancing, holding his position, or tightening his finger on the trigger to end her life.

Suddenly, a small light clicked on beneath the barrel of the pistol, and a boom of thunder echoed through the house, punctuating Render's next words.

"I've been looking for you, Kira. When I found out you were the one who escaped the city, I made it my mission to find you. I haven't slept in six days, so my trigger finger's a little twitchy. Better drop your weapon before it slips."

Kira's gaze locked onto the beam of light from his pistol, her body rigid and unable to move. The light only grazed half of Render's face, casting shadows that made him look like a sinister figure about to tell a ghost story around a campfire.

It was difficult to reconcile the man standing before her with the one she had gone on a double date with just two weeks ago. She remembered how Emma had clung to him, as if he were a trophy she couldn't afford to lose.

Render's voice snapped her back to the present, his anger palpable. "Did you hear what I said?" he barked. "You think I won't shoot you? I've done things you can't even imagine, sweetheart. Drop your weapon."

Confusion clouded Kira's thoughts. She had no idea what Render was talking about.

Weapon? What weapon?

Then it hit her—the flashlight in her hand.

In the attic, it had been a formidable weapon. A tool she could use to defend herself against an intruder. But now, facing a Patrol soldier armed with a gun, it seemed laughably inadequate.

Kira's fingers loosened around the light, preparing to drop it.

Aunt Reeva.

The old woman was asleep one floor below, unaware of the danger lurking a few feet above her head. And that's how it needed to stay.

With a shaky hand, Kira set the flashlight down on the dusty floor.

Silently.

When she straightened up, Render wagged the pistol at the kitchen table. "Sit."

She obeyed, sinking into the nearest chair, struggling to remain calm despite the fear racing through her. Not long after she'd first met Will, he had told her about a young woman—Deena—who had been searching for supplies when she was captured and murdered by a Patrol soldier. Before she was killed, she had sliced the soldier's arm with her knife. The same knife he later used to end her life.

The next evening, Kira had gone on the double date, the

memory of Will's story still haunting her mind. When she'd noticed a bandage on Render's arm and questioned him about it, the answer he gave her hadn't matched the story he'd told Emma earlier. That's when she'd known—deep down, on a gut level—that she was having dinner with Deena's murderer.

With his free hand, Render reached for his tactical vest and produced a pair of handcuffs. He approached Kira with the pistol trained on her stomach and circled behind her, roughly yanking her hands behind her back and snapping the cuffs around her wrists with practiced efficiency. He then tightened them until it felt like the metal had sliced through her skin and carved deep grooves into her bones.

The pain brought hot tears to Kira's eyes, but she did not cry out. Whatever happened—whatever Render did to her— Aunt Reeva needed to stay in that basement, asleep and unaware of the danger above.

Without Aunt Reeva, the group would fall apart.

Render loomed over her. "I didn't make the cuffs too tight, did I? Nah. Didn't think so."

The rain outside had slowed to a soft patter against the porch roof, and there hadn't been any lightning since the flash that had revealed Render's face. Either the storm was moving away from Emmitsburg, or her mind was blocking out every distraction so she could focus all of her attention on the Patrol soldier.

Although there were several windows in the living room and one in the kitchen above the sink, there was no ambient light in the Unregulated Zone. The street lamps had gone dark long ago and were now choked by the same climbing vines that had reclaimed much of the town for the wilderness. Even the moon had abandoned Emmitsburg on this night, chased away by the storm like a child fleeing a bully.

The only light came from the flashlight mounted on

Render's pistol. Above the beam, Kira could see the outline of a small, ominous black hole. A portal through which death could come at any moment.

Render bent down, bringing his face close to hers. "You know, I knew there was something off about you at dinner the other week. I just didn't know what it was. I think I could smell the traitor in you."

His voice was too loud, each word a potential alarm that could wake Aunt Reeva. Kira resisted the urge to tell him to lower his voice, knowing it would only give away the presence of another person in the house.

"How is Emma?" The question slipped out before she could stop it. She needed to know what had happened to her best friend after she escaped Vita Nova. Devlin must have known about Emma's involvement—after all, Kira had crashed Emma's Porsche on City Island while fleeing the city.

The uncertainty was eating away at her.

Render's smile vanished, replaced by a cold, steely glare. "She's in the Confines, along with that sanitation worker who helped your other traitor friend escape."

A strangled sound came from Kira's throat—a mixture of a cry and a gasp. She instinctively tried to cover her mouth so Aunt Reeva wouldn't hear, but her hands were cuffed behind her back, so she only succeeded in driving the handcuffs deeper into her wrists.

She barely felt the pain.

Her worst fears had been confirmed. Both Jonesy and Emma had risked everything to help her, and now they were paying the price. She couldn't imagine the horrors they must be enduring in that hellish place. No doubt Emma's father was using his considerable financial means to save his only daughter, but money couldn't buy freedom.

Not in Vita Nova.

Render studied her, scratching his ear with the barrel of his gun. "What did you expect? Treason doesn't go unpunished in Vita Nova. Their actions put the entire city at risk. You didn't think they would get away with it, did you?" He shook his head, his lips vanishing into a thin line. "It's a shame, though. Your dark-haired friend was a real beauty. I doubt she looks so good now, after a week in the Confines."

Kira lowered her head, tears spilling down her cheeks. How much time did Emma and Jonesy have? Devlin had ordered Will's execution to be carried out quickly, but typically prisoners languished in the Confines for weeks or even months before being put to death as Compulsories.

Something told her that Devlin wouldn't give them that much time. He'd want to make an example of them.

Not that it mattered. Kira couldn't save them.

But she could still save Aunt Reeva.

She lifted her tear-streaked face and met Render's gaze with as much defiance as she could muster. "So, what are you waiting for? Why are you just standing there? Take me back to Devlin and collect your blood money."

Render stared at her. "Do you think I'm an idiot?"

A trickle of sweat traveled down the curve of Kira's spine. The kitchen wasn't as hot as the attic, where the stagnant air was as thick as soup, but Render's question seemed to raise the temperature another twenty degrees. "What are you talking about?"

His eyes narrowed, dark and suspicious. "Don't play dumb with me. You've been whispering this whole time, and you placed that flashlight on the floor so carefully. There's someone else here, isn't there?" His eyes shifted to the ceiling, then snapped back to her. "Where are they? Upstairs? Or are they in the basement?"

"No!" she blurted out, panic rising in her chest. "I swear,

it's just me. That's how people stay safe out here. They spread out all over the place, everyone living in different houses, so the Patrols can't capture them all at once."

He raised an eyebrow, a smirk playing on his lips. "Interesting tactic. Thanks for the information. I'll pass it along to the rest of my team."

Kira's throat constricted, and she tried to push away the thought of how her confession could be used against the few people still hiding in Emmitsburg. She forced herself to focus. "Just take me back to the city," she urged. "Don't you want to get me to Devlin before your pal Dayton shows up? You'll have to share the glory with him."

"Still hung up on Dayton, huh?" Render's smile twisted into something darker. "For the record, he's not out here tonight. No one else is. This is what you might call a little solo mission. And let me tell you, he didn't think much of your little date. He said—and I quote—'*Kayla* was a real drag.'"

"My heart is broken into a thousand pieces," she muttered. "Can we go now?"

Render's amusement faded as he stepped closer. "You're really eager to leave, aren't you? What's the matter? Isn't the Unregulated Zone everything you'd hoped it would be when you defected? Missing your fancy townhouse and your cushy job in the Governmental Sector already? Just remember, Kira, there's no air conditioning in the Confines."

She shot out of the chair. "Take me back!"

In an instant, Render's smile disappeared, and the monster that lurked beneath his skin battled its way to the surface. He lunged at her, his hands gripping her shoulders and shoving her roughly back into the chair. Then he leaned in close, his breath hot and foul against her face. "Try that again," he hissed, pressing the barrel of the pistol against her cheek. "Please. I dare you. I would consider it an honor to dispatch you right here, you disgusting, pathetic traitor. Do you understand me?"

The handsome Patrol soldier who had whisked Emma onto the dance floor at The Grotto was gone. This was the real Render, stripped of any pretense. The man she had met on that double date had been nothing but a mask.

With the mask off, he was terrifying.

Render leaned back slightly, but kept the pistol against her face. "Tell me the truth," he demanded, his voice ice-cold. "Is. There. Someone. In. The. Basement."

Each word was punctuated by the gun digging deeper into her skin.

Kira wanted to resist, to fight back.

But he had a gun to her head.

She closed her eyes and whispered the truth.

"Yes."

Render's smile returned, triumphant. He moved the gun away from her face. "Good girl. You gave me a truthful answer, and I won't forget that. Now, I'm going to ask you one more question. Answer it truthfully, and you and I will leave this house together. Just the two of us. I'll leave your friend in the basement alone. That's a promise."

Render's promises held no weight with Kira, but there was something in his voice that made her think he might be sincere. "What is it?" she asked, her voice trembling. "What do you want to know?"

He leaned back against the kitchen table, casually crossing his legs at the ankles. "The Easton kid."

Despite the humidity in the kitchen, Kira's body went cold.

"Tell me where the kid is," Render said, "or I'll kill whoever's hiding in the basement."

Chapter Four

Teddy.

Kira knew exactly where he was—two blocks away, safe with Will, asleep in the basement of a white Cape Cod-style house. But that information was something she could never give to Render, no matter what threats he made. Even if he dragged Aunt Reeva out of the basement and put a gun to her head, Kira would not hand Teddy over to the Patrols.

She would rather die than let Render take the boy back to Vita Nova to be sacrificed as a Volunteer by his evil mother.

"Please," she whispered, hoping to appeal to any shred of humanity he might have left. "He's just a child. Besides, he's hidden far from here and well protected. You'll never get to him. Let's go back. You've got me. I'm the one Devlin wants."

"You?" Render's lips curled into a cruel smirk. "Do you actually think Mayor Devlin cares about you? You're just a defector. Devlin wants the kid. Sure, there's a bounty on your head—an extra month's pay for any Patrol soldier who brings you back, dead or alive—but it's the kid he really wants."

Dead or alive.

My father.

My own father.

Her eyes stung with unshed tears, but she clenched her teeth, refusing to let them fall.

Devlin didn't deserve her tears.

"What does the mayor want with Teddy? Doesn't he have enough innocent people to kill?"

Render tossed his cap onto the table and rubbed the stubble on his head. "The Easton kid is Devlin's prized Volunteer," he explained. "The youngest Volunteer in Vita Nova's history. I don't care how long it takes. I *will* find him. And when I bring the boy back, along with the traitor who took him, I'm sure the mayor will be happy. He might even pin a medal on me."

As Kira tried to process his words, Render reached out and squeezed her shoulder in a mock gesture of comfort. "Don't worry," he said. "Giving the kid up doesn't make you a bad person. You'd be saving the life of whoever's in the basement, and the boy gets to be a superhero for his city, just like he always wanted. It's a win-win. Besides, what kid doesn't love fireworks? Theodore Easton gets to *become* one."

Rage flared inside Kira, a white-hot fury she could barely contain. If it had been up to people like Render and her father, Teddy would already be dead. The city would have murdered him for the good of all, cremated his body, and shot it into the sky during the weekly Reverence Ceremony's fireworks display.

Just like all the other Volunteers.

If Kira's hands hadn't been cuffed behind her back, she would've wrapped them around the Patrol soldier's neck right then and there. "You're a monster. He's just a little boy, and you're talking about murdering him."

"It's not murder." Render crouched in front of her. "Don't you remember? The kid volunteered."

The smug grin on his face pushed Kira over the edge. The fury simmering inside of her came to a boil, and without considering the consequences, she slammed her foot into Render's exposed groin.

He let out a piercing howl of pain, the gun slipping from his hands as he grabbed himself. With both hands clutching his injured groin, he toppled over like a fallen tree, unable to brace himself. He crashed onto his back, rattling the kitchen window in its frame.

Without thinking, Kira threw herself on top of him. Her eyes landed on the gun lying by his right elbow, its flashlight casting a narrow beam across the kitchen. She couldn't grab the weapon—not with her hands bound—but at least she could stop Render from reaching it.

He thrashed beneath her, trying to wrench his arm free to reach for the gun, so she drove her knee into the meat of his thigh.

"Get off of me!"

Render spat the words at her, and the stench of rotten meat —likely the remains of whatever game he'd killed and consumed for dinner—filled her nostrils. She tried to knee him again, but he shifted his weight, blocking her move. With a powerful surge of strength, he bucked his hips and rolled, flipping Kira onto her back.

In an instant, he was on top of her, his knees straddling either side of her chest, her arms pinned behind her back.

She braced herself, expecting him to grab the pistol and shoot her in the face. Or pull out a knife and slit her throat.

But instead, he wrapped his thick fingers around her throat.

Pinned beneath his weight, Kira couldn't see his face in the darkness, but she could hear his grunts as he choked the life out of her. She struggled to free herself, but he was too strong, his fingers growing tighter around her neck.

Render was strangling her. There was nothing she could do to stop him.

A faint creak sounded from behind her, so soft that Render didn't notice. But Kira's nights of vigilant listening in the attic had sharpened her senses to even the faintest noises—noises that could mean danger or salvation.

She managed to tilt her head back, which only seemed to irritate Render, causing him to tighten his grip even more. But as she peered upside-down at the kitchen door, she saw it—the pale arc of light from the flashlight barely illuminating the beginning of the hallway.

Aunt Reeva stood there, half in shadow, half in light. From Kira's perspective, the old woman looked as though she were standing on the ceiling, her wispy white hair defying gravity as it hung over her shoulders. She held a hunting rifle, its muzzle aimed at Render's head.

Kira wanted to scream at Aunt Reeva not to shoot, but her throat was constricted, and no sound came out. If Render had lied about being alone in Emmitsburg, a gunshot could draw more Patrol soldiers to the house.

Then both Kira *and* Aunt Reeva would be captured or killed.

But Aunt Reeva was no fool. She hadn't survived this long in the Unregulated Zone because she was reckless. Her eyes met Kira's for a brief moment before she crept closer to Render on stealthy legs, the rifle pressing into the crook of her shoulder.

The Patrol soldier must've sensed her presence because he turned his head.

But it was too late.

Aunt Reeva swung the barrel of the rifle, striking Render's temple with a sickening crunch of metal against bone. The force of the blow sent him tumbling off Kira, his limp fingers falling away from her throat.

Kira rolled onto her stomach, coughing violently. Spittle flew from her dry lips as she struggled to catch her breath. When she could finally lift her head, Aunt Reeva was kneeling beside the Patrol soldier, rummaging through the pockets of his tactical vest. She produced a tiny metal key from one pocket and crawled over to Kira.

A second later, the cuffs were off, and Kira pushed herself into a sitting position, rubbing her sore wrists. She watched as Aunt Reeva secured Render's hands behind his back with the handcuffs. A faint moan escaped his lips, but he made no other sounds or movements.

With Render subdued, Aunt Reeva slumped back on her heels, wheezing. She wiped her forehead with the back of her hand and pressed her palm to her chest.

"Aunt Reeva?" Kira rasped, her throat raw. "Is it your heart?"

The old woman mustered a weak smile. "My ticker's fine, young lady. As steady as ever. Probably better than yours, with all that rich city food you've been eating. You're the one who looks worse for wear. That young man did quite a number on you."

Kira winced as she touched her bruised neck, feeling little nicks made by the Patrol soldier's nails. "It's nothing. Are you sure you're alright?"

"I'll be fine, dear. Nothing a cup of coffee and a dash of cinnamon won't cure." Aunt Reeva glanced at her watch and sighed. "Suppose you better get my Motorola and call the others. It's not even four yet. I hate to disrupt their sleep, but we don't have a choice."

"What should I tell them?" Kira asked.

"Tell them we've captured a Patrol soldier," Aunt Reeva said, her voice steady despite the situation. "And we need to figure out what to do with him before the sun comes up."

Chapter Five

"This is it. We're finished."

Devan Brack drove his fist into the wall of the makeshift infirmary with such force that the medicine bottles on a nearby shelf rattled, the impact sending a shower of dust and plaster raining down onto the floor. He let out a grunt—whether from anger or pain, it was hard to tell—and resumed pacing between the neatly made beds, each heavy thud of his boots echoing through the room like the relentless ticking of a giant clock.

A clock that was counting down the minutes before someone in Vita Nova noticed the Patrol soldier's absence and came searching for him.

At the far end of the room, Aunt Reeva hovered over the same hospital bed where Pastor Alwyn had drawn his last breaths a few weeks earlier. She carefully affixed a blood pressure cuff to Render's muscular arm. The soldier remained unconscious, a thin line of drool escaping his parted lips, the wound on his temple now covered with fresh gauze. Ropes secured each of his limbs to the metal bed frame.

Brack had been storming around the infirmary for the better part of an hour, tugging so hard on his beard that Kira could see small clumps of reddish-brown hair slipping between his fingers and drifting to the floor.

Trying to stay out of his way, Kira sat on one bed, her body pressed against Will's. Despite his arm wrapped protectively around her shoulders, she was still trembling.

Less than ten minutes after Kira had called him on the radio, Will had appeared at the back door of Aunt Reeva's house, a sleeping Teddy cradled in his arms. He handed the boy off to Aunt Reeva before pulling Kira into a quick embrace, then he held her at arm's length, his eyes sweeping over her face and body. "Are you hurt?"

"No, I'm fine," she said, trying to keep her chin down so he wouldn't notice her neck.

For once, Kira had been thankful for the darkness.

But then Will pulled a flashlight from his pocket and aimed it at her neck. His eyes widened as he took in the bruises left by Render's hands.

The muscles in his throat worked as he swallowed hard. "He did this to you?" he asked, shifting his gaze from Kira's neck to the unconscious Patrol soldier on the floor.

"Yes, but I'm okay now. Aunt Reeva took care of him."

"Is he dead?"

"No. Just unconscious."

"Good." He moved toward Render, grabbing him by the shoulders. "Then I'm going to kill him."

Kira grabbed his arm. "No! He's not a threat."

"As long as he's alive, he's a threat to us."

"Will, please..."

After a few moments, he released Render and ran a hand through his unkempt hair. "I should've been here," he muttered, his voice low and angry. "I should've stayed with you, no matter what anyone thought about it."

Kira wrapped her arms around Will's waist and leaned into him. She hadn't realized how desperate she'd been to have his arms around her until that moment. "If you were here, then Teddy would've been here, too. Render didn't want me. He wanted to take Teddy back to the city to die. It's a blessing you guys were somewhere else."

Will hadn't argued further, but he also hadn't left her side since his arrival at Aunt Reeva's house.

She decided not to share with Will what Render had mentioned about Jonesy and Emma's imprisonment in the Confines. Hiding the truth about Jonesy and Emma had been a deliberate decision on Kira's part. If Will knew that Jonesy—a man who was like a father to him—was locked up in the Confines, he might try to sneak back into the city to free him, and she couldn't let that happen. Most of the people arrested and sent to the Confines for offenses against Vita Nova or its government remained there for months or even years before their trials. Both Jonesy and Emma would be okay for a little while.

Well, maybe not okay, but they would at least be alive.

Kira couldn't say the same for Aunt Reeva and the others. Someone from the Patrols would inevitably come looking for Render, and Kira didn't want to think about the consequences if they discovered he had been injured by a group of Lawless.

For now, her priority was finding a safe place for Aunt Reeva, Teddy, and the others. Only then would she tell Will the truth, and they could decide together what to do about their friends in the Confines.

Brack stopped in front of the industrial sink, gripping the stainless steel, and took a deep breath. "Everyone in this room knows what needs to happen, but no one has the guts to say it."

"Why don't you say it then?" Aunt Reeva challenged, her tone sharp as she removed the blood pressure cuff from Render's arm. "Stop all your blustering and spit it out."

Brack spun around to face the group, his hands clenching into fists. But instead of smashing another hole in the wall, he grabbed the neck of his t-shirt, as if it were suddenly choking him, and stretched it even wider.

Aunt Reeva clicked her tongue in disapproval. "Destroying a perfectly good shirt out of anger," she scolded. "You're reminding me more of Samson every day, Brack—except without the hair. What's next? Should we light foxes on fire and send them across the bridge into the city?"

"It's not a bad idea," he muttered. "If I could catch them, I would."

Kira wasn't sure who Samson was or what Aunt Reeva meant about burning foxes, but describing Brack's shirt as "perfectly good" was a bit of an exaggeration. The tattered fabric barely clung to his body, the sleeves straining to contain his enormous biceps, and the stretched-out neck revealing more of his hairy chest than anyone needed to see.

Brack's wife, Grace, sat on another bed, one hand resting on her five-month-pregnant belly, the other on Teddy's shoulder. The little boy was tucked into the bed beside her, trying to sleep through Brack's tantrum. "Feel better now, honey?"

"Not much," Brack grunted.

Kira had only exchanged a few words with Grace, but the young woman seemed to perfectly embody her name. Where Brack was rough, Grace was gentle. When he fumed and blustered, she spoke in calm, measured tones. Her beauty was both delicate and fierce, with small, finely sculpted features framed by a wild cascade of strawberry-blonde curls that tumbled to her waist. She never bothered to tie her hair back, letting it flow freely around her face.

"She washes it in rainwater," Aunt Reeva had once explained to Kira. "If you're curious about how she keeps it looking so nice out here, that's the secret. She collects rainwater and washes it twice a week. Grace is a lovely young woman—far too good for that ogre Brack—but trust me, you don't want to be around her in the winter or during a dry spell. Without her rainwater, that sweet girl can turn into a real spitfire."

Though Grace didn't seem bothered by Brack's outburst, Kira had a feeling that she could end it anytime she wanted with just a subtle nod or a few choice words.

"All I'm saying," Brack said, his tone more controlled, "is that we shouldn't have brought him here. We should've left him in the house and hightailed it out of town like we planned."

"So he would die alone on my kitchen floor?" Aunt Reeva asked, crossing her arms. "Is that what you're suggesting? You want to make a murderer out of me?"

Brack glowered at the woman. "Come on, Reeva. He won't die from a little bump on the head. He'll wake up in a few hours with a bad headache, but that's about it. And let's be real. Who cares if he dies? Did you forget he tried to kill Liebert?"

"Tried is the operative word. Kira's just fine. This young man, on the other hand, could have a traumatic brain injury. Leaving him in that house would've been akin to a death sentence."

"A death sentence? Like the one he imposed on Deena when he slit her throat?"

At the other end of the room, Render let out a low moan, as if protesting the accusation.

"What if he'd killed Grace instead of Deena?" Brack continued, red splotches blooming on his tanned cheeks. "Because he would have if Deena hadn't sacrificed herself so Grace could get away. If this piece of human filth had killed my wife, I wouldn't have left him on your kitchen floor to die a peaceful death. I would've sent him to hell myself."

"*Enough.*"

All eyes turned to Grace, who leaned forward on the bed, her hands gripping the edge of the mattress. "Enough," she repeated, her voice softening. "Enough shouting and stomping around like a crazy person. It's not impressing anyone."

Brack lowered his head like a dog that had been scolded by its master. "Sorry, Tumblebug."

"Aren't you always telling me to trust in God? After everything that happened with Deena, and now that we're expecting a baby, haven't you been saying that we need to trust in Him because he always takes care of us?"

Brack's jaw tightened as he raised his eyes to meet hers. "That's true, Tumblebug. He's protected us so far, but I'm not sure He'll keep doing that if we take unnecessary risks, like turning our basement into a field hospital for injured Patrol soldiers."

Grace shook her head, her curls bouncing. "He's not a threat to our group, at least not anymore. And as Christians, we have a duty to care for him."

"You don't think he's a threat? For all we know, the Patrols could be tracking him right now."

"Didn't you take his gear off of him at the house?"

"Sure, but the tracker could be *internal,* Tumblebug." Brack turned toward the soldier, his hand moving toward the hunting knife on his belt. "I guess we could start cutting until we find it."

"Take your hand off that knife," Aunt Reeva growled, and Brack reluctantly complied.

Kira leaned close to Will, their heads almost touching. "Why does Brack call Grace Tumblebug?"

"It's a nickname," he whispered back. "Tumblebugs are

beetles that roll their...uh...dung into little balls and bury them. It's kind of endearing, I guess."

"I'm pretty sure Grace doesn't know what it means."

"Yeah, I doubt it." Will turned his attention back to the group, raising his voice. "What about the bridge? We could drop him off near the Market Street Bridge so the Patrols will find him."

"That's eight miles from here, Foster!" Brack snapped. "Are you volunteering to haul this sack of garbage eight miles? Because I'm not."

Teddy's little body jerked beneath the covers at the sound of Brack's voice. He rolled over and buried himself deeper underneath the blankets, whimpering softly.

Rubbing Teddy's back, Grace shot her husband a stern look. "Quit your shouting right now," she said, her voice carrying a slight backcountry twang, a remnant of her rural upbringing. "I'm not going to ask you again."

Brack's voice dropped to a whisper as he tried to plead his case. "Even if I were willing to carry this guy back to the city—which I'm not—we have to consider how long it'll take for me to hike there and back. You can forget about leaving today."

Grace wrapped one of her curls so tightly around her finger that the tip turned red from the pressure. "Even if Brack could get back in time for us to leave today, it's too dangerous. Since the mayor announced his little search-and-destroy mission, the entire area has been crawling with Patrol soldiers. We can't risk it."

Will removed his arm from Kira's shoulder and slid off the bed, his boots hitting the floor with a thud. "So, what are we supposed to do? Wait here until he recovers? We don't know how long that will take or if he will even recover. We've already waited too long."

Grace nodded. "Will's right. We have to leave today, no matter what."

The room fell into a tense silence, broken only by Render's labored breathing and Teddy's soft whimpers as he drifted back to sleep.

Until Aunt Reeva's voice cut through the silence, pulling all the air from the room.

"I'm staying behind."

Chapter Six

A faint whistle escaped Render's mouth, as if Aunt Reeva's declaration had caught him off-guard.

Will shook his head. "No way."

Grace let go of her hair, the deep-red tinge on her fingertip vanishing as the curl unraveled and fell back into place. "That's not even an option."

"It absolutely is," Aunt Reeva countered, waving a dismissive hand at Grace. "In fact, it's the only option that makes sense. Think about it. I'm the only nurse in this group.
"

"Exactly," Brack agreed. "You're the only one with medical training. Which is why we need you with us on the road."

"I'm the one responsible for this man's injury," Aunt Reeva continued, ignoring Brack as if he hadn't spoken. "Which makes it my responsibility to care for him. Besides, I'm too old to make this trip, and you all know it. My stomach has been acting up all week, and I've got less energy than a dehydrated raccoon trapped in an empty dumpster. The last thing you'll need out there is an old woman who has to stop every twenty paces for a bathroom break, slowing you down. Besides, who will water my dahlias if I go?"

Her words had the cadence of a rehearsed speech, and Kira couldn't shake the suspicion that Aunt Reeva had never truly intended to leave Emmitsburg with the rest of the group. Perhaps she had played along with their plan until they were too committed to turn back. And now, Render's injury had given her the perfect reason to stay.

Will crossed the room, stopping just a few paces from Aunt Reeva. The muscles in his forearms tensed as he stood there, seemingly torn between the urge to embrace her and the instinct to drag her out of the church against her will. "I'm sorry, Reeva, but I can't let you stay behind."

Defiance flashed in Aunt Reeva's eyes. "You're not going to *let* me do anything, Will Foster. I may be old and half-senile, but I'm still capable of making decisions without your help. I managed just fine before you came along, and I'll manage again. End of discussion."

Kira knew better than to argue with Aunt Reeva. The woman was as stubborn as a mule, and once her mind was made up, there was no changing it. "I'm staying with you."

Will spun around to face her. "You're what?"

She looked past him, focused on convincing Aunt Reeva. "The Patrols will be looking for me, not the rest of you. I hope they don't find us, but if they do, I might be able to distract them and keep them from pursuing the rest of you. That gives you a better chance at finding safety."

Aunt Reeva shook her head. "I'm sorry, honey, but I can't allow that."

"It's not up to you," Kira replied, folding her arms over her chest. "I've made my decision. End of discussion."

She couldn't help but feel a small sense of satisfaction at parroting Aunt Reeva's words back to her.

But instead of responding with her usual spunk, Aunt Reeva gave Kira a gentle smile. "God works in mysterious ways, and I'm so grateful that He brought you into our little dysfunctional family. You've been such a blessing to me. As much as I've loved having you here, it's time for you to go."

"Reeva, I'm not—"

"The boy needs you," Aunt Reeva interrupted, her eyes flicking to Will—not Teddy—for a moment before returning to Kira. "It's obvious he loves you, and it would break his heart if you stayed behind. We can't send him on a journey with a broken heart, can we? Not after everything he's been through."

Kira opened her mouth to argue, but the words wouldn't come. Will was a natural-born survivor, and he would be fine without her, but she hadn't considered what her staying behind would mean for Teddy. Before the staff at Rolling Meadows could euthanize him, Kira had convinced the little boy to leave the lodge—and his narcissistic mother—by making him a promise. She had promised him they would stay awake together. She had promised him an adventure outside the barricade.

She'd brought him too far to abandon him now.

"Then it's settled," Aunt Reeva said, taking Kira's silence as agreement. "The sun's rising. Time to get moving."

The group lingered in the vestibule, exchanging hugs, tears, and goodbyes with Aunt Reeva.

Kira couldn't bring herself to say goodbye to the woman, so she grabbed a metal bucket and moved around the perimeter of the sanctuary, watering the beautiful dahlias one last time. It was a familiar task—she had spent many hours helping Aunt Reeva care for the flowers, listening to her hum Christian hymns and explain the intricacies of growing dahlias indoors.

As she emptied a little river water onto each plant, Kira realized that Aunt Reeva would soon be solely responsible for caring for an entire churchful of dahlias—and an injured Patrol soldier.

When she set the empty bucket down, Kira noticed she was standing in the exact spot where she had first met Aunt Reeva a little over two weeks earlier. It seemed like a lifetime had passed since that rainy Tuesday afternoon, when she was still living in the city and working as a volunteer advocate. Back then, she had feared the Lawless—those terrifying inhabitants of the Unregulated Zone—so much that she used to have nightmares of them capturing her and dragging her into the river.

Now, she was living in the Unregulated Zone, the Lawless were her allies, and the Patrols were hunting her. In just a few days, her entire life had been turned upside down, and as she stood in the spot where it all began, she realized it was about to change even more.

She turned to see Aunt Reeva kneeling before Teddy, holding a stuffed brown bear with a missing button eye clutched in her arthritic fingers. "I found this guy in my attic a few months back," she said. "Isn't he a handsome fella? When I told him you lost your friend, Pandy, in the river, he asked if he could be your new best friend."

Teddy's eye widened as he accepted the bear, his small fingers tracing the missing eye. "He's mine? For real?"

"For real," Aunt Reeva nodded. "Just promise to take good care of him. And give him a name, of course. I thought about calling him Teddy, but that name's already taken. Then I thought about giving him a pirate name, like Eye-Patch Eddie, but that's kind of dumb. I was hoping you could come up with something better."

Teddy thought for a moment, then his face lit up with excitement. "Can I call him Randy?"

Aunt Reeva chuckled, her wrinkles deepening around her mouth. "Randy, it is. That's a good, strong name for a brave little bear."

The boy threw his arms around her shoulders. "Thank you, Reeva!"

"You're most welcome, sweet boy."

Aunt Reeva's old bones creaked as she pushed herself to her feet. Leaving the others in the vestibule, she shuffled into the sanctuary. "That was nice of you to water my flowers one more time, honey. My lower back thanks you."

"Your lower back is welcome."

Aunt Reeva pulled Kira into an embrace so tight that she could feel every vertebra in the woman's spine. "I appreciate your offer to stay," she whispered. "But I know those boys out there need you more than I do. You're a rare one, with a noble heart and strong character. I only wish we could've known each other longer before you had to leave."

The finality in Aunt Reeva's words made Kira uneasy. "You're talking like I'm not coming back. This isn't goodbye. We're coming back for you."

"Oh, I know you are, honey. Others have made the same promise, but you're different from the others, aren't you?" The old woman rubbed Kira's back in slow, soothing circles, a gesture that reminded Kira of her mother. "But don't lose sight of your true purpose. God has a plan for you, even if it's not clear yet. He doesn't want you to waste time fretting over a grumpy old lady and her flowers. God is sending you into the wilderness for something far greater than me, and I believe His plan is for you to face the tumult head-on."

"I don't know what good I'll be to God," Kira said. "I'm not brave or strong. I'm the complete opposite—scared and weak."

Aunt Reeva pulled her closer. "You jumped off a bridge to save that little boy. That sounds pretty brave to me. And you might not be as strong as Brack, but remember: 'God has chosen what is weak in the world to shame the strong.'"

Soft light filtered into the sanctuary, illuminating the tears on Aunt Reeva's cheeks. Both women turned to see Brack holding the church's heavy wooden door open, signaling that it was time to leave.

The others waved their final goodbyes to Aunt Reeva before disappearing into the pale morning light, leaving only Kira and Aunt Reeva in the church.

Kira picked up her rucksack and slung it over her shoulder. It wasn't as heavy as the packs carried by the men, but it still weighed heavily on her slight frame. The straps dug into her shoulders, but it was the sharp pain in the center of her chest—where her sternum was still healing—that brought tears to her eyes.

Or maybe it was Aunt Reeva.

The woman used her sleeve to wipe Kira's cheeks. "Don't cry, honey. God will be with you every step of the way, and I'll be back here praying for you every day."

"Don't bother unpacking your bags," Kira said, barely able to choke out the words. "Because I'm coming back for you."

Chapter Seven

The group left Emmitsburg at eight in the morning, only faint traces of light seeping through the thick clouds, which hung low over the crumbling buildings like a sodden blanket. Kira walked in silence, her boots splashing through puddles that formed tiny mirrors, reflecting the dreary gray sky above. Beads of cold rain dripped from the thick canopy of leaves overhead, as if Emmitsburg itself were mourning their departure, shedding silent tears for the small band of travelers it expected would never return.

Before the distance grew too great, she stole a glance back at Aunt Reeva. The woman stood on the overgrown sidewalk in front of the church, looking small and fragile in her bib overalls, like a child pretending to be an adult. She raised her hand in a silent wave.

You're never going to see her again.

Kira waved back, banishing the insidious thought from her mind.

She would see Reeva again.

The next time she looked back, both the woman and the

church had disappeared, swallowed up by the weeping jungle of green.

They headed north out of Emmitsburg, abandoning the highway for the old railroad tracks that ran parallel to the Susquehanna River. Sunbaked vehicles clogged both lanes of Highway 15, making it impossible to keep a good pace. The tracks, however, were mostly clear, save for the occasional downed tree, and offered the group easy access to fresh fish and water to filter for drinking. The tracks also provided better cover, hidden down a steep embankment from the highway. According to Brack, they could follow this stretch all the way to Pittsburgh if they wanted, though Kira could tell from his tone that he didn't think they had much chance of making it that far.

They had decided to travel north. Going south would've led them into Carlisle and York, once densely populated areas now best avoided. Heading east presented a similar problem, taking them into Lancaster County, which was once known for its idyllic farmland but had transformed into a major urban area rivaling Harrisburg in the years before the virus.

Traveling away from populated areas sounded counterintuitive—they wanted to *find* help, not run from it. But the other groups that had left Emmitsburg heading south or east had not returned.

In the end, the choice was between heading west or north, and after much discussion, they settled on north. Both directions led to rural areas, but the terrain north of Emmitsburg was mountainous and difficult to navigate. A few towns lay scattered along the riverbank, but none were as large as the cities located south and east of Vita Nova, making them less likely to be covered by the Patrols.

But what no one was saying—and what Kira only knew because Will had mentioned it to her days earlier—was that the last group to leave Emmitsburg had gone north based on a similar hypothesis and had not returned.

As Kira trudged along the railroad tracks, one thought kept nagging at her: the faraway look in Will's eyes when he mentioned that last group. He had rattled off details about previous expeditions, speaking matter-of-factly about the number of people and their intended destinations. But his demeanor shifted when he spoke of the last group—the one that went north. His expression had glazed over and hardened, and Kira couldn't help but wonder if someone important to him had been in that group.

Why are we really heading north? she wanted to ask him. *To find safety from Vita Nova or to find someone you lost?*

Eventually, the sun broke through the thick clouds, casting light on the swollen, meandering river, making the dark surface shimmer as if littered with diamonds. The air smelled fresh after the storm, and by mid-morning, the temperature had risen into the low eighties.

As Kira walked along the overgrown railroad tracks, the rusted rails seemed to stretch endlessly before her. The tree branches above formed a natural canopy, allowing slivers of sunlight to filter through and illuminate patches of decaying metal. The desolate landscape—so different from the city— held a strange beauty, as if she had stepped into another world.

Following the tracks quickly proved challenging. Thick layers of moss and lichen clung to the rails, making them slick. She tried to match her steps to each wooden railroad tie, but it soon became too awkward, and she ended up walking on the gravel between the tracks. Even with sturdy hiking boots, after several hours of trudging over rough gravel, everyone was complaining of sore feet.

Everyone except Teddy, who happily rode on Brack's broad shoulders, pointing out every squirrel and chipmunk he spotted along the way.

The tiny pebbles that lined the railroad tracks crunched beneath Kira's boots, drowning out all sounds except the incessant buzzing of mosquitoes in her ears. Walking on those rocks was strange and unnatural, and with each step, Kira imagined that the rocks weren't rocks at all, but the brittle bones of people who had succumbed to the virus years earlier.

Water, she reminded herself. *Those kinds of morbid thoughts mean you need to drink more water.*

Kira reached into a side pocket of her rucksack and pulled out a water bottle with an attached carbon filter—a gift from Will. He and Brack had stumbled upon a small box of unopened water bottles in the storage room of an old hiking store south of Emmitsburg. Aunt Reeva had called it a blessing from God to make their journey easier. But there had only been five bottles in the box, not six. At the time, Kira didn't know what to make of that. If God was taking care of them, why hadn't He provided enough bottles for the entire group?

Then Render showed up in Emmitsburg, and their group of six had become five.

Kira took a long swig of water, her gaze falling on Will, their silent leader. He walked a few yards ahead of the rest of the group, carrying a rucksack with a tent strapped on top and a black Weatherby hunting rifle slung over his shoulder.

Brack followed, carrying another tent and a rucksack that was twice as swollen as everyone else's. Teddy sat atop the rolled tent, his stuffed teddy bear tucked under one arm, prattling on about anything and everything that came to his mind. Brack occasionally responded with a disinterested grunt, but the lack of a two-way conversation didn't seem to bother Teddy, who kept talking.

Kira and Grace brought up the rear of the group, walking on opposite sides of the tracks, as if subconsciously leaving enough space between them for Aunt Reeva. They both carried rucksacks and Glock 19 pistols on their hips.

Although Kira wasn't comfortable with guns, Will had insisted she carry something for protection. Most of the weapons and ammunition they carried had been scavenged years ago from an old army weapons depot just south of Emmitsburg—a lucky discovery that had left their group armed with enough firepower to rival a small militia.

Kira had practiced shooting the Glock the previous Saturday, with Will setting up targets in the woods outside of Emmitsburg. He had stood behind her, his arms around her, and showed her how to use her non-dominant hand to stabilize the weapon. He had also tried to teach her how to control her breathing to minimize movement before firing.

"Breathe in, exhale, and fire," he had whispered in her ear, his breath tickling the back of her neck.

He hadn't meant to make it harder for her to control her breathing, but that's exactly what happened.

Shooting hadn't come naturally to Kira. No matter how hard she tried to follow Will's instructions, she hadn't hit the target once. Most of her shots had gone wild, whizzing off into the woods, never to be seen again. Frustration had bubbled inside her until she finally gave up, crossing her arms and refusing to shoot another round.

Will had just laughed and pulled her close, kissing away her irritation and telling her how cute she looked when she was angry.

And with that, their shooting practice had come to an abrupt end.

After a few miles, Brack slowed his pace to let Kira and Grace catch up.

"Kira!" Teddy exclaimed when he saw her. "Did you see that huge snake in the weeds? I've never seen a real one before."

"The huge—? *What?*"

Grace laughed. "I didn't say anything because I didn't want to freak you out, but you came within a foot away of stepping on its head."

"Are you serious?" Goosebumps erupted on Kira's arms, and she scanned the foliage near her boots for hidden dangers. "There are snakes out here?"

Brack rolled his eyes. "City girl," he muttered, before turning his attention to his wife. "How are you feeling, Tumblebug?"

"Fine, babe. You know I can handle this."

"Any pain or cramps?"

"I said I was fine, Devan."

"I heard what you said." Brack reached into his rucksack, pulled out his water bottle, and passed it to her. "Drink something. It's getting hot."

Grace pushed the bottle away. "I have my own water."

"But you're not drinking it." He cast a dark gaze at Kira. "Why are women always so difficult?"

"When I'm thirsty, I'll drink, okay?" Grace grabbed his forearm and squeezed. "You need to relax, babe. This isn't my first time outside of Emmitsburg."

"I know, but—"

"And you know I wouldn't do anything to harm our baby, right?"

"Of course."

"Yes, I'm pregnant," she continued, "but I'm also in excellent shape. I drank a ton of water before we left the church, and it's not that hot walking under these trees. I haven't even broken a sweat yet. But I promise you, the second I get thirsty, I'll empty the whole bottle and throw it at your head so you'll know I'm finished. Okay? Will that do?"

Kira covered her mouth to stifle a laugh.

Brack pursed his lips as if considering his wife's proposal, then nodded. "That'll do."

Brack and Grace walked ahead, their laughter echoing through the forest, making everything seem a little lighter. Kira smiled as she watched them, allowing herself to feel a glimmer of hope that they might actually make it to safety. But as her eyes drifted to the river, the feeling faded, replaced by the grim reality of what was still happening on the other side.

Even if their group succeeded and found a safe place to settle, Vita Nova—that relentless machine of death that claimed more innocent victims every day—would never stop. Volunteers were still living out their Final Weeks, and Compulsories were still being put to death.

And while she was free, Jonesy and Emma remained imprisoned in the Confines.

And Kira was leaving them all behind.

Chapter Eight

North of Emmitsburg, a concrete path veered away from the railroad tracks, sloping down to an old boat launch. The river lapped at the shoreline, where bloated clumps of algae floated on the surface like dead fish. The algae emitted a noxious odor—Kira pegged it somewhere between sewage and decay—but the stench couldn't diminish the awe she felt as she took in the sight of the Rockville Bridge.

The railroad bridge stretched across the Susquehanna, its forty-eight stone arches having withstood a century and a half of heavy winds, flash floods, and brutal ice floes. In the early days of the virus, the bridge had also escaped destruction by the local Army engineer unit, which had blown most of the bridges in the Harrisburg area. Situated five miles north of the city, on the far side of the barricade, the Rockville Bridge must have been deemed unworthy of the effort or the explosives.

A freight train still rested on the bridge, its jet-black engine frozen midway across the river. Graffiti, faded by years of exposure to the elements, covered almost every container. Three containers had toppled over, likely from the wind, but only one had taken the long plunge into the river below. It lay crumpled on its side, a white island in a sea of muddy green.

"The baby's sleeping."

Kira turned to look at Grace. "What?"

The young woman tossed her strawberry-blonde curls over her shoulder. "She sleeps so much during the day. I think the movement lulls her to sleep. But then she's up all night, twirling around like a ballerina when I'm trying to rest." She put a hand on her belly. "You wouldn't think there'd be enough room in there for pirouettes and plies, but this little one manages."

The image of Grace's baby as a tiny, redheaded ballerina brought a smile to Kira's face. "How do you know it's going to be a girl?"

"I just know in my heart, and it's *not* wishful thinking," Grace insisted, as if Kira had suggested otherwise. "Honestly, I would've preferred a boy if I had a choice. Boys are more useful." She gave Kira a rueful smile. "That probably sounds harsh, but that's the world we live in now. Plus, I think Brack would've been happier with a son. Most men want sons, even if they won't admit it. Brack goes on and on about the things he's going to teach his son. I know this is probably my pregnancy hormones talking, but sometimes I wonder if he'll stick around when this baby turns out to be a girl."

Victor Devlin's pockmarked face flashed in Kira's mind, and she wondered if Grace was right. Would things have been different for her mother if she'd had a son instead of a daughter? Would Devlin have married her instead of leaving her to raise their child on her own?

"My father left my mother as soon as he found out she was pregnant with me," Kira admitted, her voice quiet. "He didn't care that she was alone and scared. He made her all kinds of promises, and then he just walked away, leaving her to deal with everything by herself. I hated him for that, and for a long time, I assumed all men were like him—ready to abandon you when things got hard. If I were to psychoanalyze myself, I'd say that's probably why I never had a boyfriend before Will."

Grace gave her a small, sad smile. "Who could blame you? That really sucks. For you and your mom."

Kira glanced at Brack, who was carrying Teddy a few paces ahead. When she'd first met him, Kira had been terrified. With his massive build, full beard, and partially shaved head, he looked like the embodiment of the brutal Lawless men she'd imagined occupied the Unregulated Zone—like the faceless man from her nightmares. But those fears had been shaped by years of Vita Nova's broadcasts and propaganda. After watching Brack interact with Grace and Teddy, Kira realized how wrong her first impression had been.

He would die for anyone in their group, including her.

"But Brack is nothing like my father," Kira said. "He's solid. He's not perfect, but he's the kind of man who sticks around, who fights for the people he loves. Even if he secretly wants a son, as soon as he meets his daughter, she'll have him wrapped around her little finger. Especially since she's going to be a miniature version of her momma."

Tears welled in Grace's hazel eyes. "Thank you, Kira. I appreciate that." She lowered her gaze to the ground. "If I tell you something, do you promise not to say anything to Brack?"

Despite the seriousness of the conversation, Kira couldn't help but laugh at the absurdity of the request. "Don't worry, your husband and I don't exactly have heart-to-heart chats."

Grace brushed a strand of hair from her mouth with her pinky finger, leaving a faint smudge of dirt on her cheek. She stepped over the railroad ties to join Kira on the opposite side of the tracks. "When I found out I was pregnant," she said, her voice almost too low to hear. "I didn't want the baby."

Kira was taken aback by the confession. Brack and Grace seemed so excited about the baby. "Why not?"

A pained expression crossed Grace's face. "Neither one of us wanted to bring a child into this world. We tried to be careful, but accidents happen, and I knew right away I was pregnant. Everything felt different—*I* felt different—and I just knew. It's not that I didn't want her, but I couldn't bear the thought of bringing a child into a life like ours. Always on the run. Always in danger. Never enough food. That's no kind of life for a baby. Can you understand that?"

Kira placed a hand on Grace's back. "I completely understand."

Although Will was her first boyfriend, Kira's work as a volunteer advocate had forced her to think deeply about what she would do if she ever got married. No matter how much she loved her husband, she knew she could never have children. The thought of bringing a child into a world where it could be ripped from her arms and murdered by the city was unbearable.

In Vita Nova, every prenatal ultrasound was a gamble—potentially a death sentence. If any birth defects or health conditions were found, abortion was mandatory under city law. After all, what was the point of carrying a child to term only to have the government put it to death as a Compulsory? Wasn't it better to never meet the child at all? Even if no health issues were detected, abortion was encouraged as a means of controlling the city's overpopulation problem.

Tears slid down Grace's face, soaking into her black tank top. "Nights are the worst. I can't get my mind to shut down. All I do is lay there in bed, wondering if I'm going to die in childbirth," she whispered, her voice trembling. "Other times, I'm terrified of surviving the birth but losing the baby. And if we both survive, there'll be one more person in the world for me to worry about losing. One more person whose death would break me. I mean, what chance does a baby have out here? What if the Patrols hear her crying and find us? Or what if the virus isn't really gone like we thought, and she gets sick and dies like everyone else?"

Kira intertwined her fingers with Grace's, squeezing them gently. "You have every right to be scared. But you're not doing this alone, Grace. You have Brack, who loves you more than anything, and you have the rest of us. We're your family, and whatever happens, we're going to be right there with you."

Grace nodded, sniffing. "I know you will."

"And this baby is already luckier than the babies in Vita Nova because she'll be free. No one will take her from you if she gets sick. Her life won't be perfect, but it'll be hers. And you'll have a spunky little redheaded daughter who, hopefully, looks and acts a lot more like her momma than her daddy."

Grace used her free hand to wipe the tears from her cheeks, somehow looking even more beautiful after her cry. "This might sound bad," she said with a laugh, "but I'm glad Will tried to kidnap you."

"Me too, I guess."

Brack glanced back at them, his massive hands clutching Teddy's skinny legs. His gaze fell on their interlaced hands, and he narrowed his eyes in disapproval.

"You two make me nervous," he muttered before turning away.

That only made them laugh harder.

Chapter Nine

A few miles north of Emmitsburg, Teddy tugged on Brack's beard. "Can we stop soon? I have to go pee."

Brack groaned. "We haven't even been walking for two hours yet, kid. We'll stop for lunch in a little while. Can you hold it until then?"

"Uh, okay."

Grace came up beside him, placing a hand on his shoulder. "Babe, just remember, if this little guy has an accident, it's going to be on your shoulders. And your shirt's already had a rough day."

With a reluctant nod, Brack handed the boy off to his wife.

Grace took Teddy's hand and led him toward a cluster of trees to their left, where the ground sloped up to meet the highway. A low retaining wall composed of mismatched brown and gray stones sat at the top of the embankment, blocking their view of the road while also offering concealment from anyone who might be passing by.

They hadn't heard any Patrol vehicles all morning, and Kira hoped it would stay that way.

As Teddy and Grace disappeared into the trees, Will approached Kira and offered her his filtered water bottle. "Are you drinking enough? You should drink whenever we stop. You don't want to get dehydrated out here."

Kira couldn't help but smile at his overprotectiveness. Will was always looking out for her, just like Brack looked out for Grace. "I've got my own, remember?" she said, gesturing to the bottle tucked into her rucksack. She playfully nudged his arm with her elbow. "And I'm not going to become dehydrated. I know you still think of me as a pampered city girl, but I'm a tough Unregulated Zone girl now."

Will's lopsided dimples, the ones Kira had grown to love, made an appearance. "Yeah? Well, even tough Unregulated Zone girls need water to stay alive." He took a few swallows from his bottle, his gaze drifting to the river. "Hey, can I show you something?"

"Sure."

Leaving their rucksacks on the tracks, Will and Kira joined hands and descended the slope toward the river's edge.

Will pointed at the water. "See? Over there."

Kira followed his finger to the center of the river, where a replica of the Statue of Liberty stood atop an old railroad bridge piling. The statue was a whitish gray rather than the iconic green, and though it was much smaller than its famous counterpart in New York City, it still had to be at least twenty-five feet tall. The statue towered over the crumbling bridge piling, her long skirt and sandaled feet seeming to anchor her in place. Behind her, on the opposite shore, a lush green mountain rose up, forming a sharp peak over her head.

"That's the Dauphin Narrows Statue of Liberty," Will explained. "My dad used to point her out whenever we drove up this way. A local guy built her in the 1980s using fiberglass and Venetian blinds. He and his friends snuck out in boats one night to put her up, and it supposedly caused a bunch of traffic problems the next morning. The original statue was destroyed by weather, but the city eventually built a sturdier replacement." He paused to take another sip of water. "It's hard to believe Vita Nova ever cared about freedom."

Kira nodded, though she was barely listening. The statue had triggered a memory—one she hadn't thought of in years. A long-ago Saturday morning car ride with her mother behind the wheel of their little red sedan. The windows were down, and her mother's blonde hair whipped and danced around her face. Madison Liebert had worn a dress that day—one Kira had never seen before. Dark green with little white flecks, like snowflakes on grass. She'd even painted her nails to match.

They were going somewhere special, but Kira couldn't quite remember where.

Along the way, her mother pulled over and pointed out the statue in the middle of the river. Kira remembered staring at it, awestruck, goosebumps prickling her arms. To her childish mind, this smaller Statue of Liberty was every bit as impressive as the real thing—perhaps even more so because it didn't belong to New York City.

It belonged to her.

She couldn't recall how old she'd been at the time—maybe six or seven—but it was before the virus, before everything changed.

Her mother had been so happy that day. She couldn't stop smiling.

Where had they been going?

Will's eyebrows knit together as he studied Kira's face. "What is it?"

She shook her head, trying to clear the memory from her mind. Now wasn't the time to dwell on thoughts of her mother. She had to stay focused. "Just a memory of my mom and me at this statue a long time ago. We were going somewhere important, I think, but I can't remember where. I don't remember much from before the barricade."

Will wrapped his arm around her shoulders and drew her closer, his lips brushing against her temple. Kira breathed in his dandelion-woodsy scent—the smell of life and freedom. "I wish I could've met her."

Kira leaned into his embrace, one arm slipping behind his back, the other around his waist. She pressed her hands against the soft fabric of his shirt, feeling the strength of his body beneath. "She would've loved you."

When Teddy returned from his bathroom break, Will took him down to the river's edge to show him the statue. As Brack stood scowling on the tracks, clearly annoyed by the delay, Will spent a few minutes explaining the statue's history.

"That's cool," Teddy said, more interested in the pebbles at the feet than the lady on the bridge piling. He scooped up a handful of stones and lobbed them into the water, laughing as they sent tiny ripples across the river.

Kira locked eyes with Will over Teddy's head, and the sadness in his gaze mirrored her own. The statue meant nothing to Teddy—not because he didn't care, but because he was too young to grasp its significance.

She couldn't blame him. He hadn't been taught to value freedom, liberty, or life.

Like everyone else in Vita Nova, Teddy had been taught to value death.

Chapter Ten

An hour later, they came upon a gas station.

Following the railroad tracks had kept them out of sight of the highway for most of the morning, but after their brief stop at the Statue of Liberty, the ground beneath the tracks had begun a steady, gradual ascent, carrying them away from the river. The dense cover of the forest had given way to an open field running parallel to the highway, which was clogged with broken-down vehicles—rusted metal reminders of lives that had come to a sudden halt.

The gas station sat at the edge of the field, near the road, its once-bright red exterior faded to a dull pink with the passage of time. Thick weeds punched through the cracked asphalt of the parking lot, and two of the three pumps lay toppled on their sides, resembling ancient grave markers slowly being consumed by the grass. Only one vehicle remained in the parking lot—a white Ford pickup haphazardly parked near a gas pump.

Kira wondered what had become of the driver. Had he left his truck at the pump while he went inside to pay for his gas or grab supplies during the chaos of the viral outbreak? If so, why hadn't he returned?

"We should check it out," Will suggested, nodding toward the gas station. "There might still be something useful inside."

"There won't be anything left," Brack muttered. "Whatever the looters didn't get, the Patrols would have taken back to the city years ago."

"We won't know unless we look, right?" Will glanced at his watch. "Plus, it's lunchtime. I don't know about you, but I'd rather eat inside than out here in the open."

Brack lifted Teddy from his shoulders and set him on the ground. "Whatever, man. Just make sure it's clear first."

Kira knew what Brack meant by "clear."

Make sure there are no dead bodies inside.

Any bodies would be skeletons by now, but Kira still didn't love the idea of eating lunch with them.

As they approached the entrance, a flicker of movement caught Kira's eye. She glanced up at the power lines stretching along the highway. Thick vines had overtaken the wires, causing them to droop toward the ground. A lone red-winged blackbird perched on one wire, its wings extended as it preened the dirt and parasites from its feathers. As they passed beneath the line, the bird tilted its head to one side, its beady eyes briefly tracking their progress before resuming its grooming, indifferent to the five humans intruding on its world.

Just outside the entrance, they gathered around a squat white machine with two metal sliding doors. The red letters beneath the doors had long since faded, so Kira could make out the ghostly outline of the word *ICE* in block letters.

Will tugged at one of the doors, but it wouldn't budge.

"You think you're going to find ice in there, Foster?" Brack chuckled. "No electricity, remember?"

Will ignored him, continuing to struggle with the rusty

door until it finally gave way with a metallic screech that sent the blackbird flapping away into the distance.

Kira placed a hand on his shoulder and peered inside the cooler. The inside was stale and musty, and she realized this was probably the first time anyone had opened the doors in more than a decade. Dozens of empty plastic bags littered the bottom of the machine, each still tied shut.

"I thought it'd be filled with water," Kira said. "Old, nasty water, but water."

Will pointed at the bottom of the cooler. "There's probably a drain underneath. Whatever water didn't leak out would've evaporated years ago."

For reasons she couldn't quite explain, the sight of those shriveled plastic bags made Kira's heart ache. Not so long ago, people would have stopped at this gas station to grab a bag of ice for a weekend getaway, having no idea that their world was on the brink of disaster. Before the barricade, people had taken everything for granted—the power grid, the abundant food supply, the ice in their drinks. All of it so tenuous. So fragile. Humanity had existed on the razor's edge of extinction, completely unaware of how precarious their situation truly was.

Then, in a matter of weeks, a virus swept across the globe and snatched it all away. Now, all that remained of that old world was a bunch of empty plastic bags at the bottom of a cooler.

Brack clapped his hands. "Come on, Foster. We're wasting daylight staring at a broken cooler. Let's do a quick sweep inside, make sure it's clear, and then we'll eat."

"Sounds good."

The two men headed for the gas station's main door.

"I'm coming with you," Kira blurted out before she realized

what she was saying. Her feet moved on their own, carrying her toward the entrance.

Both men turned to stare at her, surprise evident on their faces.

"No," Brack said firmly. "You and Grace stay outside with Teddy until we call for you."

Kira straightened her back, trying to project confidence. "Grace and Teddy can wait outside, but I'm coming with you. Three people are better than two. If something goes wrong, you might need help."

What am I doing? What am I trying to prove?

Brack raised an eyebrow. "It's a deserted gas station, Liebert. The worst thing we're going to find is the skeleton of the attendant slumped over the cash register."

"Exactly. So, there's no reason for me to wait outside." Kira turned to Will for support. "Right?"

Will looked like he would rather shoot himself in the foot than let her go inside, but he also knew she wouldn't back down easily. "Fine," he conceded. "But let's make it quick."

Shaking his head, Brack turned away and pulled his pistol from his belt. He grabbed the handle of the station's main door and yanked it open. The stiff hinges groaned with a high-pitched squeal—an almost human sound that made Kira flinch and stumble backward into Grace.

"It's okay," Grace whispered, steadying her with a firm grip on her shoulders. "Anything that could hurt you is long dead. Just keep your pistol aimed at the floor. Don't point it at anything unless you mean to kill it."

Brack positioned himself in the doorway, holding it open with his body as he aimed his pistol into the darkness. He nodded at Will, who slipped past him, raised his rifle, and disappeared into the shadows.

Grace held the door to keep it from swinging closed as Brack entered the store, heading in the opposite direction from Will. Both men moved swiftly and silently, their movements well-practiced from clearing countless buildings in Emmitsburg.

Kira pulled the pistol from her hip. With the gun in her shaking hands, she felt both dangerous and absurd at the same time.

"What do I do?" she whispered to Grace.

"They both turned, so you go straight ahead," Grace replied. "Just remember to keep your gun aimed at the floor. And please, try not to shoot my husband."

With a gentle nudge from Grace, Kira stepped inside the gas station.

Chapter Eleven

The interior of the gas station was shrouded in darkness, with only faint light filtering through the grimy windows. Time-worn signs advertising hot dog lunch combos clung to the glass, but most had peeled away, leaving large expanses of exposed, filthy glass. A thick layer of grime coated the floor, obscuring whatever color the tiles had once been. Mold crept up the walls behind the main counter, a patchwork of green and black streaks weaving a sickly pattern. The entire place reeked of dampness and decay—like a long-forgotten basement—but at least it didn't smell of human decomposition. If anything had died here, it had done so a long time ago.

Kira stood just inside the door, beside a set of wire racks that had once held newspapers. Only one remained on the bottom shelf, its pages yellow and brittle with age. She resisted the urge to touch it, fearing that it would disintegrate in her hands. But the bold headline was still visible:

IS THIS THE END?

Kira sensed rather than saw the vague shapes of Will and

Brack moving through the darkness, their movements fluid and silent. She tried to imitate them, heading for the aisles in the center of the store, but her steps were clumsy and loud in comparison with the quiet, gliding motions of the guys.

At the center of the store, rows of toppled shelves formed a jumbled maze of broken glass and twisted metal. She awkwardly climbed over one, the unfamiliar weight of the gun in her hand making her movements even more cumbersome.

Just as she reached the end of the aisle, a muffled sound caught her attention. It came from a closed door behind the store's main counter, where customers once lined up to pay for their gas and snacks.

Will appeared at her side, his eyes locked on the door.

He'd heard it, too.

The main counter was in disarray. The glass cases that once held cigarettes were shattered and empty, and the cash register was missing. The only evidence of its existence was a frayed wire that hung off the counter like a dead snake.

Steeling herself, Kira followed Will behind the counter. The floor was empty—no sign of the mummified remains Brack had suggested they might find. Kira's grip tightened on her gun as Will positioned himself in front of the door, his hand reaching for the metal doorknob.

The wooden door, like everything else in the store, was rotting and covered with mold. There was no lock. She leaned closer, straining to hear any sounds from within, but there was nothing.

Will turned the doorknob, and the door swung open.

Light filled the room, far brighter than the gloom she'd grown accustomed to in the store. She raised her hand instinctively, squinting as her mind raced to make sense of its source. Could there still be power in this back room? An old generator that somehow still worked?

No. That was impossible. Any generator would've run out of gas years ago.

"Will? Where is that light coming from?"

Before he could answer, her eyes adjusted, and she realized the light was natural, streaming in from a half-open door at the far end of the room. A rear exit that opened into the back parking lot. The door swung lazily in the breeze, letting in sunlight and fresh air. Long-dead leaves had blown in, forming a crunchy brown carpet near the exit. The warmth of the sun on her skin was a stark contrast to the store's chilly interior.

She let out a nervous laugh. The sound she'd heard was just the door's noisy hinges.

Will turned to grin at her. "For a second there, I thought—"

A large shape charged out of the shadows toward them.

Kira gasped and fumbled to aim her Glock at the thing—whatever it was—her finger curling around the trigger and applying pressure. But just as she was about to shoot, Will stepped in front of her with the rifle, blocking her line of fire.

Ice-cold terror shot through her, and she snatched her finger away from the trigger.

All she saw were colors—tan, brown, and white—blending into a solid, charging mass.

A loud snort cut through the air.

Kira screamed as her legs tangled beneath her, sending her crashing to the ground. She fell backward out of the room, landing hard on her backside. The pistol slipped from her grasp and skidded away on the grimy floor.

I almost shot him.

I almost shot Will.

She lifted her head to see a dark silhouette framed in the doorway she'd just fallen through. But it wasn't a man.

It was a white-tailed deer.

A buck—a *big* one—with massive antlers that could gore her to death and hooves that could trample her.

Running footsteps rang out behind her, and the deer lifted its head, its coal-black eyes locking onto what it perceived as its next threat.

Kira turned to see Brack standing at the end of the counter, his eyes bulging, and his pistol dangling uselessly from his right hand.

Will stepped out of the office, his hunting rifle aimed at the buck's throat, his finger steady on the trigger.

"Shoot it, Foster!" Brack shouted.

Kira squeezed her eyes shut, bracing for the loud crack of the rifle. But there was only silence.

She opened her eyes.

Everything seemed to move in slow motion. The buck snorted, lifting a hoof, a mist of liquid spraying from its dark nostrils, and then it launched itself into the air. The animal seemed almost weightless as it soared over Kira's head, its coat a blur of white and brown, its white tail streaming behind it like a banner.

Brack scrambled out of the way as the deer landed inches from where he'd been standing, its hooves clattering on the tile floor. "Foster! What are you waiting for?"

But Will still didn't fire.

Not even when the deer bounded toward the nearest window and crashed through the glass.

Kira scrambled to her feet, grabbing a rack of cheap sunglasses for support. She stumbled toward the shattered window, dreading what she might find outside. Would the animal be lying dead in a pool of blood, or would it still be alive and suffering? Something had stopped Will from pulling the trigger when the buck loomed over her, but now he would have no choice.

But when she looked out the window, the deer wasn't on the ground.

It stood among the shards of glass, its glossy eyes fixed on the broken window. There was no sign of blood or injury on its body. No indication that it had harmed itself with its daring leap through the window. As Kira watched, it lowered its head, displaying its massive antlers, as if daring them to come outside and face it on its own turf.

Then, with a final snort and a flick of its tail, it bounded off into the woods.

Chapter Twelve

"Did you see that rack? I counted eight points."

Brack sat on the floor, legs stretched out in front of him, a half-empty can of kidney beans in one hand. For the past half hour, he had alternated between excitement over the size of the deer and frustration at Will for not shooting it so they could have eaten it for lunch.

Grace lounged nearby on a pile of flattened cardboard boxes, inspecting an overripe blackberry for any stray bugs. Aunt Reeva had included the berries with their food supplies, and they had divided them up for lunch. Satisfied that it was bug-free, Grace popped the berry into her mouth. "You're exaggerating, as usual. I only saw four points. Four measly little points."

"Four points?" Brack's spoon hovered midway between the aluminum can and his open mouth. "Remind me, Tumblebug, did you come face-to-face with that beast inside the gas station? Because I did. It practically jumped into my arms. I could feel its breath on my face. I think I got a better look at it than you did."

"That may be true, but you've also got a knack for embell-ishment." She smirked and reached for another berry. "Remember last year when you claimed to have pulled a fifty-pound catfish out of the Susquehanna, only to have it slip out of your hands and swim away?"

"At least fifty pounds," Brack muttered. "How else do you think it got away?"

Near the entrance of the storage room, Will and Kira sat cross-legged, their knees touching, an old can of French-cut green beans between them. They took turns scooping out spoonfuls of watery beans, washing them down with sips of lukewarm water from their bottles.

Teddy had already finished his meal—pinto beans and blackberries—and was now playing with six toy cars he'd found under a toppled rack. His new bear—Randy—was propped up against a shelf, watching Teddy with its one good eye.

Kira wrinkled her nose at the spoonful of green beans. Cold green beans weren't high on her list of favorite vegetables, but then again, she had never been a fan of the fresh green beans sold by the vendors at the Broad Street Market in Vita Nova, either. Those were always too tough and fibrous for her taste. Emma had once told her that the workers in the Agricultural Sector often harvested the produce before it was fully ripe, but Emma was also notoriously picky.

Emma.

Kira stirred the remaining beans with her spoon, studying the faded label as if it held an answer she desperately needed. The thought of her best friend languishing in the Confines brought on another wave of guilt. While she sat here, enjoying a simple meal with her boyfriend, Emma was likely going hungry. Prisoners were given food, but it wasn't anything like what Emma was used to.

"Are you okay?"

She looked up to find Will watching her.

"Yeah," she replied, forcing a smile. "I think I'm still rattled by that deer. The way it charged at us." Her voice trailed off, and she shuddered at the memory of the animal's white underbelly sailing over her head. "I can't believe it survived that leap through the glass."

"You'd be surprised how tough those things are."

Will pulled out his pocket knife, its dark blue handle worn from years of use, and used it to slice through a green apple. One of the last pieces of food he'd managed to smuggle out of Vita Nova before the start of his Final Week. Sunlight from outside glinted off the blade as he handed Kira a slice.

She took it, their fingers brushing. "Why didn't you shoot it?" she asked, genuinely curious. "You had the rifle in your hands, and you're an amazing shot. It would've been easy."

Will lowered his eyes, fiddling with a tiny string protruding from the hem of his pants. "Because you were right there," he finally admitted, pulling the string until it broke. "I didn't want you to watch it die."

She stared at him, the apple slice forgotten in her hand. "But I already know you hunt for food. There's nothing wrong with that."

Will raked his fingers through his messy hair. "Yeah, but it's more than just hunting. When you take a life, even for survival, it changes something inside you." He paused for a moment before continuing. "It's never easy to see something die, especially if you're the one responsible. No matter how many times you do it, no matter how much you tell yourself it was necessary, there's always a part of you that wishes it could've gone another way."

Kira had no idea what to say. She didn't understand how watching Will shoot a deer could change how she felt about him. But she sensed there was more to his reluctance—something deeper he wasn't saying.

Will broke the tense silence. "I'm not hungry anymore," he said, passing the apple slices to her. "You can have the rest."

"But you hardly ate anything."

He unzipped his rucksack and stuck his spoon inside. "I had plenty. I wasn't all that hungry to begin with."

Kira watched him closely, trying to read between the lines, trying to figure out what he wasn't telling her. And then, before she could stop herself, she blurted out the question that had been nagging at her since they left Emmitsburg. "Will? What are we really looking for out here?"

He held her gaze for so long that she thought he might actually tell her the truth. But then he blinked and shook his head. "You know what we're looking for, Kira. We're looking for a safe place."

"But you pushed for going north," she pressed, trying to keep her voice steady. "I remember how it went down. We talked about heading west, toward Pittsburgh, but you kept steering the conversation back to north. Why?"

"Kira—"

"Is it because the last group went north?" And then, before she could stop herself, she asked, "Was there someone in that group? Someone you're looking for?"

Will's mouth fell open, and that was all the confirmation Kira needed. Her gut feeling had been correct.

He was looking for someone.

Someone who wasn't Kira.

Deep inside her chest, something broke.

After a few moments, Will pushed himself to his feet. "We can talk more later, but right now, we need to keep moving, or we'll end up camping here tonight."

"Will, please," she pleaded, looking up at him. "Just talk to me."

He hesitated, his hands clenched into fists at his side, and Kira waited for him to say something. To give her the answers she so desperately wanted, even if it hurt.

But then he swallowed hard and shook his head.

"I'm sorry, Kira."

Then he walked away.

Chapter Thirteen

Kira walked with her head bowed, the golden light of the setting sun stretching her shadow across the abandoned tracks. Wild purple asters sprang up around her, their delicate fragrance filling the air. She tried to focus on counting the wooden ties beneath her feet, but her thoughts kept drifting back to Will. Every step took her farther from Vita Nova, the only home she'd ever known.

And she was doing it for Will—a man she wasn't sure she could trust anymore.

A hand gripped her upper arm, startling her. She looked up to find Grace beside her, but the young woman's eyes were fixed on something ahead.

"Look!" Grace whispered, pointing down the tracks.

Kira followed her gaze and saw a massive raccoon wrestling its way out of the tangled vegetation at the edge of the tracks. Once free, it lumbered onto the railway, positioning itself squarely between Will and the rest of the group.

The others froze, staring at the creature that blocked their path, but Will kept walking, oblivious to what was happening behind him.

"Aww!" Teddy bounced on Brack's shoulder. "A raccoon!"

"Quiet," Brack growled under his breath.

Teddy stopped bouncing and hugged Randy.

Kira opened her mouth to scold Brack—it was just a stupid raccoon, after all, not something truly dangerous like a bear or a wolf. But she hesitated. Something about the animal was off. Growing up behind the barricade, the only wild animals she had encountered were birds, chipmunks, and the occasional gray squirrel. But she'd seen enough pictures in books to know what a raccoon was supposed to look like—fluffy fur, a masked face, an adorable little bandit.

This one was anything but.

The raccoon staggered in slow, erratic circles, hissing and growling, its mouth foaming with thick, white saliva. Blood seeped from deep scratches on its face, darkening the clumps of matted fur. It clawed frantically at the ground with blackened paws, as if trying to escape the viscous liquid oozing from its eyes.

The stench of disease and decay hit Kira's nostrils, making her stomach churn. What was wrong with the animal? Had it been caught in barbed wire and gotten an infection? Or had it been mauled in a fight with another animal? And why—despite being smeared in blood and gore—did it show no fear of the humans standing in its path?

Grace answered her unspoken question.

"Careful, Brack. That nasty thing's rabid."

"Thanks, Tumblebug. I figured that out."

Rabies. The word conjured images of bats, not raccoons. She knew little about the disease, except for one thing: without prompt medical treatment, it was almost always fatal. The realization sent a fear coursing through her as she watched Brack and Teddy, still frozen on the tracks, with only a few feet separating them from the snarling, foaming creature.

Grace grabbed Kira's elbow, and they backed away, clambering over the next set of tracks.

"Are rabid animals aggressive?" Kira whispered.

"Some are. Some aren't," Grace said. "But raccoons are meaner than junkyard dogs on a good day. And this one is definitely not having a good day."

The raccoon lowered its head, sniffing at the railroad ties as it wobbled unsteadily, inching closer to Brack and Teddy.

Grace cupped her hands around her mouth. "Brack! Don't let it get too close!"

"Tumblebug..." Brack muttered. "Do we shout around rabid—?"

Before he could finish, the raccoon lunged at him, spittle flying from its mouth. It swiped wildly at his legs with its sharp claws, barely missing him. Brack let out a high-pitched yelp and hopped back a few steps, nearly toppling over with Teddy in his arms.

In that split second, Kira's mind filled with a horrifying image: Brack falling to the ground, landing on his back, and before he could scramble to his feet, the rabid animal sinking its teeth into his soft flesh...and into Teddy's.

By some miracle, Brack managed to stay upright.

But the raccoon wasn't finished yet. It charged again, snarling, now just a few feet away, and moving faster than any sick animal should. Driven by a single purpose: to pass its death sentence onto someone else.

The uneven railroad ties made it difficult for Brack to move quickly, and with Teddy perched on his shoulders, he struggled to maintain his balance. The boy slipped to one side, and Brack had to lurch to keep him from falling, the sudden shift almost sending them both crashing to the ground.

The raccoon closed the distance between them.

"Brack!" Kira cried. "Watch out!"

A deafening crack shattered the silence of the forest. The rabid animal came to an abrupt halt, as if it had struck an invisible barrier. It slumped onto its side, its legs going rigid in the air. A small red dot blossomed in the matted fur just below its neck, blood seeping into the gravel between the railroad ties.

Kira lifted her eyes from the raccoon and saw Will standing a few yards away, rifle in hand, his expression cold and unyielding. He met her gaze, and in that moment, he seemed like a stranger—nothing like the Will she'd first met in her office back in Vita Nova. That Will had been sweet, funny, and mischievous. But this Will—the one she was only beginning to know outside the barricade—was different. He was stronger, quieter, and more dangerous. The kind of man who could kill a rabid animal with a single shot without hesitating.

This, she realized, *is the Will who survived a month alone in the Unregulated Zone after his parents were murdered.*

This is what he meant back at the gas station.

He tore his eyes away from hers, as if it hurt him to look at her, and continued walking down the tracks.

They continued on in silence, leaving the dead raccoon where it had fallen.

THE GROUP HAD HOPED TO COVER A MILE EVERY THIRTY TO forty minutes on their first day, considering the weight of their gear and the uneven terrain. Kira had thought it a cautious estimate, but their pace turned out to be much slower than planned. An hour-long lunch break at the gas station, countless bathroom stops for Teddy, and the raccoon encounter had all eaten away at their time. By seven o'clock, they had covered less than ten miles and were already searching for a place to camp for the night.

Leaving the tracks behind, they ventured onto the highway and found themselves in the blink-and-you'll-miss-it village of Wagner. The small town offered little more than a smattering of small businesses: a gas station, a dollar store, an auto repair shop, and a long-abandoned Chinese restaurant called The Hot Wok.

A faded sign on the restaurant's window displayed a mouthwatering plate piled high with fried rice and crispy noodles.

Brack's eyes lingered on the image. "We sure could use a meal like that right now," he said. "Think there's anything left inside?"

Grace tugged him toward the door. "Worth a look, don't you think?"

While Brack and Grace—and Teddy, still perched on Brack's shoulders—disappeared into the Chinese restaurant in search of long-expired rice, Kira and Will continued another quarter-mile down the road to the crumbling parking lot of the dollar store. A few sun-bleached vehicles sat abandoned in the lot, their faded paint peeling away. A sign in the store's front window hung askew like a crooked grin, boasting cheap prices and a wide selection of food items.

Kira broke the uneasy silence. "They might be right about the prices, but I bet the selection is pretty lousy by now."

Will managed a smile at her weak attempt to lighten the mood. Avoiding her gaze, he knelt and pulled a flashlight from his rucksack. "Try to be quick," he said, handing it to her. "Grab anything useful—canned food, batteries, medical supplies. As much as you can carry."

She stared at him. "You're not coming with me?"

Will kept his focus on tightening the drawstring of his pack. "Do you want me to?"

Yes, she wanted to shout. The thought of walking through a dark and abandoned store alone—especially after the gas station incident—filled her with dread. Why would Will ask her to do such a thing? But instead of arguing, she reminded herself that she wanted to be useful on this journey. She wanted to be like Grace, not a helpless city girl who needed her boyfriend to protect her. "No, I'm good," she said, trying to keep the fear out of her voice. "I can handle it. But what are you going to do?"

Will stood, slinging the rucksack over his shoulder. "We've got less than an hour before dark. The highway's pretty clear around here—not as many abandoned vehicles as there were in Emmitsburg." He nodded toward a used car across the road, where a dozen vehicles sat in a row, their window markings smeared and unreadable. "Before I drove the disposal vans, Jonesy taught me how to work on them—and how to hot-wire them. Keys aren't an issue. If I can get one of those vehicles running, we might not have to walk tomorrow."

"But won't the batteries be dead?"

"Probably." Will rubbed his eyes, looking more exhausted than she'd ever seen him. He gestured to a squat building farther down the road. "But there is an auto repair shop over there. We might get lucky and find a battery with some charge left."

"Maybe." Kira thumped the heavy flashlight against her thigh, struggling to find something else to say. She turned toward the dollar store. It looked darker than the gas station. More rundown. "Well, good luck out here."

She began walking toward the store when Will's voice stopped her. "You know what? Maybe I should check it out with you. It'll only take a minute. Besides, if there's any kind of deadly or dangerous animal living in there, I'm sure you'll try to fight with it."

In different circumstances—if Will had been honest with her at the gas station and eased her fears—Kira would have gladly accepted his offer. She had no desire to explore any of these decaying buildings alone. But Will's evasiveness about his real motives for this trip had shattered her trust, leaving her with something to prove.

If Will found the person he was looking for, he would be done with Kira. She would be on her own. Just as her mother had been after Kira's father left—alone and unable to rely on anyone but herself.

She turned slightly, just enough to speak over her shoulder without looking at him. "I'll be fine," she said, keeping her voice light and airy. "You worry about getting a car running, and I'll be back in a few minutes with more dry pasta and toilet paper than you can shake a stick at."

Another weak attempt at humor was met with silence.

"Be careful," he said. "If anything seems off, get out of there."

What do you care? she wanted to say. *You're just going to leave. Like they all do.*

Instead, she forced a smile and said, "You got it."

Then, with a quick wave over her shoulder, she headed for the store.

Chapter Fourteen

The dollar store, like the gas station before it, was a hollow shell of its former self. The metal shelves, long since stripped of essentials, stood barren and rusted, clinging to their empty frames. Though the shelves hadn't been toppled like those at the gas station, there was nothing useful left—no food, no toilet paper, no clothing, no medical supplies. Not even a pack of bandages had escaped the frenzy of looting that followed the viral outbreak.

Yet Kira scoured every aisle with her flashlight, unwilling to overlook anything that might have fallen from the shelves. She examined every inch of space, from the grimy floor to the stained drop ceiling. Shards of glass glinted in the faint light seeping through the store's dirt-encrusted front windows. The air inside the store reeked of dust, decay, and mildew, and she instinctively pulled her jacket sleeve over her nose and mouth to block out the smell.

All that remained was junk—outdated daily planners, half-melted birthday candles, expired makeup kits, peeling scratch-and-sniff stickers, coloring books, old maps, and forgotten

Halloween decorations. Useless things, remnants of a world that no longer existed.

She considered grabbing a superhero coloring book for Teddy—he adored superheroes—but she couldn't find any crayons among the items strewn on the floor. What good was a coloring book without crayons?

Before leaving, she checked behind the counter, hoping other looters might have overlooked something valuable. But the low shelves beneath the cash register yielded only an old stapler, a few dried-up markers, and an empty tape dispenser—nothing worth taking.

As she turned from the counter, the tip of her boot nudged something that rattled as it rolled away. Crouching down, she aimed her flashlight at the source of the noise and saw two bottles of generic aspirin on the floor. She picked them up and examined them. One was open and half-full, the other sealed. She tucked both into her rucksack.

At least she wouldn't leave empty-handed.

Kira straightened up and headed for the front entrance, her meager treasures in tow. But as she pushed the door open, a thought struck her—she hadn't checked the storeroom.

There had to be one. Every store had a place to keep overflow stock.

Raising her flashlight, she scanned the rear of the store. The beam settled on a door she hadn't noticed before—a swinging door with a small, square window. No light shone through the glass, suggesting the room had no windows.

She made her way down the center aisle, the store growing darker as she left the front windows behind. Broken glass crunched beneath her boots, the noise sending an unseen army of mice scurrying for safety. Kira let out a little yelp and froze, listening to the sound of tiny claws skittering across the tile floor.

When the noise finally subsided, she hurried to the door, determined to search the storeroom quickly and leave. She stood on her tiptoes to peer through the small window, but saw only darkness. Pressing her flashlight against the window didn't help much; she could only make out the vague outlines of what might be boxes.

Taking a deep breath, she pushed the door open, the rusty hinges screeching in protest. She propped the door with her body and aimed her flashlight into the room, half-expecting to see the glowing eyes of a nocturnal creature.

But there were no animals.

Only boxes. Lots of them.

Plastic bins and cardboard boxes, varying in shape and size, were stacked in a small tower in the room's center, as if someone had deliberately placed them there.

Kira stepped inside, letting the door close behind her, and approached the boxes, her heart pounding with cautious hope.

The first box she opened contained individually wrapped rolls of paper towels and yellowed packs of toilet paper. Another held cleaning supplies, hand sanitizer, and bars of soap. She covered her mouth to stifle a squeal of joy. Real soap! She hadn't bathed with actual soap since leaving Vita Nova. She picked up a wrapped bar and inhaled its faint floral scent.

Moving on to the next set of boxes—hard plastic bins with lids—Kira pried the top off one, and the bar of soap slipped from her hand, thudding onto the floor.

She didn't bother to pick it up.

The bin was filled with canned goods. Dozens of them. Super-sweet corn. French-cut green beans. Italian-diced tomatoes. There were even cans of an odd canned potato salad Kira had never heard of. Two other bins held more cans of various sizes, some with labels, others without.

Another smaller box was filled with luxuries Kira hadn't

seen in years: bags of potato chips, breakfast pastries in single-serve packets, and a bulk-sized pack of gummy candies. All long-expired, of course, but treasures nonetheless. These were things that no longer existed in this world, not even in Vita Nova.

Why would such valuable supplies be left untouched in an abandoned store? They didn't appear to have been picked through by looters—no looter would leave behind gummy candies or potato chips, expired or not. Was it possible that no one who had previously ransacked the store had thought to check the storeroom?

Possible, but unlikely.

The storeroom was the most obvious place to check for hidden supplies.

Besides, the boxes had been carefully packed, organized, and arranged in the center of the room, as if someone had deliberately put them there. Someone who intended to return.

The realization dulled Kira's excitement. It wasn't right to steal someone else's food stash. But then again, whoever had gathered this food had likely stolen it themselves. It wasn't fair for someone to hoard so much while Kira was trying to feed a hungry child and a pregnant woman.

They could be dead.

As soon as the idea occurred to her, Kira clung to it, refusing to let it go. Yes, that had to be it. Whoever packed these supplies must be long dead by now. Why else would they leave such precious items unguarded? If Kira didn't take the food, it would rot or be devoured by the store's resident rodents.

All while Teddy and Grace grew weaker.

That settled it. Kira dropped her rucksack to the floor and knelt beside it, setting the flashlight down so that its beam bounced off the opposite wall, providing just enough light to see. Crawling over to the box of canned goods, she began stuffing them into her pack, knowing that when it was full, she'd have to find the others and share the load. Food was their most urgent need—she didn't bother with the cleaning supplies or the toilet paper—but she slipped two bars of soap into her bag, the idea of washing away the grime of the past few days too tempting to resist.

With her rucksack now loaded, Kira heaved it onto her shoulders, grunting under the strain. She knew immediately that she'd packed too much. If she tried to hike with this much weight, she doubted she'd make it a mile before collapsing. But she had to try—there was no telling when they would find more supplies.

Just as she turned toward the door, she realized she'd forgotten the flashlight. Pivoting back, her foot nudged it, causing the beam to swing around and illuminate a part of the storeroom she hadn't noticed before.

The dull yellow light revealed a row of cots, three of them lined up side-by-side with blankets and pillows.

Kira's hand flew to her mouth.

Someone lives here.

Chapter Fifteen

Every one of Kira's instincts screamed at her to run, to bolt out of the suffocating darkness of the store and into the safety of daylight. But her body refused to obey. She stood rooted in place, staring in disbelief at the heaps of discarded men's clothing strewn across the floor between the cots. Filthy jeans, riddled with holes. Socks, once white, now brown and stiff with dirt. Shirts reduced to rags, bearing faded logos of sports teams whose players had likely succumbed to the virus years earlier.

The Lawless.

Kira tried to push the thought away. Her father had invented the concept of the Lawless to scare people into staying within the walls of his barricaded city. They weren't real.

But the cots are real, her mind argued. *The clothing is real.*

Maybe they were decent men, like Will and Brack. Men who would share their food with strangers.

But the stifling, musty room filled with dirty clothing and hoarded supplies didn't feel like the domain of decent men.

Perhaps it was intuition—or something deeper, something

Will and Aunt Reeva might attribute to God—but Kira knew with certainty that whoever lived in this storeroom would be enraged if they found her taking what was theirs.

I'll put it back. I'll just put it all back.

And then I'll leave.

Yes, that was the safest option. Returning the food wasn't just the right thing to do; it was her only choice. She would replace everything, slip out of the store, and never breathe a word to the others about what she'd found.

But just as Kira started to shrug off her rucksack, a new smell invaded her nostrils—one that hadn't been there before.

The unmistakable stench of unwashed bodies.

She glanced at the cots. Could the smell be coming from the discarded clothing? It seemed possible—no human being could possibly smell that bad—but why hadn't she noticed it earlier? That foul odor should've hit her the moment she entered the storeroom.

Her answer came in the form of a sound—the screeching of old hinges.

Someone was coming.

Kira dove behind the boxes of toilet paper, her fingers shaking as she fiddled with her flashlight, desperately searching for the off switch. She finally managed to turn it off, plunging the room into darkness.

The silence that followed was endless.

Kira squeezed her eyes shut and prayed to hear Will's voice. She'd been gone so long—it only made sense for him to come looking for her.

But that awful smell—it was getting stronger.

Will?" she squeaked, her voice barely audible, like the frightened cry of a mouse.

Then a deep voice—eerily similar to the one that haunted her nightmares—spoke up in the darkness.

"I can be Will, if that's who you want me to be."

Kira clapped a hand over her mouth to stifle a scream.

Laughter followed—a high-pitched, maniacal cackle. Another voice added, "Where there's a will, there's a way."

No. No. No. No.

The scream died in her throat. Her hand remained frozen over her mouth, but she no longer needed it.

She wasn't even breathing anymore.

"Do you think she's playing hide-and-seek with us, Frank?"

"She might be. Girlie must know we like games. We've got a few of our own to play whenever she's ready, don't we, Chet?"

"Oh, we sure do."

A new voice, colder and more menacing than the other two, cut through the darkness. "We've got excellent night vision, young lady. You develop it by living in the dark the way we do. So, if you don't want Chet here to put a bullet in that pretty head of yours, you better come out from behind those boxes and show yourself."

Kira's frantic mind raced for options. She had a pistol on her hip. She could fire blindly into the darkness, hoping to hit something. But the men would shoot back, and she feared their aim would be far more precise.

Her escape options were just as grim. The door leading back to the main store was blocked by the men, and even if there was a rear exit somewhere in the storeroom, she had no idea where it was. Even if she found it, they'd shoot her down before she made it outside.

Her only chance was to come out of hiding and try to explain herself. Maybe the men were just angry because she'd tried to steal their supplies. Maybe she could reason with them.

Slowly, Kira rose to her feet, revealing herself to the men.

"Good decision. Now, take that gun off your hip and place it on the ground. Same with the flashlight. Do it carefully."

She did as she was told, setting the flashlight and pistol down at her feet.

"Good. Drop your bag and put your hands in the air."

She let the rucksack slide off her shoulders and thud onto the floor, the cans inside clanging against each other, betraying her secrets to the men.

"Please," she whispered. "Don't shoot me."

The steady voice responded, "Go ahead, Frank. Turn it on."

A flashlight beam seared her vision.

Kira cried out in surprise, raising an arm to shield her eyes. As she blinked away the bright spots from her vision, she peeked under her arm to see three pairs of legs in frayed pants and scuffed boots. She focused on those legs, praying they wouldn't step any closer.

Not being able to see the men's faces had been horrible. But as her eyes adjusted to the light, she lowered her arm and realized that seeing them was so much worse.

Three filthy men with thick beards stood before her, their skin browned from years spent under the sun. Their tattered clothes matched the rags lying on the floor between the cots, and their boots were wrapped in duct tape, probably to keep the soles from falling apart.

The one holding the flashlight—Frank—was even more muscular and menacing than Brack, with a snake tattoo winding around his thick neck and slithering up onto his bald head. Another had a long blond ponytail and a grotesque overbite, which he emphasized with a leering grin. The third man had greasy hair and cold, dark eyes.

But it wasn't their appearances that terrified Kira the most. It was the rifles slung over their shoulders and the assortment of hunting knives strapped to their belts.

The Lawless are real. Kira's heart pounded as she looked

from one man to the next, each of them the embodiment of her worst nightmares. *They've always been real.*

Two more flashlights clicked on in the other men's hands. They propped them on the nearest box, with the beams aimed at the ceiling.

The added light did nothing to ease Kira's fears.

She almost wished it were still dark.

The one with the blond ponytail squinted at her, then nodded approvingly. "Not half bad, is she?" he said, revealing himself as Chet, the one with the cackling laugh. "I've seen and done much worse out here."

The man with the greasy hair—*their leader*, Kira realized—glared at her, strands of oily hair falling across his face. He brushed the hair aside with a grimy hand, his eyes locking onto Kira's rucksack. "What's in the bag? Open it and show us."

A tiny seed of hope sprouted in Kira's chest. Maybe this was just about the supplies. Maybe if she apologized and returned the food, they would let her go.

"What are you waiting for?" Frank growled, stroking the snake on his neck. "Didn't you hear what Rufus said? Do it. Now."

Kira knelt and began pulling cans from her rucksack, lining them up on the floor next to the box. "I'm so sorry," she stammered. "I didn't realize the food belonged to anyone. I just thought... I got lucky."

Chet's laugh echoed in the storeroom. "Oh, you're about to get lucky, sweetie."

Frank's eyes narrowed into dark slits, like the snake's pupils tattooed on his skull. "Everything in this room belongs to us, girlie," he said. "And now that you're here, so do you."

Chapter Sixteen

Kira knelt on the ground as the three men formed a tight circle around her, blocking her exit. The stench of sewage, body odor, and stale smoke clung to them like a second skin, and their eyes gleamed with a vile mix of desire and contempt.

She fixed her gaze on the man with greasy hair—Rufus. "Please. All your food is still here. I haven't taken anything. Just let me go."

"Let you go?" The bald one—Frank—scoffed, a twisted grin spreading across his face. "Why would we want to do that?"

"Because I haven't wronged you."

"You're trespassing in our home." Rufus knelt in front of her, leaning in so close that his breath—a sour mix as foul as his body—assaulted her nostrils. He picked her Glock off the floor and tucked it into the waistband of his belt. "Your friends are out there right now, trespassing in our town, taking what they want, leaving nothing for us."

In her shock at encountering the Lawless men, Kira had momentarily forgotten about the others. Brack and Grace were at the other end of town, but Will wasn't far away. She couldn't take on all three men alone, but if she screamed loud enough, Will might hear her.

Rufus pointed an accusatory finger at her. "I know what you're thinking, but calling for help won't save you. If you scream and your friends come running, we won't kill you. Not right away. Instead, we'll dispatch them one by one as they come through that door. All of them. The pregnant woman. Even the kid."

Kira didn't doubt for a second that these men would follow through on their threats. "I won't scream," she said, her voice trembling. "Just leave the others alone. Please."

Frank ran a hand over his bald head, his eyes sweeping over her body in a way that made her skin crawl. "What's your name, girlie?"

She didn't bother lying. What was the point?

"Kira."

"Mmmm. And where do you come from?"

What would happen if she told them the truth? That she was from Vita Nova, the mayor's daughter, and now a fugitive on the run? Would these Lawless men even care about her father's position? Doubtful. Victor Devlin's name held power in Vita Nova, but out here in the Unregulated Zone, it meant nothing.

"I escaped from the city," she blurted out.

Frank exchanged a quick look with the other two men before turning his attention back to Kira. "The city, huh? You mean Harrisburg?"

She nodded.

"Why'd you leave a nice place like that? Didn't like all the fireworks?"

Kira shook her head. "Not really."

"We've dealt with those city soldiers before, you know," he

said. "We keep our eyes peeled, report back on what we see, and in return, they give us food and even weapons. They ain't like any soldiers I've ever known. The stuff they do out here..." He paused, clicking his tongue on the roof of his mouth. "Girlie, it would make your blood run cold."

Kira said nothing. She didn't want to know what Frank was referring to, and she wasn't about to ask. She'd seen enough of the Patrol soldiers to have an idea.

"So, what's the real reason you ran?"

He was trying to trick her into giving information away because information was power. Kira understood that, just as she understood that it was currently the only weapon she had. As long as she kept the men talking, they weren't hurting her. She might just be able to buy herself enough time for Will and the others to show up.

"Because it wasn't safe for me there. I upset the wrong people, and they were going to kick me out anyway. That's why my friends and I are out here. We're just trying to find a safe place, far from the city."

"A...safe...place?" Rufus repeated her words slowly, as if they were foreign to him. "You should've stayed where you were. There's nothing left out here in the wilderness. Nothing but misery and death."

"It doesn't have to be that way," she said. "You don't seem like bad people. There's no reason our groups can't work together. Help each other survive."

Frank laughed, the snake tattoo on his neck appearing to slither with the movement. "You think we need your help to survive? We've managed just fine on our own. Rufus, Chet, and I—we're nomads. Always drifting, going wherever the wind blows us, never staying in one place for long. Wherever we lay our heads, that's our home until we move on. And we will defend our home to the death. So, it's a real pity that you and your friends tried to take what's ours."

"But we haven't taken anything," Kira insisted. "We were just passing through, looking for supplies in the empty shops. We didn't know anyone lived here. But now that we do, we'll leave. If my friends took anything, I'll make them put it back. We'll go right now and forget this place ever existed."

Frank shook his head. "I wish it were that simple. Problem is, we can't let people think they can steal from us and walk away. Otherwise, they might come back and do it again. That's why the punishment has to be severe." He took a step closer to Kira. "We need to make sure you never forget us."

A story from childhood flashed through Kira's mind—Goldilocks and the Three Bears. She remembered the basics: a little girl breaks into a cottage, eats the bears' porridge, sits in their chairs, and sleeps in their beds. But how did it end? Did Goldilocks escape? Did the bears adopt her?

Or did they eat her?

Frank glanced over at Chet. "What's the penalty for trespassing in our town?"

Chet's overbite jutted out as he grinned. "Ooh, it's pretty steep."

Frank turned back to Kira with a cold, cruel smile. "The only question is, are you willing to pay the whole price yourself? Or should we make your friends share it?"

Kira's heart sank. These men had no intention of letting her go. No matter how much she apologized, begged, or reasoned with them, they would do whatever they wanted to her.

And then they would kill her.

She wanted to scream for Will. He was her only chance. But if he came running, the men would hear him and gun him down the moment before he could reach her. She had no doubts about that.

She couldn't watch Will die.

Nothing these men could do to her would be worse than that.

Aunt Reeva's words echoed in her mind. They'd been walking behind the church in Emmitsburg when Kira pointed out a patch of beautiful purple wildflowers.

"Asters are hardy little things," Aunt Reeva had said. "To look at them, you might say they're pretty but dainty. Maybe even a little weak. But God, in His wisdom, designed them to survive."

If Aunt Reeva's God had designed flowers to survive—flowers that bloomed and died in months—surely He had designed Kira to survive as well.

"Come on, honey," Frank said. "It's better for everyone if you don't fight us."

Kira clenched her fists, her fingernails digging into her palms. She was a city girl from Vita Nova. She didn't know the first thing about survival. She didn't know how to fight off one man, let alone three.

But she would learn.

"I'm not afraid of you." Kira recognized the truth of the words as soon as they left her mouth. "I feel sorry for you, actually. You're pathetic. You choose to hurt people when you could be helping them."

Frank's smile faltered. He hadn't expected defiance. "You're going to regret saying that."

Kira held her ground, her heart hammering in her chest. She knew that showing fear would only feed their cruelty, and she refused to give them that satisfaction. "Maybe," she replied, her voice steady, "but when this is over, I'll still be able to look at myself in the mirror. I'll always know that, even when the world fell apart, I didn't use that as an excuse to become a monster like you."

Rufus closed the distance between them in three swift strides, grabbing Kira's arm and yanking her to her feet. His stench was overwhelming—sour dirt, cigarettes, and stale breath all rolled into one vile package that made her gag.

"That wasn't a very nice thing to say," he growled.

Kira clawed at Rufus with her free hand, but his iron grip only tightened, his hand clamping around her elbow like a vice. Frank rushed forward, grabbing her other arm, his uncut nails biting into her skin. Together, the two men forced her arms behind her back.

Rufus hooked his arm through hers, holding her tightly against his body. "I got her, Frank. She's not going anywhere. You can let go."

Frank released her arm and stepped back, his eyes flat and lifeless, like a shark's. "Got some spunk in you, huh?" He grinned as he slid a dirty finger down Kira's cheek, chuckling as she flinched. "That's okay, girlie. I like a feisty woman."

Not like this, she thought, panic rising. *I didn't escape the city just to die like this.*

With a fierce cry, Kira stomped down hard on Rufus's foot. Pain shot through her ankle, but she barely registered it as Rufus let out a grunt and his grip on her loosened—just enough.

Seizing the opportunity, she wrenched her right arm free and drove her elbow into his gut. Rufus doubled over, wheezing, greasy hair falling over his face, but his other hand remained clamped on her arm.

Not for long. She grabbed a fistful of his hair and yanked with all her strength.

Rufus howled in pain, releasing her at last.

She was free, but she knew she only had moments before Rufus recovered. She was vaguely aware of the other two men laughing behind her, still blocking the storeroom door. They weren't intervening—just watching, seeming to enjoy the sight of their friend being bested by a girl.

"You sure you got this, Ruf?" Frank taunted.

Kira's gaze dropped to Rufus's belt—to her Glock.

She lunged without thinking, snatching the pistol from his waistband.

Rufus made a wild grab for her, but she staggered back, just out of his reach. Quickly, she spun to face the other two men blocking the door, her eyes darting between them. With Rufus temporarily out of commission, she had to focus on her next biggest threat.

It wasn't hard to figure out.

The pistol trembled in her hands as she aimed it at Frank's chest.

Center mass, she reminded herself. *Just like Will said.*

The men stopped laughing.

"Don't you point that thing at me, girlie," Frank muttered. "Especially if you don't know what you're doing. Put it down, or I'll make you regret it."

"Get out of my way." Kira's voice was steady, unlike her hands. She turned slightly, trying to keep Rufus in her peripheral vision. "Let me out of this room, or I will shoot you right where you stand."

Frank squinted at her as if she were a puzzle he couldn't figure out. "You'll get one shot off, if you're lucky," he said. "For your sake, it better be a good one."

She steadied the gun with her left hand and aimed at the spot on Frank's chest where his heart should be—if he had one. "I'm not going to tell you again."

Frank opened his mouth to respond, but his eyes shifted past her to Rufus.

Kira risked a glance over her shoulder and saw Rufus still doubled over, clutching his stomach.

Her relief was short-lived.

Footsteps pounded behind her, and she spun around just in time to see Chet barreling toward her.

She pulled the trigger.

The bullet struck Chet in the shoulder, spinning him around like a rag doll. He crashed into a pile of boxes and sprawled onto the floor. Blood gushed from a hole below his left shoulder, quickly turning the front of his shirt black.

He slapped a hand over the wound, his face contorting in agony as blood leaked through his splayed fingers. "She shot me, Frank!" he screamed. "Get her!"

Kira turned just in time to see Frank charging at her like a linebacker. Before she could react, he slammed his fist down on her wrists, sending the pistol clattering to the floor, where it vanished into a pile of discarded clothes.

"Get over here!" Frank barked.

She dodged his grasp and bolted for the door. The exit was clear. No one was blocking it.

This was her only chance.

"Stop her!" Rufus roared.

But she was almost there. She was going to make it!

Kira flung herself through the doorway, only to collide with something solid. Something that hadn't been there a moment ago.

The impact sent her reeling backward, but then someone caught her arm, keeping her from falling.

Will. Relief surged through her. *Thank God, it's Will.*

But when she looked up, her breath caught in her throat—she was staring into the cold, unforgiving gaze of a fourth Lawless man.

Chapter Seventeen

The man wore black from head to toe, the lower half of his face obscured by a handkerchief, leaving only his sharp, penetrating eyes visible. Those eyes studied Kira with an intensity that suggested he was no stranger to situations like this. One arm held her firmly against his chest, while the other gripped a double-barrel shotgun, its cold steel glinting in the dim light.

Kira's body went limp against him, the fight draining out of her as she realized her one chance of escape had slipped through her fingers. She hadn't even considered that another member of Rufus's gang might be waiting outside the storeroom, and she had sprinted right into his arms.

The storeroom door swung open.

"Stay behind me," the man in black commanded, pushing Kira behind him. He leveled the shotgun at her three attackers.

Frank was the first to burst out of the storeroom, coming to an abrupt halt when he found himself staring down the twin barrels of the shotgun. His eyes flicked nervously from the weapon to the man holding it. The other two men followed quickly, nearly colliding with Frank as they stumbled through the doorway.

"What is this?" Frank sputtered, his hands slowly rising in a gesture of surrender. "Who are you?"

The man in black kept his finger on the trigger, his other hand steady on the pump. "Get out."

His voice was gritty, like sandpaper scraping across stone, and it stirred something deep inside Kira. Not quite a memory, but the shadow of one. The feeling of cool afternoon air, the sting of wind and water lashing at her skin, and the sound of her mother's laughter.

Still clutching his bleeding shoulder, Chet glanced at Rufus. "What did he say?"

"You heard me. Get out."

Frank's mouth twitched into a nervous smile, and he made a calming gesture with his raised hands. "Now, let's not be hasty, friend. We don't need to fight over her. I'm sure we can come to some kind of deal where we—"

The man in black fired his shotgun at the ceiling, sending buckshot pellets into the tiles and raining debris down on the three men. They ducked, shielding themselves from the falling plaster, though Chet struggled to do so with only one functioning arm.

In one swift motion, the man in black pumped the shotgun and aimed it directly at Frank's forehead.

"Leave."

The single word was spoken with a cold, calm authority that carried more weight than any scream or threat could have. It was the voice of someone who had nothing left to lose— someone who had killed before and wouldn't hesitate to do it again.

Kira realized in that moment that the man with the shotgun was as dangerous as the three Lawless men, if not more so.

Yet, strangely, she wasn't afraid of him.

That voice, Kira thought. *How do I know that voice?*

Frank swallowed hard, his Adam's apple bobbing. "You've already wasted one shot, friend, which means you've only got one left. In case you can't count, there are three of us."

"Yes, but the next shot is going inside your head, friend." Without taking his eyes off Frank, the man whispered over his shoulder to Kira. "Lift the back of my jacket."

She did as he asked, revealing a handgun tucked into a holster on his waistband. It wasn't exactly like her Glock—this gun had an external safety and a hammer—but Will had taught her enough about guns to understand how to use it.

"Take it," he said. "Shoot if you have to."

Kira pulled the gun from its holster, flicked off the safety, and cocked the hammer. With Frank covered by the shotgun, she aimed the pistol at Rufus's chest.

Frank let out a dry laugh. "You think he's going to protect you, girlie? Look at him—he's just like us."

The discordant creak of old hinges echoed through the aisles as the front door of the store swung open.

"Kira? Are you in here?"

"Will!" Her legs nearly buckled at the sound of his voice. Just moments ago, she was certain the three men in the storeroom were going to murder her, but now Will was here. She was safe. "I'm at the back of the store!"

Footsteps pounded down the center aisle.

"Are you okay? I thought I heard…" Will came to a halt as he rounded the corner, his eyes widening at the sight of the four men, all tense and armed. He raised his hunting rifle, shifting the barrel from one man to the next. "Kira? What's happening?"

She bolted toward Will, and he wrapped his free arm around her, pulling her tight against his chest. "Those three tried to attack me," she muttered into his shoulder, the pistol hanging loose in her grip. "But that man with the shotgun helped me."

Will gestured at Chet with his rifle. "What happened to that one's shoulder?"

"I shot him."

He squeezed her tighter. "Good job."

Kira watched as resignation dawned in her attackers' eyes. They were outmatched, facing three guns instead of one. The fight had drained out of Chet along with his blood, and Frank looked like he was itching to put as much distance as possible between himself and the double-barreled shotgun.

But not Rufus.

He was their leader for a reason, and he wasn't going to back down so easily. His narrow eyes blazed with hatred, locked on Kira as if he could burn her alive with his stare.

She pulled away from Will and leveled the pistol at him.

Frank rubbed the snake tattoo on his neck. "Look, there's no point in us killing each other when the world's already in the toilet. How about we call a truce for today? You can have this store. We'll just grab our gear from the back and be on our way."

"Your stuff stays. So do your weapons."

Rufus finally tore his eyes away from Kira to glare at the man in black. "You can't do that."

"I just did."

Deep crevasses appeared on Frank's bald head, like the earth splitting open during a seismic event. His fingers hovered over the collection of knives on his belt. "Which weapons?"

"All of them."

Behind him, Chet turned even whiter, either from blood loss or fear. "You can't do that. It ain't right to hamstring us and send us out there without—"

"You heard me," the man in black growled. "Drop your weapons on the ground before I put all three of you down like the dogs you are."

It wasn't an empty threat. He would do it. Kira could hear it in his voice.

So could the Lawless men.

Moving slowly, they began pulling knives from their belts and dropping them on the floor. It took Chet twice as long as he struggled to empty his sheaths with only one good hand. Once they were disarmed, the three men made their way to the front of the store, with Chet bringing up the rear.

As Rufus passed Kira, he muttered, "I'm going to make sure you regret this."

The man in black kept his shotgun trained on the men until they disappeared into the waning light outside. When the door closed behind them, Kira let out a shaky breath and lowered the pistol. Her legs were trembling so badly she wasn't sure they would hold her up much longer.

But she didn't need to worry because Will set his rifle down and pulled her into his arms.

Chapter Eighteen

Kira watched over Will's shoulder as the man in black walked down the aisle toward the entrance, his eyes scanning his surroundings with a practiced wariness.

Will pressed a gentle kiss to her forehead. "Are you okay?"

She nodded against his chest, although she was shaking uncontrollably and thought she might be sick. But she was alive and unharmed.

Thank you, God.

Will retrieved his rifle with one hand, the other still wrapped protectively around Kira. "I'm so sorry," he said, guiding her up the center aisle. "I should never have let you come here by yourself. I don't know what I was thinking."

"Nothing happened, Will. I'm fine."

As they reached the front of the store, the man in black turned from the door and tugged down the handkerchief, revealing a ruggedly handsome face framed by a square jaw dusted with scruff. He appeared to be in his mid-to-late forties; the dark brown hair he wore was cropped close to his scalp and streaked with the first threads of gray. Everything about him—from his corded muscles to his slightly crooked nose—conveyed barely contained violence. The kind of violence born from surviving too long in the Unregulated Zone.

And then there was the scar.

A disfiguring, jagged scar ran from the corner of his left eye to his jawline. An angry arrow of flesh that cut across his cheek like a compass rose, adding a dangerous edge to his already-intimidating features.

Kira found her voice. "Thank you for what you did. If you hadn't intervened..." She trailed off, unwilling to finish the thought or imagine what might have happened.

"It was stupid to search this place alone." His eyes bored into hers as if trying to peel away her secrets by force. The longer Kira looked at him, the more she realized it wasn't just his voice that was familiar.

It was also his face.

This man. She felt like she *knew* him.

How could that be possible? No one from Vita Nova ever left the city, and she didn't know anyone from outside the barricade except the people she'd met in Emmitsburg.

So, how could she know him?

The man seemed to sense her confusion and looked away. "What were you thinking, coming in here? Don't you know where you are?"

Heat rose in Kira's cheeks. "Of course, but I didn't realize—"

"She made a mistake," Will cut in, pulling his arm from Kira's shoulder and stepping in front of her. "We both did. We appreciate what you did, but she doesn't need a lecture."

The man's gaze hardened as it shifted to Will. "What she needs to do is go back to wherever she came from. Both of you do. And take the rest of your group with you. This is no place for a kid. You won't survive the night."

A coldness spread inside Kira, twisting her gut in its frosty grip. "Why did you help me?"

The man answered without meeting her eyes, his attention still focused on Will. "I've been tracking your group since the gas station, trying to figure out who you are and what you're doing out here. None of you knew I was there, and I had no intention of revealing myself. But then I saw you walk in here by yourself, like you didn't have a care in the world, and I knew who lived here." He shook his head and ran a hand over his close-cropped hair. "Those three were nothing compared to the people you'll run into out here. You're all way out of your depth."

Kira took a step closer to him. "What's your name?"

He stared at her for a long moment, then almost absently touched the scar on his cheek, tracing its jagged path. "Everyone calls me Ghost."

A wave of dizziness swept over Kira, and she reached for a nearby shelf, gripping the rusted metal until it bit into her palm.

Will's voice reached out to her. "Kira? Are you alright?"

Ghost's face swam back into focus, and Kira thought she saw concern etched onto his features. But it disappeared as quickly as it appeared. "I'm fine," she lied, forcing herself to take slow, deep breaths. "Just a delayed reaction to what happened in the storeroom."

"Please," Will said. "We need your help. We're trying to find a safe place. Somewhere far away from Vita Nova."

"You're from that city?"

"Yes. We're both from Vita Nova. We escaped a few—"

"Harrisburg," Ghost interrupted, his eyes flashing with

anger. "Vita Nova isn't real. Everything about that city is a lie. It was always a lie."

"We know," Will said. "That's why we left."

Ghost ignored him, his attention back on Kira. "What's your last name?"

She wiped the sheen of sweat from her forehead, her mind sluggish and slow to respond. "Liebert."

At the sound of her name, Ghost's eyes widened, and he took a small, almost imperceptible step away from her. He studied her face, the anger in his eyes softening, replaced by something that looked like sorrow.

"What about your family?" His voice was barely a whisper. "Did they leave with you?"

Kira could see the desperation in the man's eyes, as if his very existence depended on her answer.

"No," she finally managed to say. "I left on my own."

His face fell at her words, his eyes briefly filling with pain before he caught himself and masked his emotions behind a neutral expression.

And then Kira understood.

This scarred man who had saved her life. This man who seemed so strangely familiar.

He knew her.

Chapter Nineteen

"You really fell backward into this one, Liebert."

Brack knelt on the grimy linoleum of the store-room, hunger burning in his eyes. He rummaged through the totes, inspecting each item of food before tossing it into his rucksack. He paused to flash a grin at Grace, who sat on one of the cots, her arm wrapped around Teddy. "I can't believe those three idiots were sitting on this much stuff."

Kira perched on the edge of another cot, fidgeting with the zipper of her jacket. Her attention wasn't on Brack or the food —it was on the door.

Waiting for the Lawless men to return.

She had arranged flashlights around the room, hoping the light might make her less afraid. But instead of banishing her fears, the light only seems to make the shadows grow, stretching them into something larger.

More menacing.

After Brack, Grace, and Teddy finished combing through the Chinese restaurant, they joined Kira and Will at the dollar store. Brack had carried a half-empty bag of white rice above his head like a triumphant soldier returning with battle spoils. The rice smelled bad and was clearly spoiled, but Brack had taken it anyway.

Will met them in the parking lot and filled them in on Kira's encounter with the Lawless men and the stranger who had saved her. Then he had ushered them into the store and revealed the treasure trove of food Kira had found in the storeroom.

Now Brack's bag of rice lay forgotten on the floor, grains spilling out onto the linoleum.

They had decided to spend the night in the store. Kira didn't love the idea, but what choice did they have? They were all too exhausted to go any farther, and they wouldn't be any safer from the Lawless men outside. At least the store offered food, beds, and a roof.

Plus, Ghost had agreed to stay with them, and she couldn't deny that his presence made her feel safer.

"Pears!" Brack shouted, startling Kira and Grace. He tossed the can in the air and caught it with a grin. "Pears in syrup are my favorite."

Grace yawned. "That's good, honey."

"Do you guys even realize how much food is in this room?" Brack's eyes gleamed as he unearthed a six-pack of plastic soda bottles from one box. A small earthquake shook the box as smaller items tumbled into the space where the soda had been. "There's enough here to feed us for a few months if we ration it."

He twisted the cap off one bottle and took a few swigs before handing it to Teddy. The boy took a tentative sip, wincing at the taste, and then downed half of the bottle.

The soda went to Grace next, but she passed it to Kira without drinking.

Years had passed since the soda was bottled, yet there was

still a hint of carbonation, and Kira closed her eyes, relishing the sensation of tiny bubbles popping on her tongue. The acidic burn of the liquid like fire as it spilled down her throat, evoking memories of pizza parties, movie nights, and a time when the world hadn't yet fallen apart.

She finished it in three swallows.

"Check this out, little man," Brack said, tossing something to Teddy.

The boy's face lit up as he caught a red-and-white-striped peppermint lollipop in his palm. He unwrapped it and stuck it in his mouth, his eyes glazed and dreamy.

Brack handed another one to Grace. "I bet you won't say no to one of these, Tumblebug."

"You know me so well, babe. Thank you." Grace nudged Teddy with her elbow. "What do you say to Brack?"

The boy spoke around the lollipop in his mouth. "Thank you, Brack."

When Brack offered Kira a lollipop, she refused, gesturing to the door. "Why aren't they back yet? What's taking them so long?"

Ghost and Will had gone outside to make sure the Lawless men weren't lurking nearby, waiting for a chance to reclaim their supplies and weapons.

And anything else they might want to take.

Brack reached into the tote and pulled out an old box of toaster pastries. "Relax, Liebert," he said. "Your boyfriend should be back soon, as long as the scarred psycho doesn't kill him." He turned the box over in his hand, as if inspecting a rare artifact rather than stale breakfast food. "Man, I used to love these things. Do you think they're still safe to eat after twelve years?"

Grace shifted the lollipop from one side of her mouth to the other. "Those things will be dryer than dirt by now, honey.

They'll stick to your tongue like sand. Of course, that might not be a bad thing, huh? Could finally quiet you down for a bit."

Brack raised one eyebrow. "You know, I'd take offense to that if I didn't love you so much."

The storeroom door swung open, and Will entered, the hunting rifle slung over his shoulder. He didn't say a word, just leaned against the wall, eyes closed, breaths coming in ragged huffs. The sweat dripped from his forehead as if he'd just finished running a marathon.

"Glad to see you're still alive, Foster," Brack said. "I figured you were as good as dead out there with that guy."

Kira hurried to his side, placing a hand on his chest. His heart slammed against her palm, like a trapped bird trying to escape its cage. "Will? What happened out there?"

He gave her a worn-out smile. "Nothing happened. The old guy just moves really fast. I could barely keep up."

"What old guy?" Ghost muttered as he came through the door. Unlike Will, he was breathing normally and hadn't even worked up a sweat. "You need to do more cardio, son."

Brack chuckled. "Man, that's embarrassing, Foster."

"The town's empty, as far as we can see," Ghost said, shutting the door behind him. "Those three imbeciles who gave you trouble are gone, at least for now. They're probably licking their wounds tonight, or trying to find more weapons. But we'd better set up a fire watch, just in case."

"Sounds good," Kira said, lifting her hand from Will's chest. "Should we have two people standing guard at a time? Is that enough?"

Ghost didn't answer. He was scanning the room, his gaze sweeping from Teddy and Grace, the peppermint lollipops jutting from their lips, to the empty soda bottle on the floor, to Brack in the center of the room, the non-perishable food items spread around him like a buffet. "What do you think you're doing?"

Brack looked up from his box of toaster pastries. "Huh?"

Ghost squatted, so he was eye-level with Brack. "Let me make something clear to you. This isn't your food to give away. It's mine. I risked my life taking it from those idiots, and I didn't do that so you could sit here and gorge yourself."

Without warning, he snatched the box of toaster pastries from Brack's hands and hurled it against the wall.

Brack's eyes bulged, and his face turned crimson. "Are you serious?" he sputtered, leaping to his feet. But instead of attacking Ghost, he crossed the room and retrieved the dented box, clutching it against his chest.

Despite the tension, Kira almost laughed at the absurdity of it all.

Ghost turned to the rest of the group. "The rules are simple. This isn't your food. You don't eat or drink anything except what you brought with you. I'm going to check the roof now. While I'm gone, you're going to put everything back in these boxes exactly as you found it. If you've got a problem with that, we can part ways right now."

Stepping away from the wall, Will crossed the room and gently pried the ruined box of toaster pastries from Brack's grip and placed it back inside the tote. "We don't have a problem with those rules," he said. "We'll put the food back the way we found it. Won't we, Brack?"

There was something in Will's tone that left no room for argument.

Even Brack seemed to recognize it. He took a deep breath and gave a small, reluctant nod. "Yeah, sure. We will."

Ghost grabbed his rifle and cracked open the storeroom door. "I'll be back in a few minutes."

As the door swung shut behind him, Brack grumbled, "That guy's so wound up, he squeaks when he walks."

"He saved my life," Kira shot back, giving him a sharp look. "So, let's try to stay calm, keep our appetites in check, and do exactly what he says with no complaints."

"You hear me complaining, Liebert? The guy destroyed my breakfast, and he's still breathing. I'd say I handled that pretty well."

"We're not in a position to antagonize him, Brack. We need him."

"You think we need a nut job with a scar?" Brack waved the idea away with a thick hand. "Liebert, you're even crazier than he is. Has it occurred to you that a guy who looks like he wrestled a grizzly and lost might not be the best person to team up with?"

"He comes from a safe place," Will said, massaging the back of his neck. "A settlement, not far from here—less than a day's walk. He didn't share too many details, but there are a few hundred people living there. They've got a working farm, a school, and a hospital. When we were outside, he offered to let us stay for a few days until we figure out what we're going to do next. But there's one condition."

"Great," Brack grumbled. "Another dumb rule."

"I don't like rules either," Teddy agreed. "Rules are dumb."

"What's the rule?" Kira asked.

"We have to go in blindfolded."

"Blindfolded?" Grace echoed. "That's a little creepy, don't you think? Why does he want us blindfolded?"

"So we can't find it again after we leave."

A heavy silence descended over the storeroom, broken only by the soft smacking sounds of Teddy licking his lollipop.

Kira glanced from one face to another, trying to read their thoughts. "What do you think we should do, Will?"

"I think we should go with him."

Brack took a deep breath and let it out slowly. "Just hold on a minute. We have other options. We're not desperate. Yeah, we've had a few setbacks today, but it's only the first day. We don't have to put all our trust in some stranger just because he helped Kira out of a tight spot."

Kira gaped at him. "A tight spot?"

"You know what I mean. We don't know what kind of place this guy comes from. What if it's a trap? What if they lure people into their little settlement just to rob them?"

"If he wanted to rob us," Will said, "I'm pretty sure he would've done it already. Plus, we don't have anything valuable. What are they going to take?"

"How about our lives? What if they're cannibals? What if they want to have us for dinner? Have you thought of that?"

Teddy pulled the lollipop from his mouth. "What's a cannibal?"

Grace smiled and kissed the top of Teddy's head. "People with terrible table manners."

"Like, chewing with their mouths open?"

"Exactly like that."

Will's blue eyes darkened as he stared Brack down. "No one's forcing you to go. You're free to head back to Emmitsburg. I'm not going to stop you. But I'm checking out his settlement. That's why we left Emmitsburg in the first place, isn't it?"

"I remember why we left Emmitsburg."

"Good. Then you'll understand why I won't let your fear derail our mission."

Brack's eyes narrowed, and he climbed to his feet, crossing the room with slow, deliberate steps.

Kira moved to intervene, certain the two men were about to come to blows.

But then Brack extended his hand. "We stick together,

Foster. You know that. We might be a dysfunctional family—a seriously dysfunctional family—but we're still a family."

Will's shoulders relaxed, and he took Brack's hand. "Dysfunctional doesn't even begin to cover it."

As they released hands, Brack gave Will's shoulder a firm pat.

"For the record, if I end up covered in ketchup on someone's dinner plate at the end of this, I'm not going to be happy."

A FEW MINUTES LATER, GHOST RETURNED TO THE storeroom and began barking orders.

"You three," he began, pointing at Kira, Teddy, and Grace, "are sleeping on the cots tonight. But this isn't a slumber party. When you're in this room, your eyes are closed. No talking. No flashlights. Nothing. The rest of us will be sacrificing our rest to keep you alive, so show some appreciation by getting some sleep. I want you all up and ready to move at first light. Copy that?"

Kira and Grace exchanged uneasy glances, but Teddy gave the man a little salute. "Copy that."

Ghost trudged to the other end of the storeroom and pushed open a door Kira hadn't noticed before. A gust of chilly night air swept through the room, making the shadows dance across the walls. "You've got the rear entrance," he said to Will. "This is the most secure door in the building. No handle on the outside, and it locks when it closes. Do not prop it open for any reason. I want you outside all night with your eyes on those woods." He gestured at the dark cluster of trees between the dollar store and the river. "If you see anything moving out there—man or beast—shoot it. Copy that?"

Will hesitated, uncertainty in his eyes, but he nodded. "Got it."

"Good." Ghost turned to Brack and handed him the shotgun, slipping a few extra shells into his palm. "You've got the front entrance. Stay inside, and keep your eyes on the parking lot. You're the last line of defense for your friends. If anyone approaches this building, kill them. No questions asked. Can you handle that?"

Brack stared at the shotgun in his hands. "I got it."

"You going to have trouble staying awake?"

"I never do."

"Good." Ghost nudged one of their rucksacks with his boot. "Whatever junk you're carrying in these rucks, ditch most of it. Keep one change of clothes, a few pairs of socks, and any food you brought. Everything else stays behind. We'll be carrying as much of these supplies as we can on our backs tomorrow, so we need to stay light."

"What about you?" Kira asked.

"I'll be on the roof."

The words were barely out of his mouth before Kira found herself moving, drawn by a force she couldn't explain. While the others emptied their rucksacks, she slipped through the door and followed the sound of Ghost's footsteps to the store's front entrance.

"Ghost?"

He paused, one hand on the glass-paneled door, ready to push it open. His head sagged at the sound of her voice, as if her presence were too much to bear. Slowly, he turned to face her. "What do you want?"

Kira ignored the sharp edge in his tone. "Do you want me to come with you?"

She couldn't believe what she was asking, couldn't understand why she was so strangely drawn to this scarred stranger.

The last place she wanted to be was alone on a rooftop with him.

Yet, she felt a desperate need to know him. To find out how he got his scar. And why he seemed so familiar.

"Why would I want you to come with me?"

Her cheeks flushed, and her shoulders rose and fell in a weak shrug. "I thought maybe you didn't want to be alone."

For a moment, the hardness in Ghost's eyes softened, replaced by a deep, unspoken sadness. He seemed to allow her a glimpse of the broken man behind the scars.

But then the moment passed, and his expression turned hard as stone.

"I'm always alone."

With that, he stepped out into the night, the door swinging shut behind him.

Chapter Twenty

They left at first light, heading north along the railroad tracks with Ghost in the lead, setting a punishing pace.

Before they left the store, he had combed through each of their bags, searching for what he called "contraband." Since they were set to reach his settlement before sundown, they left behind tents, sleeping bags, and extra clothing to make room for more nonperishable food. Despite its funky smell, Brack had insisted on packing the white rice, and Ghost had finally relented.

It was a small victory, but victories were hard to come by in the Unregulated Zone.

Kira trailed at the rear of the group, keeping her distance from the others. Whether it was lingering anxiety from yesterday's events or the sheer exhaustion brought on by another sleepless night, every step was a struggle. She was dizzy, as if she'd spent the previous night spinning on a carnival ride rather than trying to sleep. As the cool morning air surrendered to another hot day, sweat seeped from her pores, making her clothes cling to her skin like plastic wrap.

Maybe I'm getting sick, she thought. *Maybe I'm getting the Job virus, and I'm going to die out here.*

No.

She shook off the thought. The virus was gone. There hadn't been any documented cases in years. Besides, she hadn't slept much. Only a few minutes here and there before nightmarish visions of Lawless men jolted her awake. She would bolt upright, gasping for air, convinced that the three men had returned under the cover of darkness, sneaking into the store through a hidden entrance, armed with more knives.

Coming back to reclaim their supplies.

And Kira.

By the middle of the night, she had given up on sleep entirely, rolling onto her side to stare at the dim outline of the store's rear exit. The thought of Will outside all night by himself, separated from the rest of them by a locked door, gnawed at her. He had no backup. No one to help if something went wrong.

Her tired mind conjured gruesome images of Frank sneaking up to the store, the blade in his hand gleaming in the moonlight as he raised it above his head. Will's face twisting in agony as the man buried the knife in his back.

But the night had passed without incident, and Will and Brack returned to the storeroom just before dawn, disheveled and exhausted but alive.

Kira limped along the tracks, doing her best to keep up with Ghost's pace. Her right ankle, swollen and throbbing, had barely fit into her hiking boot. On top of that, large blisters had formed on the backs of both of her heels from the previous day's march, twin hot spots of agony that burned whenever her boots rubbed against them.

As the wooden railroad ties passed beneath her feet, Kira tried to imagine what Ghost's settlement might look like. She pictured a quaint town straight out of a Norman Rockwell painting. White picket fences, tree-shaded streets, cozy cottages, and gardens overflowing with vegetables and flowers. A small corner market stocked with fresh meats and vegetables, all raised and grown in the settlement. The villagers would gather there, shopping and gossiping for hours. There would be a school where children—too young to remember the world before the virus—would learn of it in the classroom. Afterward, they would play in the streets until their parents called them home for dinner.

A tiny slice of heaven in a fallen world.

There would be no blue roses. No Reverence Ceremony. No fireworks. No Rolling Meadows. No Compulsory Clinic. No government-sponsored population control programs. In the settlement, death would come naturally and peacefully. The dead would be properly buried in a cemetery, not cremated and shot into the sky, or discarded like garbage into an unmarked burial pit.

She envisioned Ghost's home as a charming farmhouse perched high on a hill, strategically positioned to watch over the town and protect it from harm.

Soon, she told herself, allowing her sleep-deprived mind to drift deeper into the fantasy. *Only a few more hours, and we'll be safe.*

Her water bottle was missing.

She didn't realize it until the group stopped for lunch around noon. Despite feeling headachy and a little sick to her stomach, she forced herself to eat an expired granola bar and a can of peas, the mixture of salt and sugar intensifying her thirst. But when she reached into the side pocket of her rucksack, searching for her water bottle, it wasn't there. To be sure, she checked the other side pocket, but it was empty, too.

As the others prepared for the final leg of the journey, hoisting their rucksacks onto their shoulders, Kira frantically dug through her pack, shoving aside cans of fruit and boxes of stale breakfast pastries, praying she'd somehow misplaced the bottle in her rush to leave the dollar store that morning.

But it wasn't there.

I must've left it back at the dollar store, she realized, her heart sinking. *It's gone.*

Kira pressed a hand to her throbbing head, her thirst growing more insistent by the second. Under her fingers, her skin was hot and itchy, but she wasn't sweating anymore.

She wasn't sure if that was a good thing.

For a moment, she thought about telling the others she'd lost her water bottle. Brack would be annoyed with her, but it wouldn't be the first time she'd aggravated him. And someone— most likely Will—would surely share their water with her.

But she couldn't bring herself to admit it. She'd been a liability for most of the trip, stumbling from one dangerous situation to the next, and her pride kept her silent.

So, as the group set out again, Kira said nothing.

The morning gave way to the afternoon, and with it came the worst heat of the day.

Kira lagged at the back of the group, struggling to keep the dwindling forms of Brack, Grace, and Teddy in sight. The trio was at least thirty yards ahead, and Will and Ghost were even farther away, nothing more than dark smudges fading into the bright green of the forest, their lead increasing with every step.

The others didn't turn around to check on her as often

anymore, but Kira didn't blame them. They were likely absorbed in their own misery.

Kira had no idea what the temperature was, but if she had to guess, she would've placed it somewhere in the upper eighties. Too high for late September. Such heat and humidity would've been uncomfortable in Vita Nova, but out here in the Unregulated Zone—without the benefit of ice, electricity, or fans—it was unbearable.

Thirst continued to take its toll, sapping her energy and slowing her progress. Her throat was dry and scratchy, her lips cracked and peeling, her tongue glued to the roof of her mouth like a dried leaf. Swallowing what little saliva remained in her mouth did nothing to ease the fire that raged in her throat. It only made it worse, teasing the possibility of relief but offering none. Every part of her body ached, and the dull pain in her head had sharpened into a blinding headache that made it difficult to think.

The world around her started to tilt and sway, colors bleeding into one another until they became little more than bright smears in her vision.

Just a little farther, she told herself. *All I need is a little water and a good night's sleep, and I'll get both at Ghost's settlement. Just keep moving a little while longer.*

She ran a hand across her forehead, but when she glanced at her palm, it was bone-dry. Why wasn't she sweating anymore? Her skin was unnaturally hot and inflamed. She brought both hands to her cheeks, pressing her fingertips into the skin.

Her cheeks were on fire.

Was she running a fever? Was she getting sick?

The thought sparked a sudden, desperate longing for her mother. For the gentle touch of someone who loved her unconditionally. She remembered being sick as a child, running a fever so high that the thermometer felt like ice against her skin. She remembered her mother leaning over her bedside, a reassuring smile on her face as she pressed a cool washcloth against Kira's forehead.

It's okay, sweetheart. Just close your eyes and try to rest. I'll be right here all night.

A soft cry escaped Kira's throat, but no tears came.

She wiped her dry eyes, her gaze shifting to Grace and Brack. The couple continued to increase their lead on her, but something was wrong with them, too. They didn't look normal anymore. They were blurry and translucent, like ghosts gliding along the tracks. Blinking didn't help. It only made things blurrier and sent needles of pain stabbing through her eyes.

Swallowing her pride, she called out to the others.

"Hey!"

The raspy sound that slipped through her lips wasn't even close to a shout. It barely qualified as a whisper, and the others were too far ahead of her to hear it.

Okay. I just need to catch up.

She broke into a light jog, her arms pumping at her side. She wasn't going to break any world records, but at least she was gaining on the others.

The tip of her boot caught on a railroad tie, and she stumbled, nearly falling. By some miracle, she managed to catch herself before she took a nasty tumble onto the tracks.

Shouting won't work. Neither will rushing to catch up. I'll just have to wait for someone to look back.

Then it hit her—the river. It was right there. All the water she could ever want was just down the embankment a few yards away. There was no reason she couldn't slip down there, drink her fill, and climb back up to the tracks before the others even noticed she was gone. The water might not be the cleanest, but it probably wasn't dirty enough to make her sick. If she could just get a little water in her system, she'd feel a million times better, and she'd be able to finish the day without slowing everyone down.

She scrambled down the embankment toward the river. The land fell away sharply from the tracks, and negotiating the uneven, gravelly terrain wasn't as easy as she'd imagined, especially with her legs refusing to work properly. Her boots skidded on the slick gravel, and she grabbed onto a low-hanging branch to steady herself. But the branch was dead and brittle; it snapped off in her hand. She lost her footing and went down hard on her bottom, sliding toward the river's edge.

She didn't end up in the river, thankfully, but what felt like five pounds of dirt and gravel had worked their way into the depths of her boots. Even through her socks, she could feel the sharp pebbles digging into her skin. She'd have to remove her boots to clean them out, which would cost her more time.

But that could wait.

Right now, she needed water.

Badly.

Jagged rocks jutted up from the middle of the river, like broken fingers from an ancient statue. Kira imagined herself sprawled on one of those islands, water rushing past her on all sides, spraying cool mist onto her overheated skin. The river didn't look deep here. If she waded out to one of those islands, the water probably wouldn't reach past her chest.

But Kira had enough experience with the Susquehanna to know that its calm surface could be deceiving. The swift undercurrents, invisible from above, were always there, waiting to grab hold of someone's legs and drag them down to a watery grave.

She remembered the day she'd jumped into the river, and how her body had betrayed her. Her legs had stopped working, no matter how hard she'd tried to move them, and her lungs had forced her to take a breath. But instead of inhaling air, she'd inhaled mouthfuls of brackish, ice-cold water.

If she lived to be sixty, she would never forget what it felt like to drown.

Tearing her eyes away from the islands—she wouldn't risk swimming out to them, no matter how tempting they looked—she dropped her rucksack to the ground with a heavy thud.

As she approached the edge of the river, the musty scent of the water grew stronger. She couldn't wait to scoop some into her parched mouth. Crouching down, she cupped her hands together and dipped them into the water.

The first time she brought her hands to her lips, most of the water missed her mouth, splashing against her nose and cheeks, cooling her hot skin before soaking into her shirt.

But as she bent forward, cupping her hands to try again, her head dipped toward the water, and her vision blurred. Her body tipped forward, passing the point of no return. She was a ship in danger of capsizing, and she knew—in a distant, detached way—that going to the river alone had been a terrible mistake.

Warmth flooded her body, starting in her shoulder and spreading through her limbs, washing away her concerns. But instead of resisting, she surrendered to it, letting the warmth carry her out of this world of pain, death, and misery to somewhere different. Somewhere better.

And then the warmth overwhelmed her, and she tumbled into the river.

Chapter Twenty-One

Kira drifted in a strange, watery darkness, her mind tangled in a fog that made it difficult to distinguish between what was real and what was a dream.

For a time, she was in her old bedroom in Vita Nova, her mother curled up beside her in bed, still wearing the hospital gown and gray socks with treads on the bottom that she'd been given in the Compulsory Clinic.

But then something shifted, and she was no longer in the water. She was moving—no, she was being moved. The sensation was disorienting, as if the world had tipped sideways, throwing her off balance. There was pressure under her arms and under her knees, as if someone were carrying her, and she could feel her body swaying gently with each step they took.

Her head lolled to the side, one cheek brushing against rough, wet fabric. Someone's shirt—soaked through, just like her. Even as she struggled to stay awake and piece together what was happening, the sensation of someone carrying her and cradling her against their chest was strangely comforting.

As her eyes fluttered open, she caught a glimpse of the

world around her. The trees were dark silhouettes against the sky, their branches reaching out like skeletal fingers. The ground was uneven, the landscape blurring in and out of focus as she was carried through it. The coldness of the river clung to her skin, making her shiver uncontrollably, even though she was still hot and thirsty.

She tried to focus, to hold on to consciousness, but it kept slipping away like water through her fingers. The world faded in and out, each moment of clarity swiftly swallowed by the overwhelming darkness that pressed down on her. Dimly, she became aware of her descent to the ground, or perhaps it was a bed, a soft surface beneath her that carried a faint scent of earth and wood. The feeling of being wrapped in blankets followed, their rough texture brushing against her damp skin as someone tucked them around her.

There was movement around her, voices murmuring, but they were too distant to make out. Kira tried to reach out, tried to ask where she was, but her body refused to obey. The effort drained the last of her strength, and she sank into the darkness again, deeper this time, the world slipping away from her.

And then there was nothing.

***

WHEN KIRA'S EYES OPENED AGAIN, THE WORLD materialized in sharp, disjointed snapshots. Flickering light danced across a ceiling of rough-hewn dark wood, the grains and knots swirling like the remnants of her dizziness. The walls, composed of thick logs stacked and sealed with a grainy, off-white substance, seemed to close in on her. The air was thick with the scent of wood smoke, and through the lingering haze of sleep, she became aware of her body—lying on a low bed and draped in scratchy woolen blankets that made her bare skin itch.

Bare skin?

She lifted her head high enough to confirm what she could already feel: her clothes were gone. She wore only an oversized t-shirt and her underwear.

The effort of lifting her head made her dizzy, and the darkness tugged at her once again, urging her to close her eyes and surrender to its soothing embrace. She could feel it like a physical presence, its cold breath chilling the back of her neck as it waited to wrap her in its arms and carry her back to the dark place.

But Kira fought against it, forcing her eyes to open wider, refusing to return to the darkness when she was only partially clothed. As the dizziness passed and her vision cleared, she scanned the unfamiliar room, her gaze snagging on a gold candelabra perched on the windowsill. The metal was old and tarnished, as if it had been pulled from a long-buried treasure chest. Three white taper candles cast their blurry reflections on the glass, creating the illusion that some sort of three-eyed monster was peering in at her.

When she tried to move, a sharp pain shot through her right arm. She looked down to see an IV line snaking out from the crook of her elbow, held in place by a strip of medical tape. She followed the tubing to a nearly empty bag of fluid hanging from a metal pole.

A surge of adrenaline sent her heart racing, clearing the fog in her mind just enough to leave her with a single, urgent thought:

Where am I?

Her gaze returned to the candelabra, following the trail of melted wax as it oozed into the drip pan. A significant pool had already formed, leaving Kira to wonder how long the candles had been burning.

And how long have I been asleep?

She recalled leaving Wagner with the others, lured by the promise of shelter at Ghost's settlement. Somewhere along the way, she had realized her water bottle was gone. She'd probably left it on her cot in the storeroom, as she couldn't remember drinking anything after the dollar store. Too ashamed to admit her mistake to the others, she had endured the oppressive heat and humidity until dehydration set in.

Desperate, she'd gone down to the river for a quick drink. The last thing she remembered was losing her balance and falling into the cold, rushing water.

Kira's eyes darted around the room, studying her surroundings. The room was small and sparsely furnished. Aside from the bed, there was nothing else—no furnishings, no pictures on the wall. The only door was set in the wall opposite the windows, but it was closed, and she couldn't hear any sounds coming from the other side. A lantern hung next to the door, housing another small candle.

Where was Will? Teddy? Grace? Even Brack would be a welcome sight at this point.

She threw off the scratchy blankets, revealing her legs, pale and disturbingly skinnier than she remembered. Small bandages covered each of her blistered heels.

At the sight of her bandaged heels, her unease gave way to gratitude. Someone had taken the time to care for her wounds.

With considerable effort, Kira forced herself into a seated position, but the room spun wildly and her vision blurred. She held still, wrapping her arms around her knees and resting her chin on her forearm as she focused on the steady flame of a candle. Slowly, the world settled, and as her vision cleared, she swung her legs over the side of the bed, lowering her bandaged feet to the cold wood floor.

Using both hands, she pushed herself into a standing position, but her legs were useless, buckling beneath her weight. She stumbled forward and crashed to the floor, pulling the IV pole down with her. One shoulder slammed into the wall beneath the window, its impact rattling the glass and extinguishing one of the candle flames.

Footsteps echoed outside the room, and before Kira could react, she heard the squeal of unoiled hinges as the door flew open and crashed against the wall.

She grabbed the window frame. The rough, splintered wood bit into her palms as she pulled herself up to her knees, her entire body trembling with the effort. Her Glock was gone, her clothes stripped away, leaving her vulnerable and weaponless. With no other choice, she reached for the candelabra.

It was her only option.

She reached for it, curling her fingers around the tarnished metal base. The flames atop the candles flickered madly as she yanked the candelabra from the windowsill and whirled around, swinging it with all her strength. The two still-burning tapers streaked through the air in a wild, chaotic arc, wax spilling onto the floor, her arm, everywhere.

As the candelabra slashed through the air, Kira caught a fleeting glimpse of a figure—tall, with sharp features and piercing eyes—within striking distance. But before the heavy metal could connect, the figure darted to the side.

The force of the swing carried her off balance, the flames sputtering and dying as the candelabra crashed into the wall and Kira crashed to the floor.

Chapter Twenty-Two

"Whoa! Relax!"

A young woman with smooth, dark skin and almond-shaped eyes stumbled backward away from Kira, her long legs bumping against the bed frame. She threw both arms into the air, a gesture of surrender.

"It's okay! This is a safe place. Ghost brought you here. Remember him? No one is going to hurt you, Kira, I promise."

Ghost.

Kira's hand, still trembling, slowly released its grip on the candelabra.

The woman let out a slow breath, her body visibly relaxing as she wiped a glaze of sweat from her forehead. She looked young, only a few years older than Kira, and she was a natural beauty—dark curls cascading around a narrow face defined by high cheekbones and delicate features. But the most striking thing about her were her eyes. They were a vivid emerald green, naturally wide, and brimming with kindness.

She lowered herself onto the bed's edge, her lips curling into a gentle, hopeful smile—the kind of smile that belonged to someone who had experienced their fair share of hardship but still held onto the hope that everything would turn out okay.

"Who are you?" Kira whispered.

"My name is Bailey." The young woman offered Kira an awkward wave. "You're in our medical ward, believe it or not." She wrinkled her nose at the barebones room. "I know it doesn't look like much, but we do our best to make people comfortable while they're here. I'm one of the nurses—not a real RN or anything, but we don't have many of those around here. Actually," she added with a half-smile, "we don't have much of anything around here. But everyone pitches in and helps out wherever they can. I got this job because I enjoy taking care of people. Speaking of, I bandaged your feet, and I'm working on getting you rehydrated. You're free to stay here until you feel strong enough to leave."

As Bailey spoke, the weight of exhaustion settled over Kira like a heavy blanket, sapping what little energy she had left. Her body longed to sink back into the bed, to surrender to the comfort it offered. Even just sitting up took a monumental amount of effort. But she forced herself to stay awake to make sense of where she was and what had happened.

"Where are my clothes?"

"Everything was soaking wet, so I hung them to dry. In the meantime, I'll bring you something of mine to wear. I think we're close to the same size."

"This place," Kira whispered, her eyes drifting closed. "This is Ghost's settlement?"

"It sure is."

"And how did I get here?"

"That cute boyfriend of yours carried you."

Kira's eyes snapped open. "Will is here?"

Bailey's lips twitched as if she were holding back a laugh. "Of course he is, silly. Where else would he be? I had a heck of a time getting him to leave your side so he could rest. He was pretty spent after carrying you all that way."

Tears welled up in Kira's eyes as she imagined Will—exhausted from a night of no sleep—carrying her limp body for miles through the woods.

"The rest of your friends are here, too. Your group arrived just after suppertime. You were in pretty awful shape. Apparently, you'd collapsed from dehydration and heatstroke."

Heatstroke? Kira vaguely remembered the way her skin had turned hot and stopped perspiring. "Did I have a fever?"

"Your body temperature was dangerously high," Bailey explained. "Ghost and your friends did what they could for you on the way here, but once you arrived, we got some IV fluids in you and cooled you down with wet towels. You were in and out of consciousness the whole time."

Kira ran her tongue over her chapped lips. "What about my friends? Are they okay?"

"They're fine," Bailey assured her. "The couple and the little boy are sleeping down the hall, and your boyfriend is in another room." She gave Kira a playful wink. "He was in here until an hour ago, sitting by your bed and holding your hand. He didn't want to leave in case you woke up, but he kept falling asleep, so I finally told him he needed to rest. He was really worried about you."

Kira brushed away the stray tears from her cheeks, a deep sense of regret settling in her chest. She hated that her own fears and insecurities kept putting up walls between her and Will. He had done so much to prove his love for her—including saving her life multiple times—and yet she still hesitated to give him her whole heart. She knew her trust stemmed from her relationship with her father. It was just one more way Victor Devlin continued to cast his shadow over her life, controlling her even from behind the barricade.

Bailey smiled and placed a gentle hand on Kira's shoulder. "I hope you don't mind me saying this, but you're one lucky girl. Don't break his heart."

"Can you tell him I'm awake?"

Bailey's expression turned stern, her tone firm but kind. "Not for a few more hours," she said, shaking her head. "I'm sorry to be strict, but Will is exhausted, and you're still recovering from a serious condition. You both need to rest. But I promise you'll see him first thing in the morning, okay? Can I help you back into bed?"

Kira wanted to protest, but her body betrayed her. Sleep was already tugging at her mind, and her eyelids were growing impossibly heavy. She let out a small sigh of defeat. "Okay."

Bailey slid off the bed and crouched beside Kira. She slipped an arm underneath her shoulders and carefully lifted her to her feet, mindful of the IV line that trailed from her arm to the pole.

The bed welcomed Kira like an old friend, and she sank into the mattress. She couldn't remember why she had ever tried to leave it.

"You know what? I think it's time we got rid of this IV." Bailey reached for Kira's arm, her fingers gentle as she unhooked the line. "The bag's empty, and if you've got enough energy to swing at me, I'd say you're going to be just fine."

"Okay."

Bailey removed the tape holding the needle in place, then smoothly withdrew the IV from Kira's arm. She dug into her pocket and produced a small bandage, which she unwrapped and placed on the inside of Kira's elbow. "There, all done. How does that feel?"

"Thank you," Kira murmured. "For taking care of me."

"Of course." Bailey tucked the blanket around her with a tender care that spoke of long hours spent caring for others. "I'll grab some of my clothes and leave them inside the door. In the meantime, you need to rest. Everything will be okay in the morning."

"Okay."

Bailey retrieved the candelabra from the floor and set it back on the window sill before crossing the room to the door. She paused at the threshold, one hand resting on the wooden frame as she looked back at Kira. "Welcome to Heaven."

As exhaustion overtook her and her eyelids drooped shut, Kira managed a final, drowsy question. "Heaven?"

But Bailey was already gone, the door clicking shut behind her.

Chapter Twenty-Three

A loud creak nudged Kira awake.

She sat up in bed, blinking away the haze of sleep, her senses gradually coming to life. The room was still dim—dawn had yet to break outside the window—and the faint glow of the lantern near the door cast enough light to reveal that she was alone.

The sound came again—a low, deliberate creak.

She focused on the door, watching as the knob slowly turned.

She cleared her throat, intending to say Bailey's name, but before she could, the door swung open with a soft scrape against the wood floor.

"Kira?"

She recognized the whispered voice immediately, and as its owner stepped into the room, she almost sprang out of bed at the sight of him.

Will's worried expression dissolved into a relieved smile. He ran a hand through his hair, which looked more disheveled than usual, as if he had just rolled out of bed.

"I'm awake," she whispered, sliding over to make room for him on the twin-sized bed. "You can come in."

With great care, he eased the door shut behind him, clearly trying to avoid alerting Bailey. He slid off his boots, leaving them near the door, and then crossed the room in a few quick strikes. When he reached the bed, Kira lifted the blankets for him, but he shook his head and climbed on top of them.

Kira raised an eyebrow. "What are you doing? You can get under the blankets, Will. I'm not going to attack you."

"No way," he replied. "If my mother were still alive, she'd definitely have something to say about me lying under the covers with a beautiful girl. I'm not even sure she'd approve of this."

Laughing, Kira tilted her head back and brushed a hand against his cheek. The rough stubble tickled her palm. "She might change her mind if she knew I haven't bathed in three days."

"You think that matters to me? You're always a little smelly."

She playfully punched him in the arm. "Guess what?"

"What?"

"When Bailey came in earlier, I almost clocked her with a candelabra."

His eyebrows shot up. "Almost?"

"I missed, of course. What else is new? But it's a good thing I did. She's too sweet to pummel."

"That's debatable. She kicked me out of your room."

Kira shifted slightly, pulling back just enough to look into his eyes. They were a deep, vibrant blue, like the Volunteer roses. She had never seen anything so beautiful in her life.

"Do you have any idea where we are?"

"The best I can figure," Will replied, "is that we're in the state gamelands, northwest of Harrisburg. After your...accident, Ghost didn't bother blindfolding us since we were in a hurry to get help. But I'm pretty sure he took us in a few circles to throw us off. It was dark when we arrived, so there wasn't much to see, but we had to trek through a lot of woods to get here, and we passed deer fencing."

"Bailey said you carried me the entire way."

As he exhaled, Will's breath warmed her forehead. "Honestly, I don't remember much about the trip here. I guess the adrenaline kicked in. You looked bad, Kira...I thought you weren't going to make it."

His eyes drifted closed, either to hide the emotions lurking within them or because exhaustion was finally taking its toll. Kira followed his lead, resting her head against his chest and letting her own eyes close.

"I left my water bottle at the dollar store," she confessed, the shame she'd felt on the hike resurfacing. "I should've said something, but I didn't want to slow everybody down. I didn't want to be seen as a liability anymore than I already am."

"Yeah, we noticed your water bottle was missing when we unloaded your pack. I figured you lost it and didn't want to say anything. But no one is upset with you, Kira. And no one looks at you as a liability."

"I know you're tired of rescuing me," Kira said, trying to keep her tone light. "At least you didn't have to perform CPR on me this time."

She meant it as a joke, but Will didn't laugh. Instead, he pulled her closer to him, holding her as if he were afraid to let her go. "I'll never get tired of rescuing you," he said quietly. "I'll rescue you a thousand times if that's what it takes to be with you."

Tears pricked at Kira's closed eyelids. It wasn't *I love you*, exactly, but it was close. And despite the lingering concerns she had about Will and his real motives for this trip, she had the overwhelming urge to tell him she loved him.

But the words lodged themselves in her throat, and she couldn't get them out. "Do you think we're safe here?"

"I think we can trust Ghost," he said. "He saved you back at the store when he had no reason to intervene. If it was just the supplies he was after, he could've easily killed us all and taken them. And if he hadn't brought us here yesterday, I don't know if you would've made it. But..."

"But what?"

"They took our guns. We had to surrender them before they'd let us into the camp."

Kira understood the logic—Ghost wouldn't want armed strangers inside his settlement—but there was still something unsettling about not having any weapons with which to defend themselves. They were completely at the mercy of Ghost and his people.

"Do you think we can trust them?"

When Will didn't respond immediately, Kira opened her eyes to find him staring out the window. The first pale light of dawn had pierced the darkness of the small room, illuminating Will's face and highlighting the lines of worry etched deeply into his brow.

"I don't know," he finally admitted. "But we're going to find out soon enough."

Chapter Twenty-Four

Soon after Will snuck back to his own room, Kira climbed out of bed and got dressed. She slipped off the oversized t-shirt—which she only now realized was Will's—and reached for the clothes Bailey had left in a neat pile by the door: her jacket—clean and dry—along with a pair of khaki pants, a white tank top, and a beige button-down shirt.

And the thickest, most comfortable pair of socks Kira had ever worn.

Her muddy hiking boots waited like a looming threat at the foot of the bed. Even with the protection offered by the thick socks and bandages, the mere thought of sliding them back onto her blistered feet sent a shiver of dread up her spine.

But walking around barefoot all day wasn't an option.

Steeling herself, Kira gritted her teeth and tugged on the first boot. The tight leather scraped against her tender heels, making her wince. The second boot followed, and she exhaled shakily as pain flared through her swollen ankle and raw blisters. But it wasn't as intense as she'd feared. Rising from the bed, she took a few tentative steps around the room and realized that Bailey had done an amazing job bandaging her feet.

The boots didn't rub against her heels at all.

She stretched her arms over her head, trying to get the blood flowing through her sore limbs, then limped over to the window.

Even with the benefit of daylight, there wasn't much to see. The infirmary building was backed up against a dense forest, leaving only a thin strip of land between her window and the towering pines. Stacks of logs filled the small clearing—logs that looked similar to those that made up her room's walls. The smallest pile held only four logs, while the largest stood higher than her window, blotting out part of the narrow strip of cloudless sky. Turning her head, she saw piles of timber stretched out like a maze of wood, with the forest forming a dark, impenetrable wall beyond.

A soft knock drew her attention to the door.

"Come in."

The door swung open with a creak, and Bailey stepped inside, a bright smile lighting up her face.

"Hey! It's great to see you up and about," Bailey said, her eyes taking in Kira's outfit. "Oh, good—you found the clothes. Everything looks like it fits perfectly. If those boots give you trouble, just let me know. You might need a more comfortable pair of shoes until those blisters heal. You can borrow a pair of my sneakers. Can you believe we wear the same size? What are the odds of that?"

Bailey's boundless energy was almost dizzying in contrast to Kira's own bone-deep exhaustion. How did she manage to be so upbeat after what must have been only a few hours of sleep?

"How are you feeling?" Bailey asked. "Did you get any rest after I left last night?"

Kira held back a smile at the memory of Will sneaking into her room and holding her for a few stolen moments. Bailey didn't need to know about that. "Well, I'm definitely not planning on running any marathons on these feet," Kira replied, "but I do feel a little more human today. I'm not sure how much sleep I actually got, though. I was in and out all night."

Bailey slipped her arm through Kira's and guided her out of the room.

The hallway stretched out before her, a narrow spine of rough-hewn wood that seemed to go on forever, the bark still clinging to the logs in patches. Hand-chiseled beams arched overhead, their surfaces marked by the uneven strokes of axes and saws. A dozen doors lined the hallway—six on each side, each slightly different in size and shape.

The wood still smelled faintly of sap.

The building was alive, a living, breathing thing, built with care but rough around the edges, and still as much a part of the forest as the towering pines outside.

"My first night here was rough, too. That was almost eight years ago now, but I still remember it like it was yesterday. I'm originally from York, and before I came here, I was used to long, loud nights filled with awful noises. But I'd learned to sleep through it. The constant sound was comforting, in a way. When things got really quiet, that's when you started to worry. When I first got to Haven, I didn't sleep for a week. The quiet can be overwhelming at first, but you'll get used to it."

Haven?

Kira wanted to ask what Haven was, but Bailey kept talking. "You're going to meet up with Ghost later this morning. But first, though, I'm going to get you breakfast. Are you hungry? I think ham and eggs are on the menu this morning, but I haven't been to the mess hall yet."

The phrase *mess hall* conjured up images of a cold and impersonal military dining facility, where people shoveled food into their mouths as quickly as possible under the watchful eyes of strict drill sergeants.

That wasn't surprising, given what she knew about Ghost.

"Your friends are already waiting outside," Bailey added, gesturing to a door at the end of the hallway. "Oh, and the little boy—"

"Teddy."

"Yes! He's so sweet," Bailey said, opening the door for her. "He's at the playground, running around with the other children."

Kira stepped outside, her breath catching in her throat.

She stood at the edge of a vast, grassy meadow with a gravel road stretching out in front of her. Calling it a road was generous—it was barely wide enough for a small car, and there wasn't a single vehicle in sight. On either side of the road, tiny log cabins—shacks, really—lined up like soldiers, all featuring the same rough logs and sloping gable roofs. Thin tendrils of smoke drifted from their chimneys, twisting and curling before dissipating in the morning air. A series of well-worn paths connected the cabins, carved into the landscape by countless feet rather than machines.

"Incredible," Kira whispered, too low for Bailey to hear.

The previous days had been hot, the air thick with humidity. But overnight, the temperature had dropped sharply, as if September had suddenly remembered its true nature as the beginning of autumn. The oppressive heat had lifted, replaced by a refreshing chill that made Kira grateful for her jacket.

All around her, the world was alive with sound. She could hear the rustling of leaves in the cool breeze, the cacophony of insects hidden in the tall grass, the distinct trilling of crickets who hadn't yet retired their nightly songs, and the low, rhythmic mooing of cattle coming from a distant barn at the other end of the village.

There were no cabins in that part of the village—just the barn and a few smaller outbuildings, surrounded by fenced-in fields.

"It's perfect, isn't it?" Bailey beamed at Kira. "I'm not sure who came up with the name 'Haven,' but it fits. It's always so peaceful here. What do you think?"

Kira nodded slowly, still absorbing everything around her, unable to find the right words. She couldn't believe a place like this actually existed. It was so far removed from her grim imaginings of the Unregulated Zone. While the citizens of Vita Nova crammed onto crowded city buses, saluted Volunteers, and made the long trek to City Island for the weekly Reverence Ceremony, the people of Haven lived a quiet, almost idyllic life.

The two places were less than twenty miles apart, yet they might as well have existed in different worlds.

"It won't be long until we're entirely self-sufficient," Bailey continued, guiding Kira along a second pathway that appeared to wind behind the infirmary building. "We still have to send people out to search for medicine. That's our biggest need. We've lost quite a few people over the years because we didn't have the right medicine. Insulin is a big one. And antibiotics. But we grow all of our own food now. We've got cows, goats, pigs, and plenty of chickens, so we've got more than enough milk and fresh meat. There's a pond down by the farm for the animals, and it's stocked with fish, so we even get fresh fish for dinner occasionally."

As Kira and Bailey stepped around the corner of the building, the path opened up to reveal another cluster of buildings nestled against the tree line.

"This part of the village is where you'll find the common

areas." Bailey listed them off with her fingers. "The infirmary, the mess hall, the schoolhouse, and the church."

Above her were several large rectangular log structures, each significantly larger—and by the looks of it, sturdier—than the little cabins below. To her left was a long building with a small playground area; the ground was littered with wood chips and dominated by a towering wooden jungle gym.

"The school doubles as an emergency shelter. If anything ever happens, get to the school."

Kira looked at her. "An emergency shelter for what?"

"Anything."

At least two-dozen children in tattered jeans and faded t-shirts darted around the playground, squealing with laughter as they engaged in a boisterous game of tag. A group of girls sat under the shade of a sprawling oak tree, their backs pressed against the trunk, each immersed in their own book. Meanwhile, a few of the younger kids clambered over the weathered playset, which featured a clubhouse, four swings on metal chains, a metal slide, and a twisting green tube slide that looked well worn but sturdy.

Kira caught a glimpse of Teddy just as he disappeared inside the tube slide.

Bailey nodded at the playground. "He's settling in nicely. Most kids do. After everything they've been through, they crave normalcy."

Kira watched Teddy race another boy up the playset and down the slide. Teddy had been through so much in his short years. She couldn't help but wonder what tragedies these other children had endured.

When Kira finally tore her gaze away from the school, Bailey pointed out the church, its wooden cross standing tall against the pale blue sky. The church's logs were smoother and its construction more refined than those of the other buildings in the village, suggesting extra care and reverence in its construction.

"We have a church service every Sunday morning," Bailey said. "Not everyone goes, but most do. Have you ever been to church?"

Kira shook her head. "I've been inside a church, back in Emmitsburg, but I've never attended a service. We don't really have any kind of organized religion in Vita Nova." The admission made her feel guilty, as if her city's lack of faith was her fault.

"Will told me about the Reverence Ceremonies," Bailey said. "Where people sacrifice their lives in exchange for a week of fame and perks. Sounds like a religion to me—even if it's a pretty twisted one."

Kira flinched at Bailey's words, a knot tightening in her stomach. Before Will and Teddy entered her life, she hadn't dared to question the Reverence Ceremony, much less the rituals that surrounded it—they were just the way of life in Vita Nova. But it was unsettling to hear Bailey describe it as a twisted form of religion. What she had always seen as a necessary duty—a sacred obligation—now seemed like something much darker.

If the Reverence Ceremony was indeed Vita Nova's version of a religious ritual, what god were they worshipping?

Bailey reached out and patted her arm. When Kira looked up, the young woman gave her a reassuring smile. "Don't worry. You escaped from that place. You never have to go back."

She forced a smile. "I know. Thank you."

Grace rounded the corner of the infirmary with Will and Brack in tow, her face lighting up as she spotted Kira. She jogged the last few steps, throwing her arms around Kira and pulling her into a fierce hug. Leaning in close, she whispered, "This place is either the world's most charming little village or a dystopian hellscape populated by cannibals who plan to turn us into soup. I'll give you three guesses as to which one my husband thinks it is, and the first two don't count."

Over Grace's shoulder, Kira caught sight of Brack, hands shoved deep into his pockets, eyeing the surroundings like a man convinced the trees were conspiring against him. Kira almost expected him to start pacing or sniffing the air like a bloodhound on the hunt for some unseen danger.

"After the last few days," Kira replied with a weary smile, "being turned into soup doesn't sound so bad. How is Teddy doing? I haven't seen him since we got here."

"He's fine. He was pretty upset after we found you yesterday. I had a heck of a time keeping him away from you last night so you could rest. He said that he and Randy would stay up all night outside your door in the infirmary to watch for bad guys. That little boy is so protective of you."

"Really?" The thought of Teddy being concerned for her, of him insisting on sleeping outside of her room with his one-eyed bear, brought a swell of emotion that made all the bad things she'd endured over the past few weeks seem more bearable. Teddy wasn't just a child she had decided to protect—he was family. Her family.

She would do anything to keep him safe.

"You guys ready for breakfast?" Bailey asked in a cheerful voice, blissfully unaware that at least one of the new arrivals suspected her of cannibalism. "You must be starving. We should hurry before all the food is gone."

Kira glanced back at the playground. "Should I get Teddy?"

Bailey raised one eyebrow. "Teddy ate earlier, with the

other children," she said, her tone taking on a hint of reprimand. "The children always eat first."

"They do?" Grace rubbed her stomach. "Why's that?"

Bailey gave her a long, measured look, as if weighing the seriousness of the question. Then her expression softened into that of a teacher explaining a new concept.

"Because their survival is more important than ours."

Chapter Twenty-Five

The mess hall smelled like fresh-cut wood and smoked meats.

Despite its status as possibly the last city on earth, Vita Nova boasted some of the best dining spots Kira had ever known. She'd visited a few over the years, including The Riverfront. Even now, she could close her eyes and picture the blue rose pattern on The Riverfront's china, or feel the delicate stem of a wineglass between her fingers.

But as hard as she tried, she couldn't remember a single aroma from The Riverfront that could rival the mouthwatering scent that greeted her as she stepped inside the mess hall.

According to Bailey, the breakfast menu was simple—just eggs and ham, both staples she'd eaten countless times. They were hardly considered delicacies in Vita Nova. But true hunger, a physical sensation she'd only recently come to know, had a way of making even the simplest foods smell as if they had been crafted in heaven.

The mess hall was divided into two sections—one for food prep, the other for dining. A tall counter separated the two, and people were gathered around it, metal plates in hand, waiting to receive their breakfasts.

Bailey passed Kira a plate, along with a knife and fork. Then she led her to a grandmotherly woman in a polka-dotted apron, who scooped a generous portion of scrambled eggs onto Kira's plate.

She gave the woman a polite nod. "Thank you."

The woman retrieved a thick slice of ham from a different pan and placed it atop her eggs. "God bless you, dear."

As she looked past the woman's shoulder, Kira noticed three others huddled over a trio of gas camping stoves, singing softly as they scrambled more eggs. Their voices blended together in a hauntingly beautiful song.

"And though this world, with devils filled, should threaten to undo us, we will not fear, for God has willed his truth to triumph through us. The prince of darkness grim, we tremble not for him; his rage we can endure, for lo! his doom is sure; one little word shall fell him."

Kira had never heard the song before, but the words drew her in. She paused to listen, her plate resting on the counter. *One little word shall fell him.* What did that mean? And how could only three women produce such a powerful harmony?

"It's a hymn."

Bailey's voice snapped her back to reality.

"What?"

"They're singing *A Mighty Fortress is Our God.* It's an old Christian hymn. They've got incredible voices, don't they? If you think they sound good now, you should hear them in church. But, uh, you're kind of holding up the line."

Kira glanced back and saw her friends—and a few strangers —waiting behind her, trays in hand. Brack looked irritated, but that was nothing new. To her surprise, none of the strangers seemed annoyed at the delay. Most of them smiled and nodded at her.

Feeling her cheeks flush, she quickly picked up her plate and muttered, "Sorry."

"No worries," Bailey said. "Don't forget to grab a drink before you sit down."

Will was waiting at the end of the line. He must've slipped past her when she was caught up in the music. A row of metal cups lined the counter behind him. As Kira approached, he picked one up and handed it to her.

"Make sure you finish it," he said with a grin. "My arms are too sore to be carrying you around the village."

"Very funny."

Just as the aroma of the food had woken her hunger, the sight of water made her suddenly, almost painfully, thirsty. The cup wasn't cold, which meant the water wasn't either, but she knew that if she started drinking now, she'd down the whole cup in two gulps.

Kira fumbled through her jacket pockets, hoping to find a spare dollar or two to offer in payment for her breakfast. But she had no money. Everything she owned had been left behind in Vita Nova. And even if she'd had money, no one was waiting at the end of the serving line to accept payment.

The food was free.

Kira and Will stood off to the side, waiting as Grace and Brack received their food. The woman behind the counter winked at Grace before adding an extra scoop of eggs and a second slice of ham to her plate.

"Thank you so much," Grace said, her eyes lighting up at the extra portions.

Brack stepped forward next, and the woman gave him the standard portion of eggs and ham. He hesitated, plate extended, waiting for the extra helpings. But the woman simply raised an eyebrow and stared at him, her expression somewhere between amused and unimpressed.

"Not pregnant, are you?" she asked.

Brack lowered his plate. "Can't blame a guy for trying."

They followed Bailey into the dining section, where nine kerosene lamps with bulging glass globes swayed overhead, casting their soft light on the diners below. Wisps of smoke swirled along the ceiling before escaping through the open door at the other end of the mess hall. The area was filled with four long wooden tables, each made up of three smaller wooden tables with matching benches. People sat in small groups, their voices filling the room with conversation, laughter, and the clatter of silverware.

It took Kira a moment to notice how many elderly people were in the mess hall. At least half of those gathered around the tables looked to be over sixty, while others were much older. One woman in particular—a tiny figure with bone-white hair who sat alone at the end of a table—had to be in her nineties. Kira couldn't remember ever seeing someone that old before.

"Will?" She leaned close to him to be heard over the noise. "Do you see how many there are?"

"Yeah, I see them. They're lucky to be here."

He was right.

If this were Vita Nova, every one of them would be dead.

"Is this okay?" Bailey asked when they had reached the far end of the first table. "It's as far away from everyone else as we can get, so hopefully we'll be able to hear each other."

"This is fine." Grace placed her plate on the table and swung a leg over the bench. Brack lowered himself down beside her. "I'd eat off the floor like a dog if I had to, as long as I get to shovel this food into my mouth as fast as possible."

Bailey took a seat on Grace's other side and looked across the table at Kira. "Would you like to say the prayer?"

"Me?" Kira tensed and leaned back on the bench, as if trying to distance herself from both Bailey and her request. She didn't know how to pray—at least, not out loud. She'd spoken to God in her head a few times, but never with other people listening. She didn't even know how to start. Her fingers tightened around the spoon beside her plate as she struggled to recall the prayers Will and the others had said at mealtimes back in Emmitsburg, but her mind was blank.

Thankfully, Will stepped in to rescue her. "I'd like to say the prayer, if that's okay with you, Kira?"

Her relief was so overwhelming she could've kissed him. "Not at all."

He bowed his head, and the others followed suit. "Kind Heavenly Father, thank you for bringing us here to this place of safety and for providing us with this wonderful food."

As Will prayed, Kira's eyes drifted to the slice of glistening ham on her plate. Something shiny gave it an enticing sheen. Honey? She inhaled deeply, savoring the sweet aroma, and her stomach growled loudly in response. She pressed her eyelids shut and bit her lip, her face burning with embarrassment.

She couldn't even say a prayer in front of people if her life depended on it. And now her traitorous body had disrupted Will's beautiful prayer.

"In Jesus' name, Amen."

"Amen," the others echoed.

Bailey brought a forkful of eggs to her lips. "Beautiful prayer, Will," she half-shouted. "I'm sorry it's so noisy in here. It's always like this at mealtimes. But most people are finishing up, so it should quiet down soon."

"We don't mind the noise," Grace replied, carving her ham slices into small, bite-sized pieces. "And we're very thankful for the food."

The meal was incredible. Kira devoured everything on her

plate within minutes, unable to shake the nagging fear that someone might take it away if she didn't eat it fast enough. When Will noticed she was done, he cut his ham down the middle and slid one half onto her plate.

"No." She stabbed the ham with her fork and returned it to his plate. "I'm not going to eat your food."

"I'm full."

She knew he was lying. Will ate like a horse, and he'd been shoveling food into his mouth just as voraciously as she had a moment ago. "I was dehydrated yesterday, not starving, and I had plenty to eat. Please, just finish your breakfast."

Bailey picked up her water glass, a knowing smile on her lips. "You two are adorable. How long have you been a couple?"

Kira glanced at Will, who chose that moment to pop a large piece of ham into his mouth. He pointed at his lips with his fork and shook his head as if to say, *Sorry. Can't talk with my mouth full.*

"I mean, we're not really..." Her voice trailed off as she noticed Will staring at her. She had no idea how to define their relationship. She knew she loved him, but she couldn't admit that to him. Not until she knew how he felt. And not until she knew what secrets he was keeping from her.

"I mean, we've only known each other for a few weeks," she continued. "But a lot has happened in that short amount of time."

Bailey giggled. "Oh, I can only imagine. Do you mind if I ask how you two met?"

Brack let out a gruff laugh. "This should be good."

Kira's water glass shook as she brought it to her lips. How could she explain to someone like Bailey that she used to help people kill themselves?

"I'll sum it up," Will said, his mouth finally, mercifully,

empty. His hand found Kira's underneath the table, and his thumb stroked hers in a reassuring motion. "But I should warn you... It's a little dark. You see, I volunteered to kill myself for the good of a corrupt and evil city, and Kira's job was to keep me happy during my Final Week so that—when the time came —I'd be okay with dying." He glanced at Kira. "I guess she did her job a little too well, because instead of making it easier for me to die, she made me want to live. And then she really messed up by saving my life."

Bailey pressed a hand to her chest, her face erupting into a wide smile. "That's the most romantic thing I've ever heard."

"Romantic?" Brack coughed. "You think that's romantic?"

"Well, sure, it's a little morbid for a love story, but that's what makes it so charming."

Will smiled. "Thanks. There was also a kidnapping attempt, a city-wide car chase, and two near-drownings, but we won't bore you with the details."

Bailey's gaze shifted to the front of the mess hall, her smile fading. She looked back at Kira and lowered her voice. "Ghost is here."

Kira and Will twisted in their seats, their hands slipping apart.

Ghost stood at the entrance to the mess hall, looking very different from the man they had met in the Unregulated Zone. He'd cleaned himself up, shaved the dark stubble from his chin, and traded his all-black ensemble for jeans and a battered flannel jacket. But exhaustion had hollowed out his cheeks, and the dark bags under his eyes made him look as if he hadn't slept in weeks.

Kira thought he looked like a man carrying the weight of the world on his shoulders.

A few people greeted him as they left the mess hall. He

responded with a curt nod, his dark eyes scanning the room before locking on Kira.

She swallowed hard, her breakfast churning in her stomach.

A memory flickered in her mind, a fleeting image that disappeared before she could grasp it.

Her fingers, sticky with ice cream, clung to a wooden railing as she stared out over the water, sunlight warming her face. She inhaled the pungent river smell—underwritten with the scent of fresh paint—and listened to the hypnotizing sound of paddles cutting through the water and churning it into a froth. A thick mist hovered above the water's surface, as if trying to slow everything down so she could remember.

Remember.

And then she did.

A boat. She nearly said the word out loud. *I've been on a boat with him.*

No. That wasn't possible.

Was it?

As if sensing her thoughts, Ghost began to walk in her direction.

"Morning," Bailey said as he approached the table. "I thought I'd make sure our guests got a tasty breakfast before they—"

He cut her off, his eyes boring into Kira's. "We need to talk," he said. "Right now."

Chapter Twenty-Six

Will and Kira followed Ghost across the meadow, heading towards the edge of the woods. Ghost wasn't running but moving with long-legged, purposeful strides, devouring the distance with each step. Occasionally, he pulled so far ahead that they had to jog to keep up.

"It was like this all day yesterday," Will muttered under his breath to Kira. "The guy is a machine."

Kira did her best to match Ghost's pace, still fighting against the lingering effects of her bout with heat stroke. Each step was an act of defiance against her own body's weakness. She knew very little about Ghost, but she could tell he valued strength, and after passing out in the river yesterday, she was determined to show a little.

"We found this place by accident," Ghost called over his shoulder. "That was about ten years ago."

The landscape unfolded before them, a vast expanse of rippling grass dotted with purple asters—Aunt Reeva's favorite wildflower. The ground was damp and springy beneath Kira's boots, urging her forward, and the breeze carried the sweet scent of hay. Glancing down, she noticed tiny brown burs clinging to her pants, hitching a ride. The faint, joyful tinkling of a piano came from somewhere in the distance. Maybe from the school or church? But in this quiet, secluded village, it was easy to imagine the melody reaching out to her from another world entirely. Or from another time.

"We built the first cabin within a month," Ghost continued. "Lived in it for nearly a year. There were only six of us back then. But every time we went out for supplies, we met more people—starving, sick people. We didn't set out to bring home more mouths to feed, but they kept coming, like someone was sending them to us."

"What is this place?" Will asked. "Why is it fenced off?"

Ghost slowed his pace a little, allowing Will and Kira to catch up and walk beside him. "This whole area used to be a nature preserve, part of a forest regeneration project by the Pennsylvania Game Commission. They fenced off three hundred acres of woodland and uncultivated fields, all of it surrounded by fencing to keep the deer out. There's only one gate into the preserve, and it's well hidden and guarded at all times."

"What about the perimeter? How are you able to secure such a large area?"

"Our best defense is our isolated location," Ghost replied. "We only leave the perimeter on foot, even if we have some distance to travel. Vehicles are noisy, and they leave tracks that could lead others to us. Everyone takes a turn on perimeter duty—we've got seven armed guards walking the fence around the clock." He glanced at Kira as they entered the woods. "No exceptions for women. We expect everyone to contribute around here. That goes for your pregnant friend, too."

Will's jaw tightened at the comment, but Kira nodded.

"We'll do our part while we're here. Just let us know how we can help out."

Ghost's expression softened a bit, and a hint of sadness clouded his eyes. "You can only stay a few days," he muttered. "Until you figure out where you're going."

Kira wanted to ask him why. Why were they only allowed to stay for a few days when he'd just admitted to taking in other starving and sick strangers he'd found on his supply runs? They weren't sick, they were able-bodied, and there was clearly plenty of room in the village.

More than anything, though, she wanted to ask him why his face conjured images in her mind of ice cream and a wooden boat.

But she kept quiet.

Ghost led them deeper into the forest, his pace unwavering even as the terrain grew uneven and rocky, until a metal structure materialized out of the trees like an optical illusion coming into focus.

The chain-link fence loomed over them, at least fifteen feet tall, its once-gleaming metal now dulled by a blanket of green vines and patches of creeping brown rust. The vines wound tightly around the links, interweaving with the metal to the point that the fence appeared more like an organic part of the forest than a man-made structure. Kira squinted, trying to trace the fence's path through the trees, but it disappeared into the tangled undergrowth and shadows after a few yards, blending seamlessly with its wild surroundings.

Kira noticed several small holes near the base of the fence where animals had burrowed their way through. The edges of these openings were frayed and uneven, as if the creatures had gnawed at the metal itself, desperate to pass to the other side. In one spot, tufts of fur clung to the twisted wire, evidence of a struggle.

A reminder that no barrier was truly impenetrable.

"Most people here think that fence will protect them from the outside world," Ghost said. "But it won't. The fence isn't electrified, and it's not tall enough to keep someone determined from scaling it. That's why we have the perimeter guards." He gave Kira a pointed look. "In Haven, we put our trust in people, not fences."

"Has anyone ever gotten past your guards?" she asked.

Ghost pulled his eyes away from her and rubbed at his scar. "Not yet. That's only because we're so deep in the woods that they haven't found us. But it's only a matter of time."

Without speaking, Kira stepped past Ghost and approached the fence. She reached out, her fingers threading through the thick vines and gripping the rusted metal underneath. It was sturdy, and when she tried to give it a little shake, it did not move.

Ghost's voice cut through the silence. "How did you get out of the city?"

Her fingers tightened around the wires. "I drove onto City Island and jumped off the Walnut Street Bridge."

Ghost didn't respond immediately, and when Kira finally let go of the fence and turned around, she saw his lips pressed into a tight line, his expression one of disgust.

"What?"

He shook his head, his scar standing out against his red cheeks. "I didn't take you for the type of girl who would throw herself off a bridge."

"I wasn't trying to kill myself," Kira said, unable to keep the sharp edge of defiance out of her voice. "I would never do that. The little boy who came here with us—Teddy—his own mother volunteered him to die for the good of the city. I broke him out of Rolling Meadows, which is the place where the Volunteers go to die, and we escaped by jumping off the bridge."

One corner of Ghost's mouth twitched, as if he wanted to smile but couldn't allow himself to do so. "Well," he said, "at least that makes sense."

The words slipped out of her mouth before she could stop them. "What's your real name?"

Ghost opened his mouth, but before he could respond, a burst of static crackled through the air, followed by muffled chatter. Ghost reached behind his back and pulled out a small handheld radio, its design similar to the battery-powered Motorola Talkabouts they'd used for communication in Emmitsburg.

He brought the device to his lips and pushed the button.

"Go ahead."

"We need you over at the barn. One of the sheep doesn't look good."

"Copy. I'll be there ASAP." He shoved the radio back into his pocket. "I need to get back to work, but I'll drop you off at your cabins first. Any questions about the rules?"

Kira shook her head. She still wanted to know his real name, but the moment had passed.

When they reached the center of the village, Ghost stopped in front of a two-story log cabin. His dark eyes were unreadable, and like his scar, the deep wrinkles on his forehead looked as if they had been carved with a dull knife.

"This is where you'll be staying. There are four women here now. Five, including you." His gaze shifted to Will. "You'll be at the other end of town with the other single men. We keep separate quarters for our unmarried residents, for obvious reasons. The last thing we need is more mouths to feed. But there's a vacant cabin for your pregnant friend and her husband. It's small, but it will do for the few days that you're here. The boy can bunk with them."

Kira braced for Will to argue about the sleeping arrangements, but to her relief, he stayed silent.

"Your belongings should already be inside," Ghost continued. "We'll work you into our security rotation soon enough. For now, just settle in. Lunch is at noon, though many of us skip it to conserve resources. You might want to do the same."

It sounded less like a suggestion and more like an order.

"Let's go," he muttered to Will. "I've got other things to do today."

As Ghost stalked off toward the center of the village, Will caught Kira off-guard by pulling her into a quick embrace. She closed her eyes and buried her face in his chest, comforted by the warmth and closeness of his body. His lips brushed her cheek, just shy of the corner of her mouth, and she felt him discreetly slip something into the front pocket of her pants.

"Just in case," he whispered.

Then he was gone, jogging to catch up with Ghost.

After they disappeared from view, Kira wiped her damp palms on her jacket and turned her gaze to the cabin. The weathered logs were streaked with moss, and the roof was blanketed in fluorescent-green lichen. A tall stone chimney jutted from one side of the structure, sending tendrils of smoke curling into the air.

Keeping her eyes on the chimney, she reached into her pocket, her fingers curling around something small and hard. The shape was unfamiliar, and she couldn't immediately discern what it was. Glancing around the village to make sure she was alone, she pulled the item from her pocket and opened her palm.

It was Will's pocket knife. The one with the dark blue handle.

Whoever had confiscated their weapons upon their arrival

in Haven hadn't found it, likely because Will kept it hidden inside his sock. Now he had given it to her.

But why? Did he believe they were in danger here?

Carefully, she slid the knife from its casing, revealing a gleaming silver blade no longer than her pinky finger. It was hard and cold against her skin, with an unexpected weight that Kira found oddly comforting.

It wasn't much, but it was better than nothing.

As she headed for the cabin's door, she let the knife slide into her jacket pocket. She planned to hide it in her sock when she got the chance, but for now, it would remain where it was.

Drawing in a deep breath, she pushed open the cabin's door and stepped inside.

Chapter Twenty-Seven

From the outside, the log cabin appeared larger than most of the other homes in the village, but its main level was modest, just wide enough to contain a tan plaid couch with frayed and punctured cushions, two high-back chairs that had seen better days, and a square dining table surrounded by four wooden chairs. In the center of the table was a small metal vase filled with purple asters.

A young blonde woman knelt in front of the fireplace, balancing on the balls of her bare feet as she tossed logs into the fire. Each collision sent a spray of sparks into the air, like tiny fireworks. The woman hummed softly as she stoked the flames, her voice carrying a melancholy tune that reminded Kira of a caged bird.

She pulled her gaze from the woman to take in the rest of the room. To her right, a narrow staircase led up to the second level, where Kira assumed the women who lived here slept. A broom leaned against the wall at the base of the stairs. The unfinished wood floor was bare, without a single rug to soften it or block out the cold. Kira couldn't imagine how cold the floor must get in the dead of winter.

A gust of cold air burst into the cabin, catching the half-open door and pushing it with surprising force. Before Kira could react, the door swung wide and thudded against the opposing wall.

Startled, the blonde woman leapt to her feet, a log slipping from her hands and landing inches from her exposed toes. Her eyes narrowed as she noticed Kira standing in the doorway, her surprised expression shifting to one of suspicion.

"Who are you?" she demanded, her nostrils flaring. "What are you doing in here?"

Kira rushed to explain, holding her hands in the air to show she meant no harm. "I'm sorry I startled you. Ghost told me I'm supposed to stay here. My friends and I arrived in Haven yesterday. My name is Kira." After a brief pause, she added, "A few of us escaped from Vita Nova."

The woman's tense posture relaxed slightly, though she didn't smile. "Oh, yeah. Bailey mentioned we had new arrivals." She bent down to retrieve the fallen log and tossed it into the fire, her eyes fixated on the burning wood. "I think she put your stuff upstairs, but we don't have enough beds. You'll have to sleep down here on the couch."

Kira's eyes flicked to the old ratty couch, which looked like it had hosted its share of unwelcome rodent residents over the years. Still, it was better than sleeping outside. "That's fine. I don't mind."

The young woman turned away from the fire and approached Kira, crossing the cabin with a graceful sort of elegance that seemed at odds with her patched black overalls and tattered blue sweater. She was tall and lean, with the long legs of a dancer, a distinctive olive tint to her skin, and striking green eyes. Her hair was swept into a ponytail, held back by a white headband.

She was one of the most beautiful people Kira had ever seen.

The woman extended her hand in a lukewarm greeting, still refusing to smile. "My name is Avery. Welcome to our extremely humble abode. How long have you been out of the city?"

"Not long. Just a few weeks."

"I used to live there with my mother," she said, her voice flat as she released Kira's hand. "We moved out a few months before the virus hit. I was never happier to leave a place in my life. Are things as bad as I've heard?"

"Worse," Kira replied. "That's why I left."

Avery stared at her, as if searching for something deeper. "Any regrets about leaving?"

Kira shook her head. "I don't miss it, if that's what you mean. My mother died two years ago, and I didn't have anyone left except for my best friend." A familiar twinge of pain accompanied the thought of Emma. "But it hasn't been easy out here, either."

"Well, don't expect things to get any easier in Haven," Avery warned, her mouth forming into a sharp line. "There's no electricity here, no running water, no indoor plumbing. But if you've been in the Unregulated Zone for a few weeks, you're probably used to that by now. We have a small room upstairs with a bathtub, and we boil water from the stream so we don't have to take ice baths. It takes forever, but trust me, it's worth the effort. Of course, we have to share the bathwater, and since you're the newest, you'll be going last."

"That's fine."

"And as for the bathroom," Avery continued. "We use

outhouses around here. We're lucky enough to have one in our backyard, so you won't have to walk as far in the middle of the night. And if you're not close to the cabin and things get desperate, there's always the woods."

"How long have you been here?" Kira asked, trying to shift the conversation away from the bleakness of her new home.

"Two years. Although some days, it feels like a lot longer." She took a deep breath and wiped her hands on her thighs, leaving flecks of bark clinging to her overalls. "I should get going. It's my day to collect the eggs and deliver them to the mess hall."

"Do you need any help?"

Avery raised an eyebrow, clearly surprised by the offer. "Sure. A little help would be great, as long as you don't mind getting your boots dirty. We've got a lot of chickens."

"How many?"

Avery grinned. "A lot."

Ten minutes later, Kira stepped over a low fence into a chaotic sea of clucking chickens. They swarmed around her, hundreds of hens in every color: brown, white, red, yellow, and black. Two piebald chickens with only a few ragged feathers left bulldozed their way to the front and hopped onto Kira's boots, eyeing her with an unsettling intelligence.

Avery moved through the mass of chickens, pulling handfuls of oats from the pockets of her overalls and scattering them on the ground. The hens squawked and pecked at the dirt, shoving each other aside to get at the grain. Despite the frenzy, most of them looked well-fed and healthy—except for the piebald ones perched on Kira's boots.

"Uh, are these guys okay?" Kira asked, gesturing to the half-plucked chickens.

Avery glanced over at her. "Them? Yeah. That's just Martha and Mary. They're Barred Rocks. They always molt in September. The other hens molt too, but for some reason, the Barred Rocks look the worst doing it. If you look closely, you'll see their new feathers coming in."

"Uh, that's okay." Kira had no desire to get any closer to the chickens.

"They get really grumpy and pushy when they're molting," Avery explained, "so I try to give them more oats than the others. Just walk around and drop the oats I gave you—they'll quiet down."

Kira hesitated. The chickens refused to move from her boots, and she didn't want to trip and crush them to death if she fell. Killing a few of Ghost's chickens wouldn't exactly earn her any points in Haven.

In fact, it would probably get her kicked right out.

Avery noticed her reluctance and gave her an amused smile. "Don't worry. They'll hop off your feet, I promise. Just start walking."

Kira forced her feet to move, and she was surprised when Martha and Mary hopped off and followed her around the enclosure. The other chickens made way as she shuffled awkwardly through their midst, grabbing handfuls of oats from her pockets and sprinkling them on the ground. The two hens bent over the oats, clucking their thanks as they pecked at the dirt. With the food in front of them, they were no longer interested in swarming her.

In fact, they were almost cute.

Kira knelt to pet them, and while most of the chickens scurried away, Martha and Mary—who refused to abandon their choice spots closest to her feet—crouched down, allowing her to smooth their budding feathers.

"Don't worry," she whispered to the hens. "Your new feathers are already coming in. You'll be strong again soon."

When she stood, she noticed Avery watching her.

"What?"

"I can't believe they let you touch them. Their feathers are really sensitive when they're molting. They won't even let me touch them, and I'm out here every day."

"Really?" Kira glanced back at the two chickens. She had no idea what she'd done to earn their trust, but now she felt a sense of protectiveness over them. She thought about the Agricultural Sector back in Vita Nova. She'd never imagined herself working with animals, but it would've been a better fit than serving as a Volunteer Advocate. She certainly would've found more happiness on the farms.

But then she remembered that most of the animals in the Agricultural Sector were eventually slaughtered to feed the city—not everyone, of course, just the wealthy and powerful people who could afford to eat meat regularly.

People like her father.

The thought of bonding with animals only to sacrifice them for food was unsettling, but it still seemed a lot better than bonding with people, only to sacrifice them for nothing at all.

After they finished feeding the chickens, Avery led Kira into a small shed filled with hastily built chicken coops. Avery grabbed an empty basket from the top of one coop, opened the rear door, and began collecting eggs.

Kira moved to the next coop and picked up her own basket. "How do you keep the eggs from spoiling?" she asked as she unfastened the tiny metal latch on the door. "Don't they need to be refrigerated?"

"Actually, they don't," Avery said. "Eggs stay fresh unrefrigerated for a few weeks, as long as you don't wash them. There's a protective bloom around the egg that prevents it from spoiling, but if you wash it, the bloom goes away, and the eggs spoil quickly if they're not refrigerated. So, we don't wash them until we're ready to cook them."

By the time they'd checked each coop, they both had two baskets filled with eggs. Most of the eggs were white or brown, but a few pale blue and pale green eggs were nestled in Kira's baskets like tiny colored treasures. Until arriving in Haven, she hadn't realized that eggs came in any colors other than white and brown.

As they stepped out of the shed and headed toward the fence, Kira cast a quick glance back at the flock of colorful chickens, who were preoccupied with pecking the last of the oats from the ground.

"Now we get to deliver these to the mess hall," Avery said, "so they can start prepping for—"

Her voice faltered, trailing off into silence.

Kira turned away from the chickens and saw that Avery's face had turned as pale as the whitest egg in her basket. Her lower lip trembled, as if she were on the verge of tears, and her eyes were wide with a mixture of shock and disbelief.

Following Avery's gaze past the chickens and the shed, Kira finally noticed Will standing a few feet away, near the fence. His fingers coiled tightly around the wires, his knuckles almost as pale as Avery's skin.

Avery's voice emerged, barely more than a whisper.

"Will?"

The realization struck Kira like a bolt of lightning—Avery was the one Will had been searching for in the Unregulated Zone. Avery was the reason he had insisted on heading north, because that's the direction *she* had gone. The intensity in his eyes, the shock on Avery's face—it all suddenly made sense. Avery was the person he'd been desperate to find.

And now he'd found her.

The basket of eggs slipped from Kira's fingers and crashed to the ground, the fragile shells shattering on impact. Golden yolk seeped into the soil, precious and wasted, like something irreplaceable lost in an instant.

Chapter Twenty-Eight

"I can't believe it. I can't believe he found Avery."

Tears blurred Kira's vision until she could no longer see Grace on the other side of the dining table. It was a relief to no longer be able to see the pity in her friend's eyes. She didn't want pity, or hugs, or encouragement.

She just wanted to go home.

She raised the metal water cup to her lips and took a long sip, letting the room-temperature water soothe her throat, which was still raw from the sobs she'd choked back after leaving Avery and Will at the chicken coop. But as she swallowed, the last swallow of water went down the wrong way, triggering a fit of coughing.

Avery and Will.

Avery and Will.

The names echoed in her mind, too perfect together. Like a song that wouldn't stop playing.

Avery was stunning—far more than Kira could ever hope to be. How was she supposed to compete with someone like that?

How could she have been so naïve, so foolish, to think Will was in love with her?

"He should've told you about her," Grace continued, running her fingers along the inside of her palm. "Didn't I tell him, Brack? Didn't I tell Will that he needed to be honest with Kira?"

Brack muttered something unintelligible from the other side of the room, where he knelt in front of the fireplace, snapping twigs and tossing them onto the dry logs.

Kira set the cup down and wrapped her arms around herself. The old cabin was filthy and cold, and the chill seeped into her bones. Even if Brack got the fire going soon, there was still so much work to be done to make this place livable. She knew she shouldn't be wallowing over Will's ex-girlfriend when there were so many other things she could be doing to be getting the cabin ready for Teddy. Her eyes kept returning to the broom with the broken handle leaning against the wall near the cabin's door, but she couldn't bring herself to stand up, let alone clean.

Grace slumped back in her chair, her face a mixture of sorrow for Kira and anger at Will. She twisted a curl around her finger, shaking her head. "I promise you, Kira. I asked him to tell you the truth. Back in Emmitsburg, when you were still in the infirmary, I told him he needed to sit down with you and explain about Avery, but the moment I mentioned her name, he shut down. That's all he's done since the day she left. He refuses to talk about her with anyone."

"What happened with them?" Kira heard herself ask, even though part of her didn't want to know.

Grace sighed and lowered her gaze to her lap. "She left a few years ago with a small group. The girl is an explorer at heart. She couldn't stand just sitting around Emmitsburg, not knowing what else was out there. She begged Will to go with her, of course, but I knew he wouldn't do that to Jonesy. Besides, we relied on him for supplies from the city. He had too many responsibilities to just up and leave. I know how devastated he was when she left, not just because she chose to go but because he couldn't protect her anymore. Will is a protector by nature. You've probably figured that out by now."

Kira nodded. It was one of the qualities she admired—and loved—most about him. "How am I supposed to sleep in that cabin tonight, Grace? That's where *she* is. How am I supposed to go back there and face her?"

"You don't have to. You're going to stay right here."

Brack cleared his throat and shot his wife a side-eye look that made his opinion on the matter clear.

"You can stay here tonight," Grace repeated in a louder voice. "There are two beds, so you can sleep with Teddy." She raised a hand before Kira could protest. "You're staying here. And I won't hear another word about it."

"Okay," Kira relented. "But just for tonight."

The truth was, she had no desire to return to Avery's cabin. What would she do when Avery returned from her reunion with Will? Or worse, what if Avery *didn't* return at all tonight?

The thought made her feel physically ill.

"Where is Will? You really should talk to him."

Kira shrugged. "Still with her, I guess."

Grace's eyes widened. "You left them together?"

Kira ran a finger along the frayed hem of her jacket. "What else was I supposed to do? Grab his arm and drag him away? The whole thing caught me off-guard. As soon as I saw her face, I knew she was the person Will had been looking for since we left town. And they just stood there and stared at each other like nothing else existed."

Kira shook her head, trying to rid herself of the memory. So much had passed between them in those few seconds—a shared history, a love that had clearly once been there. "I mumbled something about looking for Teddy and ran off. I just left them standing there at the chicken coop."

"Perfect spot for a chicken like Will," Grace muttered. "I hope he slips and falls face-first into a big pile of chicken droppings."

"Grace." Brack interjected, looking up from the fireplace with raised eyebrows. "Don't drag the guy through the mud. He didn't do anything wrong."

Grace rolled her eyes. "Of course, you'd defend him. Men always stick together, don't they?"

"And women always make things bigger than they are." Brack stood, brushing his hands off on his pants. "Not wanting to talk about his ex with Kira doesn't make Will a bad guy, nor does it mean he's still in love with Avery. All it means is that Avery is a painful part of his past, and he'd rather not dig it up. Don't you have something like that?" He directed the question at Grace, but Kira knew it was meant for both of them. "Don't you have anything you keep to yourself?"

Emma and Jonesy, Kira thought. *I still haven't told Will what I know about them.*

Hypocrite.

Grace hesitated a moment too long, the curl slipping from her finger like an argument she couldn't quite hold on to. "I don't keep anything from you."

Even Kira found that hard to believe.

"Yeah, right," Brack huffed.

"Who asked you anyway?" Grace snapped. "What makes you think you're some kind of relationship expert? You can't even get the stupid fire going!"

Brack stomped toward the door, his boots kicking up dust. "Because I need more kindling. And a little fresh air wouldn't hurt, either." He spared a parting glance for his wife. "Since you two are so good at stoking fires, feel free to give it a try while I'm gone."

The door slammed behind him, its impact knocking the broom with the broken handle to the floor.

"Just ignore him," Grace muttered, using the table to help push herself up. She put her hands on her hips and looked around the dirty cabin, as if she wasn't sure of where to start. "He's been a big grump all day. I don't think he likes it here in Haven."

"Why not?"

"Well, I don't know if you've noticed or not, but Brack isn't much of a people person. And there are definitely a lot of people around here. They're all nice enough, but I think he's worried this place isn't as safe as everyone thinks it is. And I don't think he trusts Ghost."

"Ghost saved my life," Kira said, feeling strangely protective of the scarred man. Though she'd only known him for a few days, she trusted him. She couldn't explain it, but she knew he would never hurt her.

"I know he protected you back at the dollar store, but he *is* a little scary, Kira. Plus, Brack's a realist. In his mind, when something seems too good to be true, it probably is."

"Yeah." Will had taught her that lesson today. "Ghost said we're allowed to stay for a few days, but if you guys aren't comfortable here, I'm fine with the four of us moving on. It might even be for the best."

The four of us. She'd already written Will out of their group. Or maybe he'd written himself out. But if Brack and Grace wanted to leave, she would go with them. One thing was certain: she couldn't stay in Haven and watch Will rekindle his relationship with Avery.

"Kira," Grace ventured, "don't bite my head off for saying this, but you should talk to Will before you completely cut him out of your life. I'm upset with him, too, but Brack is right—he's not a bad person. He never meant to hurt you." She paused for a moment, as if choosing her next words carefully. "I know what your father did to your mom has made it hard for you to trust people, especially men, but not everyone is like him. Will isn't like him."

Kira clenched her jaw, knowing deep down that Grace had a point, but the truth of it made her uncomfortable. She didn't want to hear it, didn't want to acknowledge the painful reality Grace was hinting at: that maybe she was the one pushing Will away, not the other way around.

She stood up from the table. "I'm not going to keep talking about this. Whatever was happening between Will and I is clearly over, so there's no point in dwelling on it. We need to get this place cleaned up before Teddy gets back from the school."

Before Grace could argue, Kira grabbed the broom and began sweeping the floors, channeling all her frustration, sadness, and anger into the task. She focused on the dirt and debris that had gathered around the edges of the room, sweeping them into neat little piles. But the monotonous chore only gave her mind space to wander, and she couldn't stop imagining what Will and Avery might be doing at that very moment.

Were they still talking by the chicken coop? Or had their conversation progressed into something more? Was Avery in Will's arms right now? Was he holding her, comforting her?

Kissing her?

The thought of another woman in Will's arms made Kira's chest tighten.

But Avery wasn't the other woman, was she?

Kira was.

A soft knock sounded at the door, and Kira's heart skipped a beat. She knew who would be waiting on the other side.

As Grace crossed the room to answer the door, Kira turned away, not wanting to see his face. It wasn't just anger over his secret about Avery—it was the ache in her heart, the knowledge that those aggressively blue eyes of his would never look at her the same way again. She'd sacrificed everything for him—her life in Vita Nova, her job, her best friend, her freedom. It felt like a part of her had died—the part that had once believed she could find happiness with this man.

Now, Will was here to make it official.

To end things with her.

"Hey, Will," Grace greeted him, her voice laced with ice. "You lost or something?"

"Is she here?"

Kira peeked over her shoulder to see Grace blocking the doorway with her body, shielding Kira from view.

"She's busy right now. The cabin's a mess, and she's been helping me clean up. Sounds like you've got a whole lot on your plate, too, so you better be on your way. I'll let her know you stopped by."

Kira heard a soft thud and imagined Will's hand on the door, preventing Grace from closing it.

"I *really* need to talk to her. It won't take long, I promise."

There was an urgency in his voice that Kira hadn't expected. She'd been bracing herself for guilt or apologies, not this.

Without moving from the door, Grace spoke over her shoulder. "Kira? Do you want to talk to this guy?"

This guy. Grace's unwavering loyalty brought fresh tears to Kira's eyes. Despite only knowing each other for a short time, Grace was already treating her like a lifelong friend.

If only she could find that kind of loyalty in a man.

"I'll talk to him," Kira finally said. She would have to face Will eventually. Perhaps it was better to get it over with now rather than drawing out the pain for another day or two.

Quick, like a band-aid.

The wood floor groaned beneath Will's weight as he stepped inside, as if the cabin itself resented his presence.

"I'll help Brack with the wood."

Only after she heard Grace's footsteps heading down the porch steps did Kira turn around.

Will stood in the doorway, his skin pale and his dirty-blonde hair disheveled. He attempted a smile, but it barely touched his lips. His shoulders sagged, his expression one of pure physical and emotional exhaustion, and Kira could see in his eyes that facing her was just another burden, one more task to endure before he could finally collapse.

"Hey."

She turned her back on him, pretending to be engrossed in her sweeping, needing to focus on anything other than the man standing in front of her. She could feel Will's eyes on her, a weight that settled on the back of her neck.

"Kira." His voice was soft, almost pleading. "She's getting married."

Kira froze, the broom's bristles hovering above the floor. The words didn't register at first, lost in the angry buzzing in her head. She replayed them several times in her mind before the meaning finally sank in.

Her head snapped up, the dirt piles long forgotten. "She's... what?"

"Avery is getting married in two days." He shifted his

weight as he met Kira's gaze. "His name is Nicolas Hernandez. She met him while traveling in the Unregulated Zone, not long before they ran into Ghost and ended up in Haven. They've been together for almost two years."

He stared at her expectantly, waiting for a reaction. But what did he expect of her? For her to throw herself into his arms as if nothing had happened? To weep tears of relief that his first choice was no longer an option, so Kira could swoop in and take her place?

But Kira didn't feel like doing any of that.

All she felt was anger.

"So? What does that mean?" she demanded. "Does that mean I win by default? Now that your first choice is taken, I'm back in the game?"

He had the nerve to look frustrated. "This isn't a game to me, Kira."

"Really? Because it sure feels like one. This was always your plan all along, wasn't it? Is this why we really left Emmitsburg—so you could find the one who got away?"

"Kira, I swear, I didn't know she would be—"

"Stop lying!" Her voice shook with anger, and she didn't care about the cabin's thin walls or who might overhear their conversation. In fact, she wanted everyone in Haven to hear it —to see Will for the liar and coward he truly was before they made the mistake of trusting him. "You're telling me we didn't head north because you were hoping to find her? I remember the look in your eyes that day, Will. I knew you were hiding something from me when we left Emmitsburg, but I was too—"

She caught herself just in time.

Too head-over-heels, blindingly in love with you to say anything.

She lowered her voice. "I was too much of a coward to call you out on it."

Will leaned against the wall, arms crossed over his chest. "You're right. I pushed for heading north because that's the direction Avery and the others took when they left. Of course, I wanted to find her. We were together for a long time, and I thought I could find out if she was okay. But not because I still love her." He stepped closer to Kira, his eyes managing to be both soft and intense at the same time. "I never loved Avery. There was a time I thought I did, but I was wrong."

Kira took two steps back, clutching the broom in front of her like a shield. "That's really convenient timing, considering she's marrying someone else in two days."

His jaw tightened. "You can believe what you want, but I'm telling you the truth."

But the truth was far more complicated than the lies Will had told her, and the realization left her feeling broken and empty. Even if he wasn't in love with Avery, did it matter anymore? Will had lied to her repeatedly—about becoming a Volunteer, about his intentions at the Volunteer Ball, about trying to assassinate her father, and about Avery.

She didn't want to talk to him anymore. She just wanted him gone, so she wouldn't have to hear anymore lies.

"Go away, Will."

"Kira."

She turned her back on him. "Please. I really need you to leave me alone now."

She expected him to argue, to plead for her to hear him out, but he did neither.

"Okay."

A long silence filled the room, finally broken by the steady thud of Will's retreating footsteps and the soft click of the door closing behind him.

She drew a deep breath and released it.

Will was gone, and she was alone.

More alone than she had ever been. Even more alone than she had been during those terrible, endless days after her mother's death, when she could barely bring herself to get out of bed.

But this time, there were no tears. No strangled sobs. Her body remained calm, her heart as still and cold as stone.

With nothing else to do, she returned to her sweeping.

Chapter Twenty-Nine

"Kira. Wake up."

She jolted awake, blinking into the darkness, only to find herself staring into a pair of intense, dark eyes.

"Get up and be quiet," Ghost muttered, nodding at the other side of the bed, where Teddy lay curled into a tiny ball, his body wrapped around Randy. "I need you to come with me."

A quick glance at the fireplace confirmed that the flames had died down, leaving only a few charred logs and a single pile of glowing embers. When she'd gone to bed, the cabin had been so hot that she'd been sweating. But with no one awake to stoke the fire, it had died in the night, leaving the cabin cold and dark.

The wool blanket was bunched up at her feet. She must have been thrashing around in her sleep, troubled by a nightmare that lingered just out of reach, its details slipping away the moment she woke.

"What time is it?" she whispered, glancing at the windows. The sun hadn't yet risen.

"Early. Get up."

Kira's gaze flicked to Ghost's scar before returning to his eyes. "Why?"

The dying embers reflected in his eyes as he replied, "Because there's something you need to see."

Unease settled in her chest, a cold feeling that mirrored the temperature in the cabin. She quietly pushed the blanket aside, slipping out of bed without disturbing Teddy. Ghost stepped back, giving her space, his expression unreadable in the dim light.

Whatever he wanted to show her, she wasn't sure she was ready to see it.

GHOST'S CABIN WAS NO DIFFERENT FROM THE OTHERS, except that it sat alone at the southern tip of the village, closer to the livestock than to the people. Kira could hear the cows lowing in the barn, as well as what sounded like a pair of roosters competing to be the first to wake the people of Haven. In the open field near the chicken coop, a single withered tree stood alone against the pitch-black sky, like a sentinel watching over the settlement.

It reminded her of Ghost.

Kira followed Ghost up the porch steps and into the house, her thoughts as tangled as the tree's branches. She hadn't yet shaken off the dream about Emma, but she couldn't stop thinking about Will and Avery, either.

What would happen now that fate had brought them back together? Would Avery's wedding still go on as planned, just as Will insisted? She wanted so desperately to believe it, but she knew from experience that men didn't always keep their promises. Her own father had proven it to her time and time again.

Will is nothing like Devlin, she reminded herself.

Ghost closed the door behind them and moved across the room toward the fireplace. He grabbed two small logs and tossed them into the flames, sending sparks swirling up into the chimney.

Kira stood just inside the door, her gaze sweeping the room. The cabin's main living area was as dark and uninviting as Ghost himself. A square wooden table with a single chair sat near the only window, and in the far corner of the room, a neatly made bed didn't appear to have been slept in that night. There were no personal touches—no photographs, no rugs, no decorations. Aside from the fireplace, there was nothing to make the place feel warm or welcoming.

"Kira," Ghost's voice cut through her thoughts. "In here."

She saw him standing in a narrow doorway at the rear of the cabin, motioning for her to follow him. She passed the fireplace and stepped into a much smaller room, no bigger than the bathroom in her apartment back in Vita Nova. It was dim inside, save for the flickering of a single candle on a desk in the corner, its flame casting elongated shadows on the walls.

Kira allowed her eyes to adjust to the low light, focusing on Ghost as he hunched over an antiquated machine that seemed out of place in the rustic cabin.

"I found this relic in an old military bunker," Ghost murmured, his scarred face half-hidden in shadow. He lowered himself into a leather chair situated in front of the table where the machine sat. Aside from the beds, the chair was the only comfortable piece of furniture Kira had seen in Haven. "It's a ham radio."

Kira had no idea what he was talking about. *A ham radio?*

Her first thought was of music, the kind they sometimes played in Vita Nova between broadcasts, but she knew Ghost hadn't brought her here to listen to a song.

"What does it do?" she asked, her eyes trailing over the wires spilling out of the radio like the guts of some great mechanical beast. It looked like something that had been repeatedly taken apart and put back together.

"It's a two-way communication system."

"You're communicating?" Kira looked at him, not understanding. "With who?"

Instead of answering, Ghost flicked a switch, and the radio crackled to life, static punctuating the air like distant thunder.

A flicker of curiosity warmed Kira's chest, and she moved farther into the room, approaching the radio with caution, as if it might spring to life and bite her.

"It works without electricity?"

Ghost twisted one of the knobs with deliberate care, his black attire swallowing the weak light. "Solar panels," he explained. "Mounted on the roof of the cabin. They charge the batteries that power the radio. Necessity breeds invention."

The scar across his face seemed deeper, more pronounced than before. His strong fingers adjusted the dials with an intimacy that spoke of countless nights spent in communion with the machine.

She leaned closer. "That sound—"

"Quiet," he commanded, bringing his lips to what appeared to be a microphone. "Brannigan? Come in. Over."

Kira held her breath, waiting, but the silence seemed to last forever.

"Brannigan? This is Ghost. How copy? Over."

Finally, a voice sputtered from the speaker—a gruff, unfamiliar one, heavy with sleep, distant and fragmented, yet unmistakably human. *"Good copy, Ghost. Are you up and burning the midnight oil, or what?"*

Kira put a hand over her chest and felt her heart racing.

The man sounded so close, as if he were in the next room. But where was he?

Who was he?

"Couldn't sleep," Ghost replied, rubbing his eyes. "Figured I'd check in and see how you all are faring up there."

"We got a little snow yesterday, believe it or not. Pretty early in the year for snow, even up this way, but we got enough to cover the grass. Didn't stick around long once the sun broke through the clouds, but it still got a smile out of Maisie. I carried her outside and held her so the snowflakes could land on her cheeks. Her birthday's next week. Did I tell you that? She'll be seven."

"Is she doing any better?"

The man on the other end of the radio cleared his throat before responding. *"No, she's not good, brother. Not good at all. She's gone downhill since we talked the other morning. Can't get out of bed on her own anymore. Her legs are just too weak. She's not eating, either. Not enough to keep her going much longer. Mostly, she just sleeps now. Her mother and I take turns sitting with her. We want to make sure that one of us is there when..."*

The sentence hung in the air, unfinished, like a story cut short. Other than his name, Kira did not know this man was, and he did not know she was listening in on the conversation, sharing the weight of his pain.

"What do you think it is?" Ghost asked, his forehead creased with worry.

A long pause followed, long enough for Kira to wonder if the fragile connection between the two radios had been lost. Then the man's voice returned, quieter, more uncertain.

"I think it might be the virus."

A small gasp escaped Kira's mouth, and she stepped away from the radio, as if it could transmit both messages and diseases. *The Job virus?* Her mind was filled with images of emaciated bodies covered in pus-filled sores. Hospital emergency rooms filled to capacity, the sick forced to die alone in the streets. The virus no longer existed within the boundaries of Vita Nova, but out here, in the Unregulated Zone, there were no walls to contain it.

"I'm not sure, though. My wife says I'm wrong—Maisie doesn't have the sores—but there were kids who didn't get the sores last time, remember? I think she's just not ready to face it. Once you've seen something like that, it sticks with you. You never forget what it looks like. I keep telling her that pretending it isn't happening won't make it go away. So far, we're both feeling okay, but who knows how long that will last?"

"I haven't heard of anyone coming down with the virus in years," Ghost said. "Are any others in your town sick?"

"Not that I know of. But we've kept to ourselves, staying isolated from everyone else. Some folks know Maisie's been ill, but people get ill around here all the time. I haven't told anyone that I'm worried it might be the virus. They're good people, but I don't know what they'd do. They might put us out."

Kira's eyes darted from the radio to Ghost. *Put us out?*

Was this man and his family in another settlement somewhere? How many settlements were there?

"I understand. You have to do what—"

"Ghost? I need to go now. My wife is calling. God bless you and protect you, brother. Over and out."

The transmission cut off, leaving an unsettling silence in its wake. The radio sat silent and cold, its wires trailing like severed lifelines, and the room suddenly seemed hollow, as if the cabin had lost its air.

"There are more," Kira whispered. "How many?"

"More than you know," Ghost replied, his gaze still on the radio, as if waiting for his friend to return.

"Are they... good?"

Ghost leaned back in his chair, the leather creaking under his weight. "Some are, like Brannigan and his people. He's the only one I talk to anymore. There have been others, but I cut them off as soon as they started asking too many questions about our location. Those are the ones that keep me up at night —the ones who want to find us so badly. Now, I mostly just listen to the chatter, trying to gather whatever intel I can on the other settlements." He shifted his eyes to her. "Vita Nova is a lie run by liars, but not everything they told you about the Unregulated Zone is a lie."

Kira understood his meaning. She'd learned that lesson back at the dollar store. "These people you've spoken with... Are they all from Pennsylvania?"

"No, I've picked up chatter from as far away as Missouri," he said. "Some areas are starting to rebuild. There's a colony near Cleveland that sounds promising. But from what I can tell, most of the country is still like the Wild West. Small settlements here and there, with a few hundred people each, all looking for hope, just like you. Some groups broadcast their location for weeks, promising safety and trying to draw people in. Then they go silent, and you never hear from them again. Those three men you encountered at the dollar store? This is their country now."

"And Brannigan—where is he from?"

"I don't know. We agreed to not share our locations. I think he's somewhere in New York, based on things he's said in the past, but he's never told me, and I've never asked."

"You don't trust him?"

"I trust him," Ghost said, meeting her gaze with a hard look.

"But I don't trust anyone else who might be listening. I've been thinking about taking my people out there," he confessed, nodding toward the radio. "To Brannigan's settlement. Assuming he could find a way to tell me where it was without risking his people's safety. But getting there would be the hardest part."

Kira could feel the weight of his decision—the responsibility he carried for every soul in Haven. In so many ways, he was the opposite of her father. The people of Haven looked to Ghost for leadership, just as the people of Vita Nova looked to Victor Devlin. Their people trusted and followed them blindly, believing that their lives depended on it. For the people of Haven, that was true. Because Ghost prioritized keeping his followers alive.

Victor Devlin prioritized killing his.

She slipped her hands into the pockets of her khakis and backed away from the radio. The narrow room's walls met her sooner than expected, and she leaned against it, grateful for the support. She was utterly exhausted and downtrodden. Every part of her body ached from the physical strain of the journey, but the ache in her heart at the loss of Will was so much worse.

"You look so much like her."

It took Kira a moment to realize Ghost had spoken. She was drowning in her own miserable thoughts—of her father, of Emma and Jonesy in the Confines, of Will and Avery, reunited and rekindling their lost love.

Thoughts of giving up and returning to her life in Vita Nova.

Then his words registered, and she looked up, meeting his eyes.

"What did you say?"

He looked different, somehow—younger and sadder, as if she were seeing the man he had been ten years ago, not the one she had met at the dollar store. The lines on his forehead weren't as deep, and the scar wasn't as pronounced.

Only the misery in his eyes was the same.

"Never mind," he muttered, tearing his gaze from hers. "Forget it."

But she wouldn't forget it, not even if he begged her to. Even if he dragged her out of his cabin, she would force her way back in.

Because she had to know.

"You said I look like someone," Kira pushed. "Who do I look like?"

Ghost refused to look at her, focusing instead on the steady flame of the candle on his desk. His right hand rested on the armrest of his chair, the veins on the back of his hand standing out as his short fingernails dug into the cracked leather. He closed his eyes, then opened them again.

Finally, he spoke. "I knew your mother, Kira. A long time ago."

Although part of Kira had been expecting those exact words, she still wasn't prepared for them. She didn't know what to say or how to respond.

One of the last things her mother had said before she died flashed through her mind.

"They made him leave, Kira. He wasn't sick."

It was him, she realized. *She was talking about Ghost.*

"How?" Kira asked, her voice cracking. "How did you know her?"

A single tear broke free from his left eye, following the pathway of his scar down his cheek. He wiped it away with the back of his hand.

"I loved her."

Chapter Thirty

Ghost reached into the pocket of his jacket and pulled out a faded photograph. He cradled it tenderly in his fingers, tilting it to the side so that Kira couldn't see it.

The scar on his face twitched as he spoke. "Madison and I knew each other in high school. Well, I knew her, but she didn't know me. I was a year older, and we didn't run in the same circles. Plus, my home life wasn't the best, so I pretty much kept to myself. But your mother—Madison—was different. She was so full of life, so outgoing. Beautiful, yes, but it was more than that. It was her energy, her spirit. She was alive in a way that I never could be. Always laughing in the hallways with her friends. You could hear her laughing from a mile away."

Kira felt a pang of sadness as she listened. She didn't remember her mother as happy and carefree. There had been good times, sure, but even in her happiest moments, Madison Liebert had always seemed a little sad. Often, when they went for walks along the river, Kira would catch her mother staring across the water at the Unregulated Zone, a strange look in her eyes. When Kira asked what was wrong, her mother would say that she missed a world without walls. Then she would change the subject.

Had her mother been looking for Ghost? Was she hoping to catch a glimpse of him on the other side of the river?

"We didn't connect until years later, when you were just a little girl," Ghost continued. "I'd just gotten out of the Army a few months earlier and was in Harrisburg for a job interview. The interview didn't go well, and I was in a foul mood. I stopped at a grocery store before leaving the city, just to grab something for dinner. I was ordering chicken from the butcher when someone tapped me on the shoulder. I turn around, already annoyed, and then I see her."

Kira could see it in her mind, as if she were watching the scene unfold before her. The bustling grocery store, the smell of fresh bread and roasted chicken filling the air, and a younger version of her mother reaching out to tap a man on the shoulder. The thought of her mother—so vibrant and full of hope—reuniting with Ghost in the store stirred something deep within Kira: a longing to have known her mother in that moment, before the virus and Vita Nova had broken her spirit.

Even though Madison Liebert had been dead for more than two years, Ghost seemed to be bringing her back to life.

"'Do you remember me?'" Ghost shook his head, a hint of a smile on his lips. "Those were the first words out of her mouth. As if anyone could forget her. Madison is not the kind of girl you can ever forget." His voice faltered, the smile vanishing as quickly as it had appeared. "We started talking at the butcher counter. I think we stood there for an hour, but it could've been longer. We exchanged phone numbers, and when I drove home later, I'd completely forgotten about the interview. I knew God had brought me into the city that day for an entirely different reason."

It was the first time Ghost had mentioned God in Kira's presence. She hadn't pegged him as a religious man.

"Did she tell you about me?" she asked.

"Of course. She talked about you that first day, but it was months before she let me meet you. She was very cautious, very protective of you. She wanted to be sure of us before she brought me into your life. I respected that. But then, one day, she said it was time for us to meet."

The cool mist of water on her face.

The sticky ice cream on her fingers.

"We were on a boat," she said. "I remember being on a boat with you. Was that real?"

"It was real. It was a Saturday. We met at the Millersburg Ferry and took it across the river. You were seven, I think."

The memory came back clearer than ever before. The steady chugging of the ferry's propellers. The gentle sway as it crossed the Susquehanna. Her mother's laughter, lighter than Kira had ever heard it. A younger version of herself perched on a wooden bench, legs swinging, a scoop of vanilla ice cream melting down the cone in her hand.

A tiny droplet of melted chocolate ice cream splashed onto her wrist, and she'd looked up into the kind eyes of a man whose handsome face had not yet been marred by a scar. He held a small cone of chocolate ice cream.

"Hi Kira," he'd said, sounding nervous. "I'm—"

"Hale," she whispered, slipping back from the memory into the dim light of the cabin. "Your name is Hale, isn't it?"

Ghost nodded. "Noah Hale. Maybe it's a military thing, but everyone has always called me Hale. Even your mother."

He laid the photograph on the table. In the image, he stood at the bow of a boat, his hair cut much shorter than it was now. His arm was wrapped around Kira's mother, and she was leaning into him, her eyes closed, mouth open in laughter. Kira moved closer to the table, studying her mother's features. What had Ghost—Hale—said to make her laugh like that? The mother she remembered was always so worried, so fearful of everything.

But she looked happy on the boat.

Happy and free.

"Halfway across the river, your mother asked me if I was ready to be a father. She said that being your mother was the most important thing in her world and that she'd sacrificed a lot for you, but that she didn't regret any of it. She said she wouldn't hesitate to sacrifice her own happiness if that's what it took to protect you."

Kira reached for the photograph, half-expecting Ghost to rip it away before she could touch it. But he didn't move as she picked it up. "What did she mean?"

"She didn't want to make another mistake." He didn't elaborate, but Kira knew he was referring to her real father. "She wanted me to know that you would always be her priority. She probably thought telling me that might push me away, but it only made me love her more."

Tears stung Kira's eyes. She pressed the photograph to her chest, feeling closer to her mother than she had since that awful day at the Compulsory Clinic. As if some part of her mother was still alive and speaking to her through Ghost.

"I was going to propose to her that day. I brought the ring with me on the ferry—it was in a little pouch in my pocket. But I waited. I didn't think it was the right time." Ghost reached up to stroke the scar on his cheek. "I shouldn't have waited. I didn't realize how little time we would have together."

As Ghost spoke, Kira felt a pang of understanding. The virus had torn them apart. The timing, the circumstances—it all made sense now. Her mother and Ghost, on the brink of a future together, had been ripped away from each other by a looming disaster that neither of them could have ever expected.

"We started hearing reports of the virus soon after that day on the ferry," Ghost continued, confirming her thoughts. "Everything happened so fast. I didn't see Madison after cases started popping up. She'd taken leave from work to stay home with you. She did everything she could to keep you healthy, including not seeing me. But then I heard Harrisburg was going into lockdown. Some of my old Army buddies were engineers, and they'd been given orders to blow the bridges. I knew I needed to get into the city. I needed to be with her. With both of you."

Kira lowered her gaze to the cabin's worn floorboards, searching her mind for a time when Ghost had been inside her home. She remembered the lockdowns. Missing school. Huddling in the townhouse with her mother, hearing news reports about the hospitals filling up with sick people. Her mother trying to make it a fun time, dedicating entire days to playing board games, watching movies, and drinking hot chocolate.

Kira remembered a lot of things from those early days of the virus.

But she didn't remember Ghost.

"You changed your mind," she finally said, returning the photograph to the desk. "Why didn't you come?"

Ghost stared at the picture for a long time, his mind seemingly in a different time, replaying whatever events had kept him from her mother. As Kira watched, his brows furrowed, his expression shifting from wistful to angry.

"Devlin." He practically spat her father's name from his mouth. "He knew about me. Somehow, he knew. I'm guessing he had people watching everything your mother did. Keeping an eye on things and reporting back to him."

Kira opened her mouth to respond, the reflexive urge to defend her father rising within her. After all, Devlin had a new family and had shown no romantic interest in her mother for years. It didn't make sense that he would try to interfere with her mother's new relationship.

But the words died on her lips. This was the same man who had created the Compulsory and Volunteer programs and who had orchestrated the deaths of thousands.

He was capable of anything.

Ghost interlaced his fingers on the desk. "When I reached the city, they had already set up roadblocks on the bridges and major highways, and they were working on placing fencing along the perimeter for a temporary barricade. But there were still ways in—places that hadn't been covered yet, gaps in the fencing. My Army buddies told me where they were, and I snuck into the city early on a Sunday morning. The bridges were scheduled to be blown the next day at sunrise. The city was in total chaos—riots, fires, shootings, you name it. Devlin had weaponized the National Guard to regain control. What I didn't know was that he'd also started sending soldiers door-to-door in biohazard suits to perform health checks. If they suspected anyone in a household of being sick, they'd remove the individual and their family members from their home under the guise of getting them medical treatment. But they didn't take them to field hospitals. Instead, they transported them outside the city limits, dumped them there, and left them to die."

Ghost paused and looked at her. "He put entire families out there, Kira. Sick and healthy together. Parents with their children and infants. The elderly. People who had no chance of surviving without help. He left them out there with nothing but the clothes on their backs."

Kira lowered her eyes, unable to look at him, as if she were somehow responsible for her father's actions. Her gaze dropped to her hands, tracing the veins beneath her skin—veins that carried the blood of a monster.

Ghost's voice pulled her back. "I showed up at your mother's house long before the sun came up. There was no one on her street. It was so quiet. That's the part I'll never forget. How silent it was, compared to the rest of the city. You could hear the sirens and gunshots, but they sounded so far away. When I knocked on the door and Madison answered, I thought I'd made it. That no matter what happened, at least we would face it together."

He hesitated, staring into the flickering candle flame as if trying to find the right words. "But then we heard pounding on the front door. A squad of soldiers in biohazard suits were on the porch. I hid in the hallway closest while Madison answered the door. I hoped it was just a random health check, but it wasn't. There was nothing random about it. Devlin must've sent them, because they refused to leave and accused your mother of harboring an infected person."

Kira didn't know whether to scream or cry. It was all so unfair. Her mother had been on the brink of happiness, only to have it snatched away by the very man who had fathered her child.

"What did you do?"

He gave her a weak shrug. "What could I do? You were asleep upstairs. Madison was crying. I couldn't risk putting you both in danger. So, I stepped out of the closet with my hands in the air. They grabbed me and pulled me outside. I didn't even get to say goodbye to her." His voice trembled. "I expected them to dump me outside the city with the others, but they took me to jail instead. The whole building was empty—they must've moved the inmates out. Probably left them outside the barricade, too. I didn't have time to think about it, though, because Devlin was waiting for me."

Kira almost asked him to stop talking. She'd never wanted a story to end so badly in her life. But Ghost needed to get this out. She could see it in his eyes—the desperate need for someone to understand, to bear witness to the pain that had shaped him. "What happened with my father?"

"He told me I'd never see Madison again, that it was better that way. For both of us and for you. He said he'd let me go, but if I tried to get back into the city, he'd make sure that Madison tested positive for the virus. He'd have both of you thrown out and left to die, and I would be responsible."

Tears slid down her cheeks as she remembered her mother's final words.

"They made him leave, Kira. He wasn't sick."

Even on her deathbed, Madison Liebert had never forgotten him. In her mind, the soldiers had suspected him of being infected and removed him from the city. She couldn't have known that Devlin was behind it all. That he'd gone out of his way to destroy her only chance at happiness.

And she couldn't have known that Ghost had sacrificed everything to protect her and her daughter.

"I wasn't handcuffed," Ghost continued. "The cell door was hanging open. Devlin had two soldiers with him, so I'm sure he felt safe. He didn't think I'd do anything. But I lunged at him. I can still see the fear in his eyes. I got in one good punch before the soldiers grabbed me. Even managed to knock out his front tooth. I remember him standing there with one hand over his mouth, this look of complete shock in his eyes, the blood pouring through his fingers. That single punch was the best thing I've ever done in my life."

Confused, Kira shook her head. "But my father isn't missing any teeth."

"Oh, I'm sure he's fixed it. He has the resources. A broken tooth is easy to fix compared to what he did to me."

"What are you talking about?"

Ghost tapped the jagged scar on his face, his fingers brushing its rough edges. "One soldier handed Devlin a knife. I thought he was going to kill me, but the other two held me down while he carved up my face. Once he finished, he said, 'I've just done you a favor. Now you've got no reason to risk your life trying to come back for Madison. She won't love you anymore now that you're so ugly.'"

Kira allowed her eyes to linger on the scar, its jagged, twisted line a stark contrast to the rugged handsomeness of Ghost's face. She knew her father well enough to understand that this permanent disfigurement was about something far deeper than a tooth.

"My mother loved you," Kira said, pulling her jacket tighter around her. "You knew that. You knew she wouldn't care about your scar. Why didn't you come back for us?"

Ghost's fingers left his scar and returned to the table. "Because it was the only way to keep you both safe. I thought if I disappeared, Devlin would leave you and your mother alone. I knew how bad it was outside the city and how hard it was to survive. I couldn't stand the thought of the two of you struggling like that." He picked up the photograph from the ferry, his voice thick with regret. "Sometimes I think about how different things would be if I'd just asked her to marry me on this day. Maybe she would be safe here with me instead of trapped in that city."

The realization hit Kira like a punch in the gut.

He doesn't know. He never asked me if she was alive.

Her mind raced, caught between the instinct to shield him from the truth and the duty to be honest. Telling him now would extinguish the last bit of hope in his heart—the hope that

the woman he loved was still alive behind the barricade, that he
had somehow succeeded in protecting her, even at the cost of
his own happiness.

But he deserved to know the truth, even if it destroyed him.
Because Madison Liebert was gone, and she wasn't coming
back. She wouldn't want the man she loved to continue living
in a purgatory of false hope, clinging to a love that had already
been lost.

"Ghost," she spoke softly, the name feeling wrong on her
lips now that she knew his real name. "I'm so sorry, but my
mother passed away two years ago."

He looked at her, confusion and sorrow battling for domi-
nance in his eyes. "Two years ago? But the virus—"

"The virus didn't kill her."

Ghost's face twisted in pain—real, physical pain—his hands
clenched into tight fists, the photograph creasing under the
pressure. He closed his eyes. "How did she die?"

Kira hesitated, knowing the truth would only bring more
pain. How would he handle knowing that Vita Nova had
decided Madison Liebert's life wasn't worth saving? That she
had been put down like a sick animal in order to conserve
resources?

"How, Kira?"

A bitter taste filled her mouth, and she rolled her tongue
over her dry lips. "She got a Compulsory Notification."

His eyes snapped open. "A what?"

"A Compulsory Notification. They're letters sent out from
the Medical Sector when you're too sick or old and become a
drain on Vita Nova's resources." The words sounded absurd as
they left her lips. How had she ever bought into such madness?
"During my mother's health screening, they found signs of lung
cancer. She got a letter soon after."

"Lung cancer."

Kira nodded. "The tumor in her lung was too big to remove. We applied for an exemption, but it was denied."

Ghost swallowed hard, looking as if he might be sick. "And what happens after you get one of these... notifications?"

"They take you to a clinic where they inject you with a drug—Somnumbutal—to put you to sleep."

Ghost buried his head in his hands, his voice cracking with emotion. "Maddie. Oh, God. I'm so sorry, baby."

Kira approached the table, drawn by the shared pain between them. Ghost had loved her mother, too. After the virus, he'd been the only other person in the world who had loved her, and Kira hadn't even known it.

As she drew closer, she could hear his ragged breathing, choked with grief. She longed to comfort him, to embrace him, but she hesitated, unsure of how he might react. Instead, she reached out and placed a hand on his shoulder, his body shaking beneath her touch. I'm so sorry," she whispered, tears streaming down her cheeks. "I'd give anything to bring her back."

He lifted his head from his hands, his eyes filled with sorrow. "Was it painful? Did she suffer?"

"No." Her voice wavered as she struggled to regain her composure. "She didn't suffer at all. She just went to sleep. The drug makes the entire process very peaceful. The city doesn't want anyone to suffer."

The words were out of her mouth before she could stop them, as if she were still reciting lines from her volunteer advocate script rather than speaking to the only man who had truly loved her mother.

The pain in Ghost's eyes hardened into hatred. "And your pig of a father allowed this to happen?"

Kira thought of that day in Devlin's car, when she had confronted him about her mother's death. The same day she had first met Will. "He said he didn't know about the Compulsory Order until it was too late."

Ghost cursed under his breath and dropped the picture onto the desk. Fresh creases ran through both his and Madison's faces. He shoved the chair back and stood, as if ready to march straight to Vita Nova. But he remained where he was, taking slow, deep breaths, working to calm himself down.

When he spoke again, it was through gritted teeth, each word forced out with difficulty. "It was him, Kira."

"Who?"

"Your father. Nothing happens in that city without Devlin knowing about it."

Her eyes fell to her mother's face in the photo. So young. So happy. So in love with the handsome man beside her.

"What are you saying?"

He didn't answer immediately, but he didn't need to.

She already knew.

Deep down, she had *always* known.

"He killed her, Kira," Ghost finally said. "Devlin killed your mother."

Chapter Thirty-One

The sun pierced the mess hall windows, casting a warm golden glow on Kira's face as she whisked a large bowl of eggs. Every movement felt labored, her arms heavy, her body weighed down by the late-night conversation with Ghost.

She had gotten no sleep after she returned to Brack and Grace's cabin, her mind unable to shake the things Ghost had said about Devlin's role in her mother's death. Until last night, Kira had only considered the possibility that her father might have known about the Compulsory Order and—for whatever reason—chosen not to intervene.

But what if Ghost was right? What if the order had come directly from Devlin himself?

An even darker possibility existed.

What if her mother had never been sick?

It seemed impossible. What motive could her father have had to want her mother dead? How would it benefit him? As far as she knew, her parents barely interacted, and Devlin seemed perfectly content to let Madison shoulder all the responsibility of raising their daughter. He hadn't even tried to take her in after her mother's death, instead continuing to keep his distance as he always had.

No, it didn't make sense.

What *did* make sense was that Ghost hated Devlin—a seething, blinding hatred fueled by years of pain. Of course, he would believe Devlin was capable of ordering the death of the woman he loved.

But that didn't make it true.

All night, Kira had lain awake, wrestling with the possibilities, torn between what she knew of her father and Ghost's accusations. So, when Bailey appeared at the cabin just before six in the morning with news that Kira had been assigned breakfast duty, she had wanted to crawl back under her blanket and disappear. But the steady rhythm of whisking bowl after bowl of eggs, combined with the soothing hymns sung by the other women in the kitchen, provided just enough distraction to keep her thoughts from spiraling.

"What a friend we have in Jesus...
All our sins and griefs to bear.
What a privilege to carry everything to God in prayer."

The clatter of utensils and plates filled the air as the breakfast crew served Haven's hungry residents. The children arrived promptly at seven, escorted by their parents. Kira paused her whisking long enough to wave at Teddy and Grace as they made their way through the line. After the children had eaten, the adults filtered in, most looking as exhausted as Kira felt. Everyone finished their meals quickly and exited the crowded mess hall, leaving space at the tables for those who had yet to eat. The building buzzed with the routine of survival, with each person playing their part to ensure the community's continued existence.

So different from Vita Nova.

"He probably won't be back until this evening, you know," Bailey spoke up beside her, a half-peeled potato in her hands. "He's out beyond the fence today."

Kira blinked, pulling herself from her thoughts. "Who?"

Bailey lowered her head, her lips curling into a teasing smile. "Who do you think? Your boyfriend. He's on the hunting party—they're usually gone all day."

The ache in Kira's chest at the mention of Will's name surprised her. Yesterday, she'd allowed her anger at his dishonesty about Avery to overshadow her feelings for him. But now those feelings had come rushing back with a vengeance, and she missed him fiercely. The thought of Will being out in the woods with armed strangers while the Patrols were still out there somewhere filled her with anxiety.

"Kira?"

A soft voice interrupted her thoughts. She glanced up to see Avery standing in the entrance to the kitchen, her slender frame casting a delicate shadow on the wooden floor.

"Can we talk?"

The blood rushed to Kira's cheeks. She glanced over at Bailey, silently pleading for rescue. "Uh, I'm pretty busy right now. I don't think I can—"

"It's fine," Bailey interjected, placing her potato peeler down and reaching for the bowl of eggs. "The breakfast rush is winding down. Take a few minutes to talk, then come back to help us clean up, okay?"

But Kira clung to the bowl, reluctant to let it go—and more reluctant to have a conversation with Avery about her relationship with Will. "But I'm still on duty."

Bailey sighed and gently tugged the bowl from Kira's hands. "Listen, I am as fond of a dramatic love triangle as the next person, but this is a survival situation, ladies. Discuss it, work it out, flip a coin for Will if necessary, and then get back to work."

Kira's body sagged at the realization that the conversation was inevitable. She had always been good at compartmentalizing, at pushing aside her own feelings to focus on the task at hand. But now, standing here with Avery looking expectantly at her, she realized she had no more excuses left. The conversation was going to happen, whether she liked it or not.

Slowly, she untied her apron, folded it, and placed it on the counter. Then she followed Avery out of the kitchen.

The crisp morning air greeted them as they stepped outside, the dew-kissed grass crunching beneath their boots as they walked toward the church. Children's laughter echoed from the playground, and she found herself wondering how Teddy was doing. She'd been so caught up in her own drama yesterday that she'd forgotten to ask him about school. Did he like his teacher? Had he made any friends?

Would they even stay in Haven long enough for any of it to matter?

Avery nodded at the church. "I'm getting there married tomorrow night."

Kira admired her ability to get straight to the point.

"The wedding is at seven. My fiancé's name is Nic Hernandez. I would've introduced you earlier, but he was on perimeter duty last night and isn't off-shift yet. We've been together for a few years."

"Yes, Will told me about your wedding yesterday. Congratulations."

Avery stopped walking and turned to face Kira, her expression a mixture of hurt and anger. "If you know I'm getting married, why are you still upset with me? Why are you upset with Will?"

"No, I'm not." Kira struggled to find the right words. "This isn't about you, honestly. It's about Will. He left Emmitsburg to look for you. He basically admitted that to me. So, the fact that you're getting married is great, and I'm happy for you, but that doesn't mean that Will isn't still—" She couldn't bring herself to finish the sentence, so she switched to a different one. "I mean, do you remember the look on his face when he saw you yesterday?"

"Yes, I remember it. He looked surprised."

"No, it was more than that."

Had it been, though? There had been a look of pure shock on Will's face, as if he'd just seen a ghost. But had there really been something more in his eyes when he looked at Avery? Or had Kira imagined it?

She bent and picked up a stick from the ground. It was old and brittle, snapping easily in her hands. "I don't understand why we're standing out here. You don't owe me any explanation. We don't know each other. You don't owe me anything."

When Avery spoke again, her voice was softer, more vulnerable. "We're standing here because I need to explain to you why I left Emmitsburg. When I left, I did it knowing Will wouldn't come with me. We had never talked about leaving together, and he had no idea I was thinking about going. But even before I told him, I knew he wouldn't come. He'd never leave Jonesy and Aunt Reeva. They were like parents to him after his own parents died."

Kira stared at her, waiting. "What are you saying?"

A new emotion, something close to anger, had edged its way into Avery's voice. "I think a big part of me was upset because I knew I wasn't Will's first priority. That sounds really childish and selfish, but it's the truth." Avery nibbled on one fingernail briefly before tucking her hand back into her pocket. "Maybe I was testing Will's love by threatening to leave. Maybe I wanted to see if he would give up everyone else to come with me. And he called my bluff. He didn't go. We talked about it a little, but I could tell it was never a serious consideration for him."

Kira experienced a rush of emotions as she listened to Avery—a mixture of surprise, empathy, and a twinge of jealousy—making it hard to focus. She tried to imagine herself in Avery's place, torn between wanting to be someone's top priority and the harsh reality that she wasn't. She couldn't help but feel a sense of validation, knowing that even Avery, with all her beauty and charm, had struggled with feeling second-best in Will's life.

"Since I'm being completely honest," Avery continued, "I might as well admit that I'm a little jealous of you."

Kira gaped at her. "*You're* jealous of *me?*"

"Of course I am. Don't you see? He wouldn't leave Jonesy and Aunt Reeva for me, but he left them for you."

"No," Kira shook her head. "He didn't. Aunt Reeva was supposed to come with us."

"I know. Will told me what happened the morning you guys left. But Reeva didn't go, did she? And yet Will is still out here.... with you. I heard the guy carried you into the village in his arms, Kira. What more proof do you need that he loves you?"

Kira opened her mouth to protest, but the truth in Avery's words silenced her. Will had left Emmitsburg with her, even when Aunt Reeva hadn't been able to come. He'd carried Kira into Haven, protecting her every step of the way. But Will hadn't just been protecting her—he'd been choosing her.

Choosing her over Avery.

Choosing her over everyone else.

"Long story short," Avery continued, "give the guy a break. He wasn't totally honest with you. He made a few mistakes. Nobody's perfect. But he's one of the best guys I've ever known, and he deserves to be with the girl who truly makes him happy."

"Thank you," Kira said, genuinely meaning it. "We don't know each other—you don't owe me anything—but I appreciate you taking the time to explain how everything happened between you and Will. I guess I should've listened to him instead of flying off the handle, right?"

"I've also been known to fly off the handle on occasion. Sounds like our Will has a type," Avery said with a smile. "Anyway, now that we've gotten the awkward stuff out of the way, I wanted to invite you to my wedding."

"You wanted to...what?"

Avery laughed at Kira's reaction. "It's going to be a blast. I'm inviting all of Will's ex-girlfriends. If enough of us show up, we'll form our own conga line." She slapped Kira playfully on the arm. "But seriously, the wedding won't be anything over the top, but it will still be a great party. We'll have the ceremony inside the church at seven, followed by dancing outside, as long as the weather cooperates. I understand if this whole thing is a little weird, but I'd still love it if you came."

Kira shook her head. "No, I can't."

Avery rolled her eyes. "Why not?"

Because I don't know you at all, she wanted to say. *Because you're Will's ex-girlfriend. Because it would be horribly awkward.*

But instead of voicing any of these reasons, Kira blurted out the first thing that came to her mind.

"I don't have anything to wear."

"Don't be silly." Avery waved a hand at her. "This wedding isn't going to be formal. Nothing around here ever is. Except for Nic, most of the men will be in jeans and flannels, and the women will wear whatever dresses they have that aren't stained and ripped."

"Yes, but I don't even have a *ripped* dress."

"I know, I know." Avery's eyebrows bunched together as she considered this, and then she snapped her fingers. "Mrs. Milroy!"

"Who?"

"She's the woman who sews our clothes. She patches things up, sews buttons when necessary, and just basically makes our clothes last longer. But she also creates beautiful dresses out of old, worn ones. She made my wedding gown out of three different dresses that Nic found in thrift stores when he was out looking for supplies. It's kind of last minute, but I'm sure she'll have something that will work for you. We can stop by later, after you're done with kitchen duty."

Kira glanced down at her nails. The last time she'd painted them had been a few weeks earlier, before her double date with Emma and the Patrol soldiers at the Riverfront. Only a few flecks of gray polish remained, the last vestiges of a life that seemed distant and irrelevant now.

"We can take care of your nails, too," Avery offered, as if reading Kira's mind. "I don't wear it much—there's no point out here—but I have a few different shades I save for special occasions."

Well, her nails *did* look terrible.

Wouldn't it be nice to feel beautiful again, just for an evening?

"Okay," Kira finally relented. "You won me over with the polish. I'd love to come."

Avery's face lit up, and she threw her arms around Kira's shoulders. "That makes me so happy. Truly. I promise, you won't regret it. This wedding is going to be the most fun we've had in a..."

Her voice trailed off, and she pulled away from Kira. There was a commotion over at the mess hall. A crowd had gathered, and the usually orderly lines of people had dissolved into a chaotic cluster, with everyone talking at once, their faces etched with worry and confusion.

After exchanging a quick glance, the two women hurried across the field. As they approached the gathering crowd, Kira tried to glean what she could from the numerous conversations that were happening, but none of it made any sense. Something about the perimeter fence.

Had someone cut the fence in the night and snuck into the village?

As Kira watched, a group of men suddenly broke off from the others and jogged toward the forest.

Avery approached a heavyset woman with red hair. One of the cooks who had been singing hymns that morning. "What is it, Maggie? Did someone get hurt?"

"Not hurt," the woman said, her voice shaking as she wiped the tears from her cheeks. "One of the perimeter guards is dead."

"One of the guards?"

As she watched Avery's face drain of color, Kira remembered her mentioning that her fiancé, Nic, had been assigned to the perimeter last night.

"Who, Maggie?" Avery asked, her voice trembling. "Who's dead?"

But the redheaded woman continued to ramble as if she hadn't heard the question. She walked away, her head low, muttering to herself. "I just saw him yesterday. It doesn't make any sense. He seemed so happy."

Avery grabbed the woman's arm. "*Who, Maggie?*"

The woman spun around, eyes wild. "Trevor Anderson," she blurted out, yanking her arm out of Avery's grip. "He hung himself on the perimeter fence."

Chapter Thirty-Two

Kira stood frozen, staring at the young man's body dangling from the perimeter fence like a twisted marionette, his lifeless form a stark contrast against the backdrop of tangled undergrowth and towering trees. His boots hung nearly six feet above the ground, the fraying rope tied to the top of the fence holding him in place, its other end cinched tightly around his neck.

She tore her eyes away from his face—one that, even though it now wore the mask of death, Kira could see had once been handsome.

Her heart broke for him.

Who in the village loved this young man?

Who was waking up this morning to the worst news imaginable?

Around her, dozens of Haven's residents stared at the body, whispering to each other in hushed, uneasy tones.

"How did he get up there? It's so high."

"Where there's a will, there's a way."

"But why would Trevor do this?"

"He's so young. Barely eighteen."

Kira listened to the murmured conversations, her gaze drifting away from the body to scan the anxious faces around her. Their shock suggested that suicide was rare in their community—nothing like Vita Nova, where it was a weekly and celebrated occurrence.

Avery leaned close and whispered into Kira's ear. "This wasn't a suicide."

Kira looked at her. "How do you know?"

A shadow passed over Avery's face, her eyes narrowing as she took in the huddled villagers. "Trevor would never do something like this. Not to his girlfriend, and not to the rest of us. Something else is going on."

Kira shivered, despite the warmth of the morning sun on her skin. "Like what?"

"I don't know yet. But Trevor didn't kill himself."

Their conversation was cut short by the crunch of leaves and the sound of running footsteps. Kira turned to see several men emerging from the thicket, rifles slung over their shoulders, their camouflage gear blending with the forest.

The hunting party.

Someone back in the village must've called them on the radio to tell them what had happened.

Will appeared at the rear of the group, a pair of squirrels hanging from his shoulder. Their small, gray bodies bounced against his side as he jogged toward her.

"Will," she breathed, relief flooding through her at the sight of him. She ran to him and threw her arms around his neck, clinging to him.

He dropped the squirrels to the ground, his arms wrapping around her. One hand came up to cup the back of her head, and he held it against his chest. She could hear his heart beating—strong and fast—and in that moment, all of her doubts and worries about him seemed distant and unimportant.

Nothing else mattered, as long as he was alive.

"Are you alright?" he asked.

She nodded against his chest, unwilling to let go just yet. "I'm fine. I'm just so glad you're safe."

The chattering of the villagers grew louder, the once-hushed whispers turning into open conversation. The crowd grew bolder, pressing closer to the fence, their curiosity outweighing their shock. Someone in the crowd—an older gentleman—reached out and touched the dead man's boots, as if needing to confirm what he was seeing. The others followed suit, leaning in to get a closer look, some reaching to touch the body.

Then, a voice boomed in the forest, cutting through the chatter like a knife.

"Do not touch him!"

Kira lifted her head from Will's chest to see Ghost standing at the edge of the group, the double-barrel shotgun hanging from his shoulder, his eyes wide with fury as he looked from one guilty face to another.

Everyone fell silent, clearly startled by the sudden appearance of their leader. Most backed away from the fence, hanging their heads in shame, but a few remained rooted in place, their faces hard and defiant.

"We came to cut him down," said the older gentlemen who had touched Trevor's foot. He pulled a handkerchief from his pocket to dab his leaking nose.

"There are at least thirty people standing around here, Gary," Ghost replied. "It doesn't take thirty people to cut down one boy."

"Well, no, but first we needed to—"

"What you needed to do was show some respect. Trevor was someone's son. Did you ever have a son, Gary?"

The man lowered his head but did not answer.

Ghost moved toward the body, and the crowd parted around him like water around a rock. He reached the base of the fence and stood there for almost a minute, his head tilting back as he studied the body.

When he turned to scan the crowd, his gaze settled on Will, Kira, and Avery. "You three will stay behind to help me cut him down. The rest of you head back to the village. There's plenty of work to do, and none of it is getting done while you all are standing around out here, gawking."

The villagers dispersed, some grumbling, others offering mumbled apologies. After they were gone, Avery stepped forward. "Ghost, I'm sure Trevor didn't kill himself. He wouldn't do this. Someone must have put him up there."

Ghost nodded and rubbed his face. "You three wait here. I need to check something."

He unslung his gun and rested it against a tree, and then he began to scale the fence, climbing to the left of the lifeless young man. As he approached the torso, he paused and leaned closer to examine the hands. He brushed his fingers over the torn clothing, then climbed higher, frowning as he examined Trevor's neck and face.

Kira looked away. She hadn't known Trevor, but it still hurt to see a person in such terrible condition. It struck her how strange people looked after they died. Whether their death had been peaceful or violent, they always seemed... off. She had thought the same thing when her mother passed away. Almost instantly, it had become obvious there was something missing— an absence that was hard to describe.

Ghost descended the fence, his face grave. "He was attacked," he said as soon as his boots hit the ground. "There's blood and skin under his fingernails, which could've come from him struggling with the rope after he hung himself. But he's also got two broken fingers on his right hand and bruises all over his head. I'm sure if we stripped him down, we'd find more injuries. Someone beat him badly before they hung him."

Will stared at him. "Who? An enemy? Someone from the village?"

"Trevor was a nice guy," Avery said. "He didn't have any enemies. No one in Haven could've done this."

No one in Haven.

A thought entered Kira's mind, one she didn't want to entertain but couldn't dismiss. She hesitated before speaking, nervously fidgeting with the hem of her shirt. "Do you think it was those men?

Ghost turned to her. "What men?"

"Those three men from the dollar store. The ones who attacked me."

It was too horrifying to consider—that Kira's presence in Haven might have led to this young man's death. But if Trevor didn't have any enemies and he didn't kill himself...

"What are you talking about?" Avery asked. "You were attacked?"

"They didn't hurt me. Ghost got to me in time."

"Thank God."

Ghost rubbed the dark stubble on his chin. "It could've been them. We were careful, but I suppose they could have followed us here."

He didn't look convinced.

Avery crossed her arms over her chest. "I'm going to talk to Nic. We need to cancel the wedding."

"Absolutely not." Ghost shook his head. "You know how things go around here. There will be rumors floating around the village for the rest of the day, but canceling your wedding will only make people more frightened. We're going to let everyone think Trevor committed suicide, at least until we figure out what's really going on here. No one knows the truth except you three, so if word spreads, I'll know it came from you. And I won't hesitate to put you outside the fence."

"So, what do we do now?" Will asked. "If Trevor didn't hang himself, that means there's a killer inside this village—or there was last night. We can't just ignore that. Acting like nothing happened could put everyone at risk."

Ghost retrieved his shotgun from where it leaned against the tree. "We'll step up security along the perimeter for the next few days. Double up on shifts—two-person teams at all times. You three need to keep your eyes open today. Avery, you know who belongs here. If you spot anyone unfamiliar, don't confront them, as much as I know you'll want to. Just call me on the radio."

"Where are you going?"

He gestured toward the fence. "I saw Nic on my way in. I'll find him and send him back to help you with the body. After that, I'm going to retrace our steps from the other day and see if I can find any tracks or signs that we were followed."

Before he could turn away, Kira's voice stopped him. "Why would they hang someone?" she asked. "Those men from the dollar store. Why would they do that? Trevor had nothing to do with what happened back there."

"We don't know it was them," Ghost replied. "It may not have been. For all we know, it could've been someone who lives here. Maybe Trevor got into a fight with someone."

"And they hung him? You don't really believe that, do you?"

"No, I don't," he admitted.

"So, what do you think really happened?"

For a long moment, Ghost's gaze shifted between the forest

and Kira. Finally, he said, "I think this was a warning. I think whoever did this wanted to send us a message."

Kira's stomach tightened as she forced herself to ask the next question. "What message?"

This time, he did not hesitate to answer. "The same one the leadership in that city sends every time they mail out a Compulsory Notification: I'm in control. Your life is in my hands."

Chapter Thirty-Three

Kira stood before a cracked mirror in the corner of the cabin, studying her body in the simple purple dress. It was the same rich shade of purple as the asters wilting in their vase on the table. The fabric hugged her curves as if tailored just for her, cinching at the waist before flaring into a gentle A-line that swayed with her movements. She wore black ballet flats borrowed from Avery. They were a size too large, but her feet were still swollen from her journey, so they fit perfectly.

Though she usually kept her blonde hair in a messy bun or a ponytail, today she had allowed it to flow freely. It had been Grace's idea to wear it down, and though Kira felt exposed and oddly vulnerable, there was no denying how good it looked cascading in loose waves over her shoulders. She fidgeted with the strands, tucking them nervously behind her ears, feeling as though she were wearing a costume that didn't quite fit. Even her nails, painted in an uncharacteristic pale pink, were a small but significant departure from her true self.

Meeting the eyes of her reflection, she forced herself to

smile. It was a wedding, after all—and she was supposed to be happy. But the memory of the previous day's tragedy lingered like a dark cloud that followed her everywhere. Each time she closed her eyes, she saw Trevor's lifeless body hanging on the fence. His death was unsettling enough, but what truly gnawed at her was the question of who—or what—had killed him.

A knock on the door startled her out of her thoughts. She knew who it was before she even looked. Will had promised to pick her up a little before seven, and he was never late. She took one last look in the mirror, smoothing the thin fabric over her hips, then crossed the room to open the door.

Will stood on the steps, his tousled hair and sunburnt cheeks adding a ruggedness to his usual boyish good looks. He wore faded black slacks and a wrinkled button-down white shirt—a far cry from the tailored tuxedo he'd worn to the Volunteer Ball during his Final Week—but to Kira, he had never looked more handsome. His piercing blue eyes softened as they took her in, and a smile tugged at the corners of his lips, revealing the lopsided dimples she loved so much. Despite the fears swirling in her mind, Kira smiled back.

Will's eyes widened as he took her in. "Kira," he said, gazing up at her as she stood in the open doorway. "That dress is... it's incredible. And your hair. You haven't worn it down like that since the Volunteer Ball."

"It's killing me to not pull it back," she admitted. "But Grace told me no ponytails or messy buns tonight."

"Grace was right." He reached out and took her hand. "Are you ready for this?"

She nodded. "Let's go watch your gorgeous ex-girlfriend get married."

Kira placed her hand inside his, savoring the familiar roughness of his calloused fingers. Together, they walked across the open field towards the distant silhouette of the church, its weathered steeple reaching for the sky.

As they walked, Kira's gaze drifted to the forest that bordered the village. The sun had nearly set, and shadows stretched out from the trees, like long, grasping fingers, reaching hungrily for the light that was rapidly fading. Even with the distant sounds of music and people coming from the church, Kira couldn't shake the unsettling sensation that eyes were on her, hidden somewhere within the thick underbrush. She tightened her grip on Will's hand, trying to push the unease away, but the feeling lingered, clawing at the edges of her mind.

Stop it, she told herself. *There's nothing out there.*

The sound of hurried footsteps on the gravel path interrupted Kira's thoughts, and she turned just in time to see Teddy barreling toward her. He wore an ill-fitting and mismatched suit, one-eyed Randy dangling from his hand, his face bright with excitement.

"Kira!" he shouted, launching himself into her arms. He would have knocked her off balance, but Will's steady hand on her back kept her upright.

She wrapped her arms around him and held him close. "Hey, buddy," she said, brushing a strand of hair from his forehead. "You ready for the big party tonight?"

Teddy nodded. "Randy and I want to dance with you all night! But only if Will says it's okay."

Will ruffled the boy's hair. "She's all yours, pal. But fair warning—she can be a handful."

Teddy wasn't heavy, but his weight was already testing her arms, which weren't as strong as they needed to be. Reluctantly, she put him down. "I can't wait to dance with you, buddy."

As they continued toward the church, Kira forced herself to smile as she listened to Teddy chatter about the other children he'd met at school, the new best friend he'd made, the games they played at recess, and his teacher.

But as they stepped into the warm glow of the church's lanterns, she stole a last glance over her shoulder at the darkened treeline.

The feeling of being watched hadn't disappeared.

If anything, it had only intensified.

THE WEDDING OF AVERY AND NIC WAS BEAUTIFUL, AND afterward, the residents of Haven gathered beneath the stars to celebrate. Lanterns hung from the surrounding trees and buildings, casting flickering shadows across the ground. Several long tables lined the perimeter of the reception, decorated with vases of purple asters. The women of the village had prepared a veritable feast—freshly harvested vegetables, tender-braised rabbit, and hearty stew made from wild game hunted in the surrounding woods. Loaves of crusty bread, still warm from the oven and wrapped in towels, sat next to jars of creamy butter and homemade preserves.

Kira stood at the edge of the festivities, finishing the last bites of a slice of warm bread slathered with peach preserves. Behind her, the forest was alive with sound—a symphony of rustling leaves, chirping crickets, and the occasional hoot of an owl. The cool night air caressed the bare skin of her back and shoulders, sending a shiver through her, though she barely noticed. She was mesmerized by the villagers' ability to find so much joy in so little.

In the grassy clearing in front of the church, people danced with abandon, their laughter mingling with the sweet sound of live music—two guitars and a violin—as they twirled and spun beneath the stars. Others gathered around the tables, filling metal plates and bowls with food. It was a simple celebration, especially compared to the lavish parties of Vita Nova, yet the happiness Kira saw in the eyes of Haven's residents was unlike anything she had ever witnessed in the city.

As Kira took the last bite of her bread, she noticed Brack at the food table, piling his plate impossibly high with everything in sight—stew, roasted vegetables, slices of bread. The plate was so overloaded that it looked like the metal might buckle under the strain.

When Grace caught sight of him, she marched over and swatted his arm. "Brack, you big glutton!" she scolded, reaching for the towering plate. "You can't possibly eat all that, and even if you could, what happened to leaving some for everyone else?"

But Brack dodged her attempt, holding his plate high above his head, just out of Grace's reach. "It's a wedding feast, Tumblebug," he declared, his grin widening as Grace made a playful, but futile, jump to grab the plate. "It would be rude not to celebrate properly."

Grace narrowed her eyes, clearly determined not to let him win. In a quick move, she faked another jump and then jabbed him in the stomach, catching him off guard. Brack let out a surprised grunt, lowering the plate just enough for Grace to snatch it from his hands. She smiled triumphantly and took a little bow as Brack rubbed his stomach.

"Tumblebug, that wasn't nice!"

The other people gathered around the food tables were laughing, clearly enjoying the antics of the feisty pregnant redhead and her oaf of a husband, and Kira laughed with them.

In the middle of the festivities, Avery and Nic Hernandez clung to each other, swaying slowly to the music despite its rapid tempo, oblivious to the world around them. Avery gazed up at her groom, staring deeply into his eyes, as if they held the answers to every secret in the universe. Nic pulled her closer, his arms wrapping protectively around her waist.

Kira smiled and shook her head, silently chiding herself for ever feeling jealous of this beautiful girl for her past with Will when she so obviously belonged to someone else.

So did Will.

Tearing her gaze away from the newlyweds, Kira searched the crowd until she found Will. He was dancing with a little girl, holding both her hands as he lifted one arm, guiding her into a playful spin. The girl, Harper, was only six years old—and one of Teddy's new friends. Like him, she had no memory of the world before the virus.

Kira wanted to believe that was a good thing. She wanted to believe that the world would only get better for Teddy and Harper. So much had happened in the last decade. So much death, loss, and pain. Maybe these children would have the chance to live a happier life.

And maybe this tattered little village in the middle of nowhere would be the start of it.

She scanned the area, hoping to glimpse Ghost's familiar, shadowy figure at the edge of the festivities, but he was nowhere in sight.

As the song ended, the crowd parted, and an older gentleman made his way to the center of the gathering. He wore a black dress shirt, faded blue jeans, a Harley Davidson vest, and scuffed motorcycle boots. The man walked with a slight hunch, carrying a stool in one hand and a stringed instrument Kira had never seen before in the other. When he reached the makeshift dance floor, he placed the stool on the ground and lowered himself onto it, his joints creaking loud enough for Kira to hear. His thinning hair fluttered in the breeze, creating a white halo around his head.

"This here is an Appalachian dulcimer," he said, setting the instrument face-up on his lap and pulling a pick from behind his ear. "Some of y'all have heard me play before, and some of y'all haven't. When Miss Avery asked me to play a few songs tonight, I said, 'Good thing, because I only know a few!'" He chuckled, and the crowd joined in with their own laughter. "This one's a favorite hymn of mine."

He plucked at the strings, a haunting melody resonating through the night air. Kira couldn't help but be struck by the contrast between the man's frail appearance and the strength in his music. Each note he played seemed to carry a sense of yearning, filling the air with a deep longing for something beyond the life they knew.

"It's *Nearer My God to Thee*."

Kira glanced up to see Will standing beside her. "Huh?"

He leaned closer, nodding at the man in the motorcycle vest. "The song—it's called *Nearer My God to Thee*. It's an old Christian hymn about how our hardships draw us closer to God. If you could hear the words, they talk about how our lives aren't always going to be easy or comfortable. Some of us will have to suffer. Some of us may even have to die. But the message is that, even in death, there is something better waiting for us."

There weren't any words to hear—the old man wasn't singing. But Kira closed her eyes and let the music wash over her, the steady rise and fall of the notes filling the cool night air. "Do you really believe that?" she asked, eyes still closed. "Do you really believe there's something more after we die?"

As the words left her lips, Kira felt a sudden, overwhelming need for an answer. It wasn't just the old man's hymn that had brought this to the surface, though the music had certainly opened a door. No, it was everything. The memory of Trevor Anderson—a young man who had his entire life ahead of him— hanging from the fence. The countless Volunteers she'd guided to their deaths. Did they still exist somewhere, or had they simply blinked out of existence, their lives extinguished like a flame snuffed out?

But more than anything, it was her mother she wondered about.

What had become of her?

Will didn't answer for a long time, and when he did, his voice sounded rougher, deeper than usual. "After my parents were killed, I buried them in the backyard. Did I ever tell you that part? I felt bad they couldn't be in a cemetery, but I really didn't have any choice. It needed to be done, and it was the worst thing I've ever had to do."

Kira opened her eyes and looked at Will. His face, weathered by grief and hardship, bore lines that shouldn't have been there. Lines that made him look older than he was. She thought of his job as a sanitation engineer, responsible for transporting the Compulsory bodies out of the city to the burial pits. Had some part of him—the part that eventually led him to her—been born that night, in the backyard of the house he'd shared with his parents?

"Faith was always important to my parents. They read their Bibles every day. We prayed together as a family. They took me to church." He shook his head and uttered a little laugh. "I mean, a deadly virus shut the world down, but even that didn't get us out of church. We still had a little worship service by ourselves every Sunday morning. My parents had their priorities, and they stuck to them."

Kira longed to touch him. To pull him close and give him the comfort he'd been denied all those years ago when he'd been left alone in the Unregulated Zone.

But she held back, for just a little while, to give him the room he needed to speak.

"They died on a Saturday," he continued. "I buried them

the same day. I was exhausted and sick, and I wanted to wait—I really did—but I couldn't wait. It was July. I couldn't wait."

His voice trailed off, but the pain of those days was still visible in his eyes. A raw wound that refused to heal.

"I didn't sleep at all that night. I thought the grief and exhaustion would be enough to knock me out for a few hours, but it wasn't. It was too quiet in the house. Until that night, I didn't know what it sounded like to be alone. Those comforting sounds I'd grown accustomed to were gone. My mother's slippers as she moved around the house. My father snoring. For the first time, the house was completely quiet, so my brain turned every sound that I didn't recognize into the Patrols, coming back to finish me off."

On that terrible Saturday in July, she had been tucked away safely in her own bed in the city, blissfully unaware that the boy who would eventually steal her heart was just across the river, orphaned and alone. She couldn't have known that, while she slept peacefully, her Will was digging graves with hands that had not yet developed calluses.

Will cleared his throat before continuing. "The next morning was Sunday. The sun came out, just like it always did. After I woke up, I held a church service in our living room. I was exhausted, every muscle in my body sore from digging the graves, and I had no idea how I was going to survive without them. But do you know the strangest thing I felt that morning?"

Kira didn't trust herself to speak, afraid she would begin to sob, so she shook her head.

"Happiness," he said, the pain in his eyes easing, softening into a quiet, unexpected peace. "I was happy for them, Kira. Everything else turned into this annoying background noise—kind of like static on a television. I remember sitting in the middle of the living room, reading their favorite parts of the Bible, and singing my mother's favorite hymns off-key. I cried a lot that morning because I missed them so much. But more than anything, I was happy for them because I knew their suffering was over. They were together, and they were finally getting their reward."

Kira could only stare at him, trying to grasp what he was saying. No part of her had known happiness after her mother's death—only an overwhelming sense of sadness and anger. Happiness had not been part of the equation. "I don't understand. What reward?"

"Seeing Jesus face-to-face," Will said, as if it were the most obvious thing in the world. "That's why I wasn't afraid to become a Volunteer, even though I knew if something went wrong, it could cost me my life. I felt God's hand guiding me, leading me to save others from the same fate my parents suffered. And if something happened to me along the way, then it was all part of His plan."

"You're okay with dying?" Kira said, her voice tinged with disbelief. "As long as it's part of God's plan?"

Will met her gaze, and in his eyes, she saw a certainty she had never witnessed before. "Yes. I have to follow God, no matter where He leads me. He never promised me a life free from suffering or death. In fact, true faith in Jesus always leads to suffering. It's just part of the deal. But when the worst happens, He's always there, giving us the strength to endure it. And if you keep pressing forward, He always brings good out of bad."

Kira could only stare at him, struggling to comprehend what he was saying. The idea of surrendering so completely to something beyond her control both fascinated and terrified her. She had spent her life clinging to whatever scraps of control she could grasp, especially after her mother's death. But here was Will, willing to let go of everything, even his life, if that's what God asked of him.

"God always brings good out of bad?" Kira asked, turning to face him fully. "Kind of like how he brought you into my life?"

A gentle smile tugged at his lips. "In that case, it worked out well for you and bad for me, but yeah, you get the idea."

Kira glanced at the others dancing in the center of the clearing. The old hymn had given way to a familiar tune, one of her mother's favorites—*I Can't Help Falling in Love With You* by Elvis Presley.

Will reached out to take her hand, his rough fingers curling around hers with a tenderness that made her chest tighten. "Will you dance with me?"

"Of course."

She allowed him to lead her into the center of the clearing. He pulled her close, wrapping one strong arm around her waist and holding her other hand against his chest.

As they swayed to the dulcimer's song, Will leaned in closer, his breath warm against her cheek. "Kira," he whispered. "I love you."

Her lips parted in surprise, her heart racing at the sound of those words. Words she had longed to hear from Will. Now they were finally out in the open, hanging between them, changing everything. It was as if the world had shifted, leaving her breathless and scared, standing on the edge of something both terrifying and wonderful.

"Don't feel like you have to say it back," Will added, his voice tinged with a hint of vulnerability. "I've just wanted to tell you how I felt for a long time. But it's okay if you're not ready, or if you don't feel the same way."

"No, I just..." Kira searched for the right words, but nothing seemed big enough to convey the depth of her feelings for him. Will had saved her life so many times, in so many ways, and he was more than just her best friend—he was everything. How could she put that into words?

I love you wasn't enough, but it was a start.

"Kira, I'm sorry if I made you—"

"I love you, Will Foster," she blurted out, pushing away from him slightly so she could look into his eyes. "I love you so much. I've wanted to tell you since the night we watched the fireworks together on the bridge. Maybe even before that. Maybe since the first moment we met." The words poured out of her, unstoppable now. "Look, I know I can be a mess. I don't drink water like I should, I fall into rivers, and I can be jealous and even a little crazy sometimes, especially when it comes to you. But that's just because I never want to lose—"

Will's lips silenced her, capturing her endless words in a kiss that was unlike anything they had shared before. This one was deeper, more certain, as if all the doubts and tensions between them had finally dissolved. The sounds of laughter and music faded into the background, a distant hum that barely registered in her mind. All she could feel was the warmth of his embrace, the steady beat of his heart against hers, and the undeniable strength of their connection, now more powerful than ever.

When they reluctantly pulled apart, Kira heard herself whisper, "Please don't ever leave me."

So much of her life had been defined by loss—her father, her mother, the life she once knew in Vita Nova, and even the security of a world without constant danger. She couldn't bear the thought of losing Will, too. He had become her anchor, the one person who made her believe there was still hope, still something worth fighting for.

Will's grip around her waist tightened, his gaze locking with hers. "Never Kira." He brought a hand to her face, his rough fingers tender as they caressed her cheek. "I promise."

She knew he couldn't truly promise her anything, not in this world filled with uncertainty and death. But as she stared into his eyes—those beautiful, endless blue eyes—she believed him.

"Thank you," she said, a smile forming on her lips. "Now, I need you to kiss me again. Just like last time. Only better."

Will didn't need to be asked twice.

They were still wrapped up in each other when fireworks began to explode all around them.

Chapter Thirty-Four

Fireworks.

The distant cracks drew Kira's attention upward, her eyes searching the sky for the familiar bursts of color she'd seen every Sunday night over Vita Nova since the first Volunteer Ceremony.

But this time, there were no explosions, not even a single star piercing the blackness. Still, she clung to the thought that Haven was celebrating Avery and Nic's wedding with fireworks.

But when she looked around at the faces of the villagers, she saw confusion quickly turning to fear. Glancing back at Will, she saw the dawning realization in his eyes.

"Will?" Kira searched his face, trying to understand what he already seemed to know. "What's happening?"

Before he could answer, one of the church's hanging lamps exploded, and the flame—no longer contained—jumped to the structure, setting it ablaze in an instant. As the fire took hold of the church's weathered wooden beams, smoke spiraled upward, the acrid stench of burning timber filling the air.

"The church is burning!" a woman screamed. "Someone do something!"

The elderly man in the motorcycle vest had stopped playing, his head tilted as if listening for something. His pick hovered a few inches above the dulcimer's strings, frozen mid-strum.

Another crack rang out.

A few feet away from Kira, a middle-aged man let out a strangled gasp and crumpled to the ground, fingers clutching his neck. Blood seeped from between them, his breaths coming in short, desperate gasps.

In that moment, the confusion in Kira's mind crystalized into cold, stark fear.

Not fireworks, she realized. *Those are gunshots.*

Panic seized the crowd. Some villagers scrambled for cover, hiding behind trees or tables, while others froze in place, paralyzed by the sudden violence erupting around them. Couples who had been swaying to the music only seconds earlier broke apart, running in opposite directions. The men sprinted toward the cabins, while many of the women ushered the children toward the school building.

That's when Kira remembered Bailey's words.

"The school doubles as an emergency shelter. If anything ever happens, get to the school."

The dying man disappeared from view as the crowd surged past him, fleeing the clearing for the safety of the surrounding buildings.

He would be trampled if Kira didn't do something.

She pushed through the crowd, trying to reach the spot where the man had fallen, but Will grabbed her arm and pulled her behind a massive oak tree at the edge of the clearing.

"Will, stop, he needs help!"

"We can't help him," he said, his voice steady and calm

despite the chaos. "Listen to me. You need to find Teddy and get to the school."

"I know. Bailey told me it's an emergency shelter."

"When you get to the school, turn left inside the door. It's the second door on the right. The entrance to the shelter is in that room. I'll find you later."

"You're not coming with me?"

"I have to help defend the village," he said, glancing toward the forest where the gunfire continued.

"Will, could this be the Patrols? Do you think they found us somehow?"

"I don't know," he said, but his eyes told a different story. "Listen, I'll meet you at the school as soon as I can. Just find Teddy and get there, okay?"

Before she could argue, Will ran off, sprinting to catch up with the other men who were already halfway to the cabins, likely heading to retrieve their weapons. Most of them hadn't brought their rifles or shotguns to the wedding because the defense of the village had always been left to the perimeter guards—until now.

You need to find Teddy and get to the school.

She spun around, searching the now nearly empty clearing for the little boy in his ill-fitting suit. She also searched for Harper, knowing that Teddy was never far from his new best friend. The last time she'd glimpsed them over Will's shoulder as they danced, the children had been sneaking baked goods at the food tables, but now both the children and the tables were gone, knocked over in the melee, their precious contents trampled into the ground.

The man who had been shot lay motionless in the center of the clearing, his glassy eyes staring up at the sky.

An older woman from the kitchen grabbed Kira's arm as she rushed past. "Get to the school, sweetie!"

There were no children left in the clearing, and very few adults. The bride and groom were gone. Even the old man in the motorcycle jacket had packed up his instrument and stool and was hobbling toward the cabins, likely to join the fight.

Where is Teddy?

Then she remembered Grace and Brack. They had been dancing near Teddy the last time she'd seen them. Since leaving Emmitsburg, Grace had taken on a motherly role to Teddy. The first thing she would have done when the shooting started was find him and take him to the school.

Kira had to get to the school. If Teddy was anywhere, he was already in the shelter.

Her legs unlocked, and she began to run, the purple dress catching on her knees, threatening to trip her. But she stayed on her feet, clutching the fabric in both hands as she raced past the burning church. The flames had taken hold with terrifying speed, climbing the wooden beams like hungry creatures, consuming everything in their path.

One of the windows exploded from the intense heat, sending shards of glass raining down on Kira. She screamed and covered her head, but she didn't slow down. The flames, now fed by the sudden rush of air, surged even higher, transforming the once-peaceful church into a towering inferno of heat and light.

The dark outline of the school loomed ahead, its windows dark.

Her blonde hair whipped behind her as she ran, the orange glow of the burning church lighting her path. The acrid smoke stung her eyes and throat, and she could feel the heat of the flames behind her as she made her final push up the incline to the school. The ballet flats she'd borrowed from Avery kept slipping off her feet, so she kicked them off and continued up the hill barefoot. She half-expected to feel a bullet tear through her back, but she kept going, her breath coming in ragged gasps.

Finally, she reached the school and burst through the door, her lungs burning as she coughed violently, trying to expel the smoke from her lungs. The distant sound of gunfire faded as she shoved the door closed behind her. With the door shut and no windows in the hallway, the darkness surrounded her, swallowing her whole. She forced herself to move, stumbling forward with hands outstretched, coughing, eyes watering. Even with the door closed, she could still feel the heat from the flames outside, as if they were right behind her, chasing her down, ready to engulf her at any moment.

"Turn left inside the door. Then it's the second door on the right," she whispered to herself, repeating Will's instructions.

When her reaching hands found the opposite wall, she turned to the left, running the fingers of her right hand along the rough wood and walking as fast as she dared down the hallway. The building smelled musty and deserted, as if no children had been there in years, and it was eerily quiet. So quiet she wondered if she had somehow stumbled into the wrong building.

Her fingers found the first door.

As her eyes adjusted to the darkness, she could just make out the faint outline of another door ahead. She rushed forward, grasped the cold metal handle, and pushed it down.

Unlike the hallway, the classroom had windows, allowing light to spill in from outside. Kira saw Avery's new husband, Nic Gonzalez, crouched beside a trapdoor. His suit jacket and tie were both gone, and his white dress shirt was dirty and ripped. He was helping two older women onto a wooden ladder that disappeared into a hole in the floor.

His head jerked up as Kira entered the room, body tensing for a fight. But then he seemed to recognize Kira and relaxed slightly. "Hurry. I need to get back outside with the others."

"Where's Avery?"

"I made her go down there," he said, nodding toward the hole. "She's not happy about it."

"Do you know if my friends are down there?" Kira asked as she approached the trapdoor. "Grace? She's got curly hair, and she's pregnant. There should also be a little boy, Teddy."

"Everyone is down there." Nic rose to his feet, sounding impatient. "Let's go."

Kira dropped to her knees beside the hole. She carefully lowered herself onto the ladder, her legs disappearing into the darkness below. The ancient wooden rungs creaked beneath her weight, and she wondered how far it was to the bottom.

How far would she fall if one of the rungs snapped?

"It's only twelve feet to the bottom," Nic whispered, as if reading her mind. "Keep going. You've got this."

She continued downward, one rung at a time. Then the light above her vanished as Nic closed the trapdoor, leaving her in pitch blackness. She paused on the ladder, listening to the faint dragging sound coming from above. In her mind, she could see Nic pulling something over the trapdoor—a piece of furniture or a rug—to hide it from whoever was invading the village.

The air was stale and musty, making it difficult to breathe. But she kept going until it felt less like she was climbing down into an underground shelter and more like she was descending into hell itself.

Finally, her bare feet met the cool dirt at the bottom of the ladder. She turned to see several dim lamps positioned around the area, casting long, eerie shadows against the earthen walls. Women and children had gathered around the lamps, their faces strained with fear and exhaustion.

The so-called shelter was nothing more than a crude tunnel in the ground. It was a far cry from the solid basement she had envisioned with solid walls and a floor. Instead, they were surrounded by damp, dark soil. The ground beneath her feet was packed dirt, and the walls seemed to breathe with moisture. Here and there, patches of moss clung to the walls, like nature's grim attempt at decoration.

"What's going on up there?" one of them asked. "Is there still shooting?"

"I don't know. I think so."

Avery emerged from the shadows, her bridal dress stained and dragging on the floor. Beads of sweat clung to her forehead. She ran a hand over her face, leaving a streak of dirt behind. "Is Nic still up there?"

Kira shook her head. "He closed the trapdoor after I came down. I think he left."

"I need to get up there." Avery pushed past Kira to grab the ladder. "I need to be with him."

"Avery—"

"Why should I have to stay down here?" she snapped. "Just because I'm his wife? That means he gets to know I'm safe, and I'm supposed to wait and hope he doesn't die? How is that fair?"

As Avery began to climb, Kira instinctively reached out, ready to grab her and pull her back. But she hesitated, her hands freezing midair. The truth was, Kira understood exactly how Avery felt. She didn't want to be hiding in this basement either, just waiting and hoping that Will would find his way back to her. Her hand slowly dropped to her side, and she watched as Avery continued her ascent.

"You don't even have a gun," Kira whisper-shouted as Avery shoved the trapdoor open.

"True, but I know where to find one," Avery said, pulling herself through the hole and slamming the trapdoor behind her.

Turning away from the ladder, Kira moved further into the tunnel, her eyes passing over more frightened women and children, all huddled close together, many of them crying.

The shelter offered no real comfort. No blankets, no pillows, no chairs—just a few ancient wooden beams jutting out at odd angles, their age and condition making them seem more like the frail bones of a once-living thing than structural supports. A few women leaned against them, but judging by the age and condition of the wood, the beams didn't look strong enough to support the weight of women, let alone the building above.

This isn't a basement, she thought, her heart sinking. *It's a mass grave. Just like the ones for the Compulsories.*

Kira shook her head, forcing the image from her mind.

She couldn't think like that now.

As she moved deeper into the tunnel, the space became even tighter, with the walls appearing to press closer with each step. The air was thick with the scent of earth and the sour odor of bodies crammed together. Women and children lined the tunnel, their bodies filling every available inch of space, their ragged breathing and quiet sobs adding to the oppressive atmosphere. Kira had to squeeze past them, her back brushing against the walls, her chest tightening as she imagined what would happen if any of the support beams collapsed.

"Grace?" Kira called out. "Is Grace down here?"

"Kira?"

The relief in Grace's voice was palpable as she emerged from the sea of strangers. She rushed over and pulled Kira into a tight hug. "Thank God you're here. Brack practically dragged me out of the clearing, and I was so worried when I realized you weren't down here." But as quickly as the relief came, it vanished, replaced by panic. "Please tell me you know where Teddy is."

"He's not here?" Kira scanned the area for the little boy, hoping that somehow Grace was wrong. That she'd overlooked him. "You haven't seen him?"

"I checked everywhere," Grace sobbed, tears streaming down her face. "I've walked the entire tunnel. Twice. When the attack started, I thought I saw him running toward the school with that little girl he's always with—I *know* I saw him—but she's down here, and he's not. He's still out there, Kira!"

Grace collapsed against Kira, her body wracked with sobs. She was gasping for air, on the verge of hyperventilating.

"It's okay," Kira whispered, trying to soothe her friend even as she wanted to panic herself. "Please, you have to calm down, Grace. This isn't good for the baby."

"But I have to get Teddy!" Grace's voice was frantic.

"Shhh!" An older woman stomped over to them, her eyes blazing with anger. "If you can't stay quiet, both of you need to get out."

Ignoring the woman, Kira turned back to Grace. "I'll go," she said. "You're pregnant, and right now, you need to do what's best for your baby. I'll find Teddy and bring him back."

The determination in her voice surprised even her. The last thing she wanted was to leave the safety of the tunnel, but for Teddy, she would walk through fire.

She'd already jumped off a bridge for him.

Grace must've heard her determination because she slumped against Kira, the fight draining from her body. "Maybe he ran back to the cabin... or followed Brack and the men... Oh God, please don't let him have followed Brack."

"I'll find him and bring him back," Kira repeated. "You don't have to worry."

"Please, help him," Grace whimpered, fresh tears flowing down her cheeks. "He's just a little boy."

Kira leaned in and kissed Grace on the cheek before resting her hand on the woman's swollen belly. She thought she felt the faintest flutter of movement against her palm—a glimmer of hope in the darkness.

"Keep the others calm until I get back."

Grace wiped her nose and nodded weakly.

She retraced her steps back to the beginning of the tunnel, but before she started up the ladder, she stole one last glance at the women and children. There were so many of them—their faces pale, eyes wide with fear, bodies trembling.

This village, once hidden away from the horrors of the world, was now exposed and vulnerable. Some were dying outside, while others were trapped underground, defenseless.

If Haven's attackers were Patrol soldiers, as Kira suspected, they were here because of her. Innocent people were suffering because she had brought the enemy to their doorstep.

If they overran the village, how long would it take the attackers to find the shelter?

And what would they do with the people they found hiding inside?

And Teddy... Poor Teddy was out there somewhere, alone and scared, with soldiers hunting him, just as Render had been hunting him in Emmitsburg.

They'd hunt him until they found him, and then they'd take him back to the city to die.

No.

She would die herself before she let that happen.

Kira grabbed the ladder and climbed.

Chapter Thirty-Five

Outside the school, the church continued to burn, the air thick with smoke that hung like a heavy, acrid blanket over the village. The haze blurred the trees and obscured the battle raging in the forest, turning the once peaceful night into a nightmare.

Through the dense foliage, Kira caught glimpses of dark shadows darting between the trees. Muzzle flashes pierced the darkness in harsh, blinding bursts. The steady crack of gunfire echoed through the woods, mingling with the anguished cries of the wounded.

To Kira's left, the mess hall loomed, dark and empty, its square windows like hollowed-out eyes watching her as she ran past. She continued across the grassy field toward the cabins, forcing herself to block out the gunfire and focus on her own pounding footsteps. The night air bit at her exposed skin, but she hardly noticed it. A single, desperate thought consumed her mind: finding Teddy.

When she reached Brack and Grace's cabin, Kira flung the

door open, her gaze sweeping over the dark room. The fire had gone out, leaving the space cold and lifeless.

"Teddy!"

She prayed the boy was hiding behind the bed or under the table, ready to pop up at the sound of her voice.

But there was no answer.

The silence pressed down on her like a weight.

"Where are you?" Fear clogged her throat, twisting her words into a strangled whisper. She couldn't allow herself to imagine that Teddy might be lying somewhere hurt—or worse.

No. He was too smart for that. If he somehow got separated from Grace, he would've found a hiding place.

But where would he go? There were a hundred places he could be hiding. She hadn't checked the mess hall. Or any of the other cabins. How was she supposed to find him?

Grace's voice filled her mind.

"That little boy is so protective of you."

In the confusion of the attack, would Teddy have tried to find her instead of Grace? And if he hadn't been able to locate her in the chaos, would his instinct have been to break off from the group and go to *her* cabin, not his own?

Clinging to that hope, Kira sprinted back outside and raced down the pathway toward the cabin she shared with Avery and the other women.

"Please," she whispered through gasping breaths, not sure who she was pleading with. The dark silhouette of her cabin came into view a few paces ahead. "I'm begging You. Please let him be there. Please let him—"

The sound of automatic gunfire, loud, jarring, and terrifyingly close, interrupted her prayer. She flinched as bullets ricocheted off the cabin, splintering wood and sending shards flying.

Her right foot snagged on something soft, sending her crashing to the ground. She landed hard on all fours, the cold, damp grass soaking through the fabric of her ruined dress. The coppery tang of blood filled her mouth—she'd bitten her tongue in the fall.

Pushing herself up, she turned to see what had tripped her. A lantern hanging from the porch of a nearby cabin provided very little light, but it was enough.

"Oh, please, no."

A woman lay on the ground a few feet away, her face drained of color, her once-pristine wedding dress soaked with blood.

"Avery?"

Kira crawled forward, the thin material of her dress ripping as easily as tissue paper on the rough ground as she moved closer.

Avery remained still, her face serene despite the horror of her injuries. She didn't move or react to Kira's presence. She looked like a beautiful porcelain doll in a tattered wedding dress. If there had been stars, they might have reflected in her eyes, giving the illusion of life.

But there were no stars.

There was no life.

Still, Kira leaned over Avery and pressed two fingers to her neck, searching for any hint of a faint heartbeat, but finding nothing. Just a cold, unnatural stillness.

She pulled her hand back, her fingers sticky with blood.

Avery was gone.

An image flashed through Kira's mind: Avery dancing barefoot in the clearing, laughing as her new husband lifted her off her feet and spun her around.

But the warmth of that memory was quickly replaced by a new one—sharp and clear. The three Lawless men at the dollar store. Something one of them had said, his words echoing back to her with painful clarity.

Words she'd forgotten until now.

"We've dealt with those city soldiers before, you know. We keep our eyes peeled, report back on what we see, and in return, they give us food and even weapons."

It's my fault, she realized, the weight of it settling on her shoulders like a boulder. *I forgot what they said. I never told anyone.*

Kira remained on the ground, the purple dress bunched up beneath her, willing herself to move.

"Teddy," she whispered.

Whatever mistakes she'd made, she still had to find Teddy.

As she pushed herself off the ground, prepared to check inside the cabin, something in the grass a few feet away caught her eye—a small, dark shape partially hidden in the mud at the base of the steps. She stumbled toward it, dread pooling in her stomach. She already knew what it was, but she couldn't allow herself to believe it. Didn't want to accept it.

But it was him.

Randy.

Teddy's one-eyed bear lay discarded and half-buried in the mud. The toy's tattered fur was matted with dirt, the remaining button eye staring accusingly at her, as if asking why she hadn't been there to protect its owner.

A faint scent drifted through her memories—the stale smell of Render's cigarettes, mingling with the sharp tang of cologne, and something darker, metallic, like blood. With it came the chilling words he had spoken that night after he cornered her in the kitchen.

Mayor Devlin doesn't care about you. He only wants the boy.

She dropped to her knees and reached for it, her hands trembling as she clutched the worn toy to her chest.

Teddy had been here—he had come to the cabin looking for her—and now he was gone.

Teddy was gone.

Avery was dead.

And Will.

Will may already be dead, his body lying alone in the dark woods, and she wouldn't have any idea. Just as Nic Gonzalez was out there somewhere, defending the village, with no idea that he had become a husband and a widower on the same night.

Or, worse, Will could be mortally wounded and suffering. Unable to speak loud enough to cry out for help. Dying slowly, with no one by his side.

The thought of Will dying alone, his last moments filled with pain and fear, was the worst thing she could imagine.

Kira willed herself to get up, to keep searching for Teddy in case he was out there somewhere, or to find Will, but her body would not obey. She was paralyzed, her mind and body disconnected from each other, leaving her weak, pathetic, and defeated.

Let them come, she thought. *It doesn't matter anymore. Nothing I do matters.*

A hundred yards away, the battle in the forest raged on. The sounds of gunfire and the cries of the wounded echoing through the trees, a haunting soundtrack that Kira knew would live in her nightmares for however long she had left.

She tried to remember the sound of the Appalachian dulcimer. The song the old man had been playing before the attack.

I Can't Help Falling in Love with You.

She replayed Will's whispered words in her mind: *I love*

you. Words she had longed to hear but would only hear once. She thought of her mother and the scarred man who had once loved her.

Noah Hale.

Ghost.

Had her mother felt this much pain when she realized she'd never see Noah again?

Kira held Randy tightly against her chest and curled into a ball, trying to block out the sounds of death that filled the air. She clung to the memory of those few precious moments from the wedding reception, where life had felt almost normal, if only for a short time. The sweetness of the peach preserves still lingered on her tongue, now tainted by the metallic taste of blood.

Across the field, the church continued to burn, its flames a distant, eerie glow in the darkness.

Eventually, though, it would burn itself out.

Maybe if she closed her eyes and asked God to take her, she could burn out with it.

Chapter Thirty-Six

It's so quiet.

Kira opened her eyes and tried to lift her head, but it felt as if it weighed a thousand pounds. She was still on the ground, the bear clutched in her arms, with no idea how much time had passed. At some point, the relentless sound of gunfire coming from the woods had ceased. Now, the only sound left was the soft rustle of Avery's dress as it fluttered in the breeze.

Everyone's dead, she thought, her body shivering uncontrollably, a mixture of cold and fear seeping into her bones. The ground beneath her was rough and unforgiving, with small rocks and twigs digging into her exposed skin. *Will and the others had died protecting the village, and now the Patrol soldiers will claim its spoils for Vita Nova—including the women and children hiding in the basement of the school.*

A sickening knot tightened in her stomach. What would the soldiers do when they found the women and children? What orders had her father given? Certainly not to bring them back to the city. There would be mercy, no compassion for widows or orphans.

Her father had made countless widows and orphans through his Volunteer and Compulsory programs.

The realization spurred her to move, her hands sinking into the damp earth as she struggled to stand. Her muscles ached, her legs were weak and shaky, and the ground seemed to cling to the hem of her dress, as if unwilling to let her go. But she couldn't stay on the ground. She might be the only thing standing between the innocent people in the school and the soldiers from Vita Nova.

As she finally stood, the world around her blurred, the colors of the forest melting into a dizzying swirl of greens and browns. She blinked, trying to focus her vision as the ground seemed to spin beneath her, like a carnival ride gone wrong. Her stomach churned, bile rising in the back of her throat, bitter and acidic. She swallowed it down, forcing herself to concentrate on the trees in the distance.

Then she saw them.

Figures emerged from the shadows, their weapons slung at their sides.

Patrol soldiers.

Kira froze in place, the one-eyed bear slipping from her hands and landing in the dirt. It was hatred, not fear, that coursed through her veins at the sight of the soldiers who had invaded Haven. Every muscle in her body tensed, preparing to fight them with whatever strength she had left.

One soldier glanced in her direction.

Kira didn't try to run or hide. She didn't even flinch.

The soldier broke off from the others, running toward her.

She scanned the ground nearby, searching for anything she could use as a weapon—a tree branch, a rock, anything. But there was nothing. She considered sprinting into the nearest cabin and searching for a weapon, but her legs were shaky, and she knew the soldier would catch her before she made it up the steps.

Without a weapon, she stepped between the approaching soldier and Avery's lifeless body, her trembling hands clenching and unclenching at her sides.

They were all she had.

"Go away," she growled. "Don't you touch her."

"Kira?"

How did the soldier know her name?

The man stepped into the meager light cast by the hanging lantern, revealing his haggard appearance. Dirt and sweat clung to his face, hiding a scar Kira knew was there. His hands were smeared with blood, and his weary eyes locked with hers before shifting to the crumpled bride at her feet.

"Ghost?"

He didn't respond, seemingly unable to tear his eyes from Avery's body, his head shaking almost imperceptibly. The exhaustion on his face gave way to something deeper, like anguish, but he quickly buried it, his expression hardening to stone.

"This shouldn't have happened," Ghost said, removing his jacket. He stepped around Kira and knelt down, his knees cracking as he carefully placed the jacket over Avery's head. Then he covered his face with one hand, his next words slipping through his bloodied fingers. "None of this should have happened."

Kira turned and saw more villagers emerging from the woods, their heads low and faces grim. They trudged across the field, weapons hanging over their shoulders or at their sides—a silent army heading toward the school.

She scanned their faces, searching for Will, but she couldn't see him.

She lowered herself beside Ghost, resisting the urge to touch his arm. She feared he might push her away.

Avery's death was her fault.

All of it was her fault.

Ghost removed his hand from his face and cleared his throat. "Soldiers from the city," he said, answering Kira's unasked question. "At least, that's what it looked like from the glimpses I got of their uniforms. They cut down a section of the fence and walked right through. Some of them broke through our line into the village, but most stayed close to the perimeter."

"They cut down the fence? What about the guards?"

"They're dead," he said, his face darkening. "They never had a chance. Not against a group of well-armed and well-trained soldiers from the city. Best I can tell, most of our people on the perimeter were taken out before they even knew what was happening. Most had their throats cut. Some of the bodies I saw still had their guns in their holsters. They hadn't even fired off any shots. And with the music and the dancing, we wouldn't have heard anything."

A wave of nausea rolled through Kira as she tried to process the horror of what Ghost was saying. Throats cut, guns still holstered. The celebration, the music, the laughter—it had all masked the silent slaughter happening in the forest.

"I think they killed Trevor yesterday because they knew we would increase security at the perimeter as a precaution," Ghost continued. "I should've known better. I should've been out there myself tonight."

"You couldn't have known," Kira offered, although her words felt hollow. Ghost considered it his responsibility to protect the village from outsiders, yet he'd allowed a group of strangers—including recent defectors from Vita Nova, one of whom was the Mayor's daughter—to take refuge in Haven. Was he regretting his decision?

Of course he was.

"Will," she managed to say. "He left me at the school. Is he okay?"

Uncertainty flickered in Ghost's eyes. "I don't know. I haven't seen him." He paused, then added, "But a lot of people died out there, Kira."

"How many?" she asked, though she didn't want to know the number. "How many died?"

Ghost shook his head. "I don't know for sure. Maybe twenty. We had fourteen guards on the perimeter, and then we took casualties in the fight. I don't know if we got any of them. They had body armor, better weapons. And I'm pretty sure they were using NVGs."

"NVGs?"

"Night-vision goggles."

Kira's gaze fell on Avery's pale legs. "What about Nic? Do you know if he made it?" A part of her hoped he hadn't, though the thought made her sick with guilt. But the idea of Nic finding Avery like this, of seeing his world shattered in an instant—it was too much.

"I don't know," Ghost said, lifting his eyes to meet hers, and she could see he felt the same way. "I didn't see him, either. The soldiers—the enemy—had us surrounded, but they stuck to the woods and fired whenever they could to create panic. I don't think they were trying to overrun us, even though they had plenty of opportunities. I think they were looking for something, and whatever it was, I think they found it."

Teddy.

Kira's heart sank as Ghost's words confirmed her worst fears. Teddy. They had come for Teddy, and now he was gone. The weight of it crushed her, making her feel as if the ground might give way beneath her feet. Every instinct screamed at her to do something—to fight, to fix it—but what could she do? He was gone, and there was nothing she could do to bring him back.

Suddenly, Ghost appeared beside her, wrapping an arm around her waist to steady her. "Kira? Are you okay?"

She collapsed against his chest, the tears she had been holding back finally breaking free. "They took him," she choked out. "They took Teddy."

Ghost's hand settled on the back of her head, holding her close enough to hear his heartbeat. In that moment, he was the father she never had but always dreamed of—protective, strong, and loving.

He was the only thing keeping her on her feet.

"What I can't figure out," he said, without her letting go, "is how they found us. We've never been attacked, as long as we've been here. I must've missed something."

Kira didn't know how Ghost would react if she told him the truth, but it didn't matter. She refused to keep any more secrets. Whatever he said or did to her, she deserved it. She'd made a mistake—a huge mistake—and people were dead because of it.

"You didn't miss anything," she began, pulling away from him. "Those men you rescued me from, back in Wagner—one of them mentioned doing business with Patrol soldiers in exchange for food and weapons. It was an offhanded remark, and with everything else that happened, I completely forgot about it. But I'm certain that's how they found us. They watched us leave the next morning, tracked us to your village, and reported the location to the Patrols."

Ghost's eyes narrowed as he processed her words. "So, what? You think this is your fault?"

She nodded. "I know it's my fault. I should've told you what they said, long before we left Wagner. If I had, you would've done things differently. You would've been more careful. People are dead because I screwed up... again."

She braced herself, waiting for him to explode in anger, to shove her to the ground, to tell her how worthless she was. But instead, he let out a long, weary sign and rubbed a hand across his face, wiping away some of the dirt and grime.

"This isn't on you, Kira. Even if you had told me what those men said, there's no guarantee it would've changed anything. They would've found us sooner or later." He stared at her, more understanding than blame in his gaze. "Guilt is a monster, Kira. It will eat you alive if you let it. Trust me, I've been there. We make mistakes, and we have to learn to live with them. The lucky among us are the ones who get the chance to make things right."

He didn't elaborate, but he didn't need to. Kira knew he was thinking of her mother. Of the choices he'd made that had left her and her daughter alone in the city. If he had ignored Devlin's threats and fought his way back to the woman he loved, everything might have been different.

Madison Liebert was dead, and Ghost's punishment was having to live with the burden of his mistake.

But Teddy wasn't dead.

At least not yet.

Which meant Kira might still have the chance to fix hers.

Chapter Thirty-Seven

They scoured every inch of the village, searching through the outbuildings, barns, and hidden spots only Ghost knew about. They walked the perimeter, calling out Teddy's, hoping the gunfire had driven him into hiding in the woods. Finally, they checked each empty cabin, searching underneath beds, inside cabinets, and behind couches.

But there was no sign of Teddy.

By the time they returned to the north end of the village, the sun had crept over the mountains, revealing the full extent of the devastation left behind by the attack.

Kira's heart shattered all over again as she surveyed the remnants of what had been a joyful wedding celebration. The music that had filled the night air was gone, replaced by an oppressive silence. The vases of purple asters, once bright and beautiful, now lay shattered, the flowers trampled underfoot. In the wreckage of scattered chairs and toppled tables, the man who'd been shot in the throat lay still, his expression strangely peaceful.

A few yards away, the church stood in ruins, still smoldering—a visual reminder of the horror that had unfolded in their peaceful haven. Several teenage boys, their faces smeared with soot, ran back and forth from the creek to the church, metal buckets in hand, water splashing over the sides.

Trying to salvage the unsalvageable.

As one dark-haired boy returned from the creek, Ghost left Kira's side and stepped into his path, stopping him. He placed a hand on the teen's shoulder. "It's alright, son."

And the boy—not quite a man—started to weep. Ghost gently took the buckets from his trembling hands and tossed the water on the church.

"Liebert?"

She turned at the sound of the familiar, gruff voice. Brack and Grace were walking toward her, hands intertwined, both looking dirty and exhausted. Grace leaned against her husband, as if incapable of standing without his support. But at the sight of Kira, she became alert, her eyes sweeping the area with urgent desperation.

"Where is he?" she asked. "Did you find him? Where's Teddy?"

Over Grace's shoulder, Kira saw the other women and children emerging from the basement of the school, led by the men who had left them there to fight. Most blinked in disbelief at the charred remains of their church, their faces masks of sorrow and shock. Hushed whispers filled the air, mingling with the heartwrenching sounds of mourning.

Not all the men had returned to their families.

"Kira? I asked you a question," Grace said, her voice cutting through the fog in Kira's mind. The no-nonsense, back-country accent—the one she reserved for her husband—was now aimed squarely at Kira. "You left me down in that hole and wouldn't let me come with you. Now, where is Teddy?"

Ghost appeared at Kira's side, the empty water buckets still in his hands. "We haven't found him."

"You haven't—what?"

"We checked every structure in the village. He could be hiding in the woods, but I don't believe that's the case. I think the soldiers who attacked us last night were looking for him, and the only reason they withdrew when they did is because they found him."

Grace stared at Ghost, her mouth slightly open, as if unable to process what he was saying. Slowly, her eyes darkened, and she shifted her gaze back to Kira. "You let those monsters take him?"

"I didn't—" Kira stammered, struggling to explain, but the right words wouldn't come. "I tried to find him, but he wasn't—"

"Shut up!" Grace cried, her voice breaking. "You let them take him, Kira! You promised you'd bring him back!"

"Baby, stop." Brack pulled her closer to him, one muscular arm disappearing beneath her curls. "This isn't Kira's fault. None of us protected Teddy last night. It's on all of us."

Grace collapsed against Brack's chest, sobbing uncontrollably. "But he's gone, Devan. What are we going to do without him?"

Panic gripped Kira's heart, threatening to overwhelm her. She needed Will now more than ever before—to feel his arms around her, to close her eyes and lose herself in his familiar scent. The thought of him not surviving the night and being one of the bodies Ghost had seen in the forest was too much to bear.

Because if Teddy was gone and Will was dead, then Kira might as well be dead, too.

When Grace composed herself, she wiped her leaking nose on her sleeve and surveyed the wreckage of the church. "So, that's it, then?" she said, her voice hollow, like something inside of her had shattered beyond repair. "We left everything we knew and came all this way, only to be worse off than we were in Emmitsburg. It was all for nothing."

Noise at the edge of the forest drew Kira's attention. A group of men had gathered there. More men were leaving the cabins after dropping off their families, moving back across the field to rejoin with the others.

She headed in their direction.

No one tried to stop her. No one called after her. It wouldn't have mattered if they had.

She needed to know if Will was alive.

As she drew closer to the men, Kira noticed the gray mounds on the ground at their feet. Bodies covered with gray wool blankets—more than a dozen of them. Blood had soaked through the fabric, turning it black in places.

I'm not ready, she thought. *I'm not ready to know for sure.*

Suddenly, Grace appeared beside her, followed by Brack and Ghost. She took Kira's hand and held it tight, all the anger gone from her eyes. "Don't worry," she whispered. "We're going to find him."

Please don't ever leave me.

She remembered her plea to Will the night before, just after they'd exchanged I love you's for the first time.

Never Kira.

One man turned as they approached. He was older, with a thick, handlebar mustache that looked like it belonged in an old western movie. He acknowledged Ghost with a nod.

"How many?" Ghost asked, and Kira realized he couldn't bring himself to count the covered mounds.

"Seventeen so far," the man replied. "Not counting any of the casualties in the village. But we're still looking. You want the names we've got so far?"

Ghost ran a hand through his short hair. "Not yet, Zeke. We're looking for a young man. Early twenties. One of the new arrivals."

"I couldn't tell you for sure." The man stroked his mustache and glanced at the mound closest to his feet. "Don't ring a bell, but with a few of them—it's sorta hard to tell."

Kira leaned heavily on Grace, her fingers tightly clenched around her friend's small hand. As much as she wanted to look away, she couldn't tear her eyes from the rows of bodies. She couldn't stop imagining herself lifting one of the blankets and finding Will's face beneath it.

"Do we uncover them?" Brack asked.

The question hung in the air, unanswered. No one moved to check the bodies, not even Brack. After a few moments, Zeke slipped away without another word, disappearing into the forest to check for more bodies.

It was Ghost who finally stepped forward and knelt beside the nearest body. Some mounds were longer, others were much shorter, but this one was the right size for Will. Ghost bowed his head as if praying, or perhaps steeling himself for what he was about to see. Finally, with a deep breath, he reached for the blanket and pulled it back to reveal the face of a young man with lifeless blue eyes.

Will.

A howl of pure agony split the air, more terrible than anything Kira had ever heard. The sound reminded her of the Compulsory Clinic. Of the overwhelming grief she had experienced when her mother's heart had stopped and her worst nightmare had become a reality.

It was the sound of a world ending.

Is it me? she wondered. *Am I making that terrible sound?*

Then Grace twisted away from the body on the ground, and Kira moved with her, clinging to her as if her life depended on it. They didn't stop until they were no longer facing the mounds of the dead, their eyes now turned toward the row of log cabins.

That's when Kira saw Nicolas Gonzalez, still wearing his wedding suit, lying on the ground on top of his dead wife. The older man in the motorcycle jacket—the one who'd played the Appalachian dulcimer at Nic's wedding—stood over him, trying to pull him away, but Nic refused to let go. Finally, the man gave up and backed away, and Nic lifted Avery off the ground and held her in his lap, still making that awful, wailing sound. That sound would live in Kira's mind forever, even if she lived a thousand more years.

"Kira."

She turned at the sound of her name, her gaze sweeping past Ghost and the bodies on the ground, to a figure standing at the edge of the forest. Her grief-addled brain struggled to comprehend what she was seeing.

Will stood among the trees, the hunting rifle slung over his shoulder, looking battered and worn but undeniably alive. For a fleeting moment, she wondered if she was seeing a ghost or if her desperate mind was playing tricks on her.

But then he started jogging toward her, his eyes fixed on Kira as if she were the only thing that mattered in the world.

But Will is dead, she thought, returning her gaze to the body on the ground. *He's right there. It's not possible.*

Ghost was in the process of covering the young man, but before the wool blanket slipped over his face, Kira noticed that the man's eyes weren't blue enough to be Will's. And his hair— much darker, with a tinge of red—wasn't Will's golden brown.

The dead man wasn't Will.

Will reached her a moment later, and she released Grace's hand and fell into his arms. His embrace was a lifeline when she was drowning, a rope pulling her out of the river before the current dragged her under. The warmth of his body, the solidness of his presence, made everything else fall away—everything except the fact that he was here, and he was alive.

He pulled her closer, his forehead resting against hers. "I love you, Kira. Did I tell you that yet?"

She smiled through her tears, her heart lifting despite the devastation that surrounded them. "I think you might have. But you tell so many girls it's probably hard to keep us straight."

Will pulled back slightly, just enough to look into her eyes. "I know you're joking, but for the record, I've only ever said those words to you."

The seriousness of his tone cut through the fleeting humor of their exchange. "Promise?" she whispered, needing to hear it to believe it.

He cupped her face in his hands, his thumbs brushing away the tears that had fallen. "I promise, Kira. You're the only one."

She buried her face in his chest, breathing him in, listening to his heartbeat, steady and reassuring. His arms encircled her, and she allowed herself to be held by him, even as reality pressed in on her, a heavy weight she could not ignore. Selfishly, she let the moment stretch on for a few more heartbeats, knowing that once she spoke, this fragile moment of peace would be shattered forever.

Finally, she forced herself to pull back, just enough to look into his eyes. "Teddy's gone," she said. "The soldiers took him."

The tenderness in his gaze vanished, replaced by sudden alertness. "Are you sure? How do you know he's not hiding somewhere?"

She shook her head. "We've searched everywhere. Last night's attack—it was all about Teddy. My father won't ever let him go because he's the perfect sacrifice for the city. This whole thing—it's all about control for him. If he can convince Vita

Nova to revere the death of an innocent little boy, he'll be able to convince them of anything."

Will was silent for a long time, his arms still securely wrapped around her. She could see the gears turning in his mind, following the same path of reasoning she had already traveled.

And she saw when he reached the same conclusion.

"We're not going to let that happen," he finally said, echoing the conviction she felt in her own heart.

"We're going to get him back."

Chapter Thirty-Eight

"I'm going with you."

Kira hoisted the rucksack onto her shoulders, adjusting the straps to pull it higher on her back. The weight was familiar—both comforting and unforgiving as it pressed into her spine. "We've already discussed this, Brack."

"Well, we haven't discussed it enough."

Back in Haven, people were digging graves and planning funerals, but Kira's group was standing close to the fallen perimeter fence—the same path the Patrol soldiers had used to infiltrate the village.

It was also the way they would leave.

Kira and Will each carried a rucksack, and the weapons they'd brought with them from Emmitsburg. Ghost, however, carried no rucksack, no food—nothing but the clothes on his back and his double-barrel shotgun.

Brack tugged at his beard. "You're not the only one who cares about that kid, Liebert. I carried him on my shoulders for two days, and I listened to every thought that came into his head. I've slept with his little feet in my face every night since we've been here. He's a pain in the butt, but I love that kid."

"I know you do—"

"We started this together, and we should finish it together."

"But we're not finishing it together," Kira replied gently. "Your wife is staying behind, and you need to be here to protect her. She's your priority now."

Grace stood off to the side, silent, her arms folded and resting on top of her pregnant belly. It was clear that Grace wanted to go after Teddy just as much as her husband did, but it was just too dangerous. Besides, Teddy had already been gone for a few hours. Every minute that passed decreased the likelihood that they could catch up with the soldiers who'd taken him.

Kira could feel Brack's eyes burning into her, but she ignored him, her gaze fixed on the broken section of the fence. Teddy had probably been carried through this spot only a few hours earlier. Had he been frightened? Had he cried out for Kira?

Her heart broke at the thought.

Will stepped forward. "Brack, you know she's right. What if the Patrols come back? We don't know if they're planning more attacks. You have to stay here to protect Grace. We'll find Teddy."

Brack's shoulders slumped in defeat. "Fine," he relented, releasing his beard. "But you three better find that kid."

Ghost hovered at the edge of the group, hands clasped at his waist, his scarred face impassive as always. Waiting patiently while Kira and Will said their goodbyes.

He had no goodbyes to say.

Kira felt a surge of gratitude toward him. Despite the danger, she felt safer with Ghost by her side. He had no obligation to go after Teddy—his people needed him as much, if not more, than she did—but he was going with her, anyway.

Her mother loved this man until the day she died, and Kira was starting to understand why.

She exchanged a glance with Grace, who stood by with tears shimmering in her eyes. She longed to embrace her friend, but she didn't want to make Grace more emotional than she already was. "Check on Nic Gonzalez later today, okay? Bring him food. He won't eat anything, but take it to him anyway."

"You know we will," Grace said. "I'll head over there as soon as I get back to the village."

"Thanks." Kira turned to Will, whose eyes were searching her face for any hint of hesitation. It was the same expression he'd worn to his first appearance in her office, when he'd requested to become a Volunteer. He'd been sizing her up, trying to figure out how much trouble she would be when he eventually kidnapped her.

Now he was sizing her up again, debating whether he should try to convince her to stay with Brack and Grace. She could see the conflict raging within him, the desire to protect her warring with the necessity of their mission. If it were up to Will, she would stay behind in Haven, and Brack would go after Teddy in her place.

But it wasn't up to Will.

"You ready?" he asked.

She didn't hesitate. "Ready."

Will took the lead, striding toward the gap in the fence. Kira watched him step over the twisted metal—the last remnants of another barricade that had failed to protect its people.

Ghost appeared beside her, his presence solid and unwavering, like a shadow that refused to leave her side. She stole a glance at him, noticing the rugged lines of his face, the hardened intensity in his eyes, and the weight of a lifetime of battles etched into every wrinkle and scar on his weathered skin.

"Your mom would be proud," he said.

With those words hanging in the air between them, Ghost disappeared through the gap in the fence, leaving Kira standing alone with tears in her eyes.

Chapter Thirty-Nine

Kira moved through the forest, her eyes locked on the back of Ghost's head. He led them through the dense thicket, moving silently and blending easily into the surrounding wilderness, as if he were a part of the forest itself.

Even as she struggled to keep up, she couldn't help but marvel at the grace with which he moved, as if he belonged to the wilderness in a way that she never could. For hours, they maintained this relentless pace—not quite running, but certainly not walking—a rhythm Ghost referred to as a "range walk."

It wouldn't be long before Kira would come to hate those words.

Ghost's range walk was worse than running, especially for Kira, with her shorter legs. Keeping up with him was nearly impossible, but she refused to complain. No matter how hot or exhausted she became, she wouldn't let her body betray her again. Her muscles ached with every step, and she could feel fresh blisters forming on her feet, but she pushed through it all.

She ignored the stabbing pain in her still-healing right ankle, focusing entirely on staying on Ghost's heels and not slowing him down.

Will jogged behind her, his head on a constant swivel as he checked their surroundings for hidden threats. Unlike Kira, he wasn't even breathing hard, and she made a silent pact with herself that if she survived this mission, she would get herself into better shape.

Every so often, Ghost would come to a sudden halt, ordering Kira and Will to take a five-minute break to drink water or share a granola bar. While they rested, he would stand with his arms crossed, staring off into the distance—usually in the direction of Vita Nova—his expression unreadable.

Kira noticed that during these breaks, Ghost would occasionally take a sip from his canteen but never sit down or eat any food. He seemed impervious to hunger, fatigue, or even the need to rest, making Kira wonder if he was something more than human—something greater.

As soon as they finished, he would bark out the words, "Range walk," and they would resume their grueling run-walk pace for another hour or so, leaving Kira to pray that her body would hold out until their next rest stop.

After hours of pushing through the woods, they finally emerged onto the highway. Kira found herself staring across the overgrown road at the dollar store, where they had taken refuge after first meeting Ghost. That night seemed like a lifetime ago.

Today is Saturday, Kira realized. *We left Emmitsburg on Monday.*

In less than a week, everything had changed.

They continued down the highway, moving faster now that they were no longer forced to navigate around large rocks and fallen trees. The only obstacles in their way were the broken-down vehicles left behind on the highway, rusted and faded after a decade spent decaying in the sun. All the while, Ghost's pace never faltered, his determination a stark contrast to the exhaustion Kira felt deep in her bones.

What was driving him? Was it his desire to save Teddy?

Or something else?

They reached Emmitsburg in the late afternoon, and Kira felt a growing sense of unease as she took in the familiar houses and buildings. Instead of welcoming her home, the dilapidated structures seemed to loom over her like silent sentinels, their windows like dark eyes tracking her every move. The eerie silence was only broken by the occasional creak of a rusty sign swaying in the breeze.

The town seemed different somehow.

Quieter.

Emptier.

She'd been gone less than a week, but something had shifted in Emmitsburg during her absence.

She glanced at Will, who returned her look with a quick nod and a half-smile. It was meant to be reassuring but only made her more nervous. Something wasn't right, and even in that brief exchange, she could tell that Will sensed it too.

Instinctively, she reached for the Glock on her hip, her fingers sliding across the cold metal.

Making sure it was still there, just in case.

As they moved further into the town, Kira saw Ghost's gaze lingering on certain buildings longer than others, a flicker of recognition in his eyes. Had he spent time with Kira's mother in this town? Had they shared a meal at one of the long-abandoned restaurants along the river?

She jogged forward and fell into step beside him. He didn't

acknowledge her presence, instead continuing to scan their surroundings with a sharpness that unnerved her.

"You haven't been back here since—?" She stopped herself before she could finish the question. She didn't want Ghost thinking about her father anymore than he already was. This mission wasn't about revenge; it was about saving Teddy. "Since you left the city?"

Ghost's jaw clenched at Kira's words, his scar pulling taut against his skin. "Left the city," he repeated, his voice deeper than usual. "That's one way to put it, I guess. No, I haven't been back since then. Didn't see much reason to come back. To be honest, I'd have been happy to go to my grave without ever setting foot here again."

She knew better than to press him further, and the tense silence between them seemed to stretch on for miles, as endless as the streets they now walked. Streets that were lined with empty homes, the spray-painted red numbers on their doors like tombstones, sober reminders of the entire families who had once lived there.

People like Will's parents.

People who had died staring across the river at a wall erected by Kira's father.

Chapter Forty

As they passed by a collapsed storefront, Kira caught a glimpse of her reflection in the shattered glass. Her face was dirty, streaked with sweat and grime from their journey. She barely recognized herself anymore. She was a far cry from the girl who had lived and worked as a volunteer advocate in the safety of the city.

Seeing her own broken reflection in the jagged glass shook something loose inside of her.

"Why are we doing this?"

She hadn't meant to say it aloud, but the words slipped out before she could stop them.

Ghost glanced at her. "What do you mean?"

"We're never going to find him," she said, her voice low enough to keep Will from hearing. "Teddy. Not like this. The Patrols have already taken him back to the city. Even if we'd left Haven the moment the attack ended, we still wouldn't have caught up with them on foot." She turned to look at him. "Right?"

His expression remained impassive. "Right."

"So... What are we doing here? Why are *you* here?"

Ghost's scar seemed to deepen as he considered her question. "I'm not looking for the boy."

His admission nearly stopped Kira in her tracks, but she forced herself to keep pace, knowing Will was only a few yards back, likely watching them.

In the distance, a low, ominous rumble echoed through the air, like the growl of a sleeping beast beginning to stir.

There was a storm coming.

"I'm doing what I should've done a decade ago," Ghost continued. "I'm looking for a way to fight back. A way to defy your father and the twisted world he's created. When Devlin threatened to throw you and your mother out of the city if I returned, I thought I was doing the noble thing by leaving quietly. I thought I was protecting her—and you—but I wasn't. I left her there thinking she'd be safe, and he killed her anyway."

Ghost's suspicions about her mother's death clawed at Kira's heart. The Compulsory Notification. The countless messages she had left at her father's office, pleading with him to help her mother get a waiver. Devlin had claimed he hadn't received them until it was too late. He'd sworn on his children's lives, and Kira had believed him. She'd wanted to believe him—needed to believe him—because the alternative was too terrible to comprehend.

But was it true?

Had Devlin personally ordered her mother's death?

A loud shriek drew Kira's attention upward, where a bald eagle circled overhead, its powerful wings beating at the air. The bird suddenly dipped toward the glassy surface of the river, its body barely skimming the water before rising again, a fish clutched in its talons.

Predator and prey.

"Did you ever love anyone else?"

The question spilled out of her, and although it wasn't a fair question to ask and it wasn't any of her business, she had to know the answer. More than anything, she wanted to hear that her mother was the most important person in the world to someone other than her.

Ghost's eyes were glistening, a rare crack in his rough exterior, but he didn't let any tears fall. "No one ever compared to your mother, Kira. After we were together, I never wanted anyone else. So, I shut myself off. Pushed anyone who tried to get close to me away. I couldn't risk losing someone like that again. I wasn't meant for happiness, Kira."

The words hung in the air between them, heavy and suffocating. She wasn't sure she believed in God, but if He was real and she could ask Him anything, she would ask Him why He had chosen to make Victor Devlin her father. Why couldn't this man—the wounded, haunted man walking beside her, the man who had truly loved her mother—have been her father?

He cleared his throat. "After Devlin banished me from the city, and I knew I would never see you or your mother again, I thought of a thousand ways to kill myself. It became one of my favorite pastimes. Eventually, I settled on what I thought was a good day to die—it was the anniversary of the day I should've proposed to your mother on the ferry."

The tears came without warning, slipping down her cheeks, the realization hitting her like a punch in the stomach. It all made sense now. The photograph he carried with him— the one from the ferry. That day had been more than just a memory; it had been the turning point in his life, the moment when everything had changed.

Instead of a husband and father, Noah Hale had become a

ghost—a man living in the shadows, haunted by his past, always on the verge of disappearing forever.

"I counted down the days until I could end it all. When that day came, I was ready. No second thoughts, no fear. I planned to do it at nightfall, as the sun set. But then, around lunchtime, I stumbled across a group of people wandering around the forest. They were dehydrated, starving. They needed help. So, I delayed my plans for one year, until the next anniversary. Why not? I had all the time in the world, right? So, I hunted game for them, and eventually we found a nature preserve, and I built them a few cabins."

It was the most he'd ever spoken to Kira since that night in his cabin. She could see the layers of pain and loneliness he carried with him, the vulnerability he'd tried so hard to hide. When he didn't continue, she said, "And then what happened?"

"Year after year, more people showed up, usually right around or on the anniversary. So, I built them cabins, too. They asked for a church, so we built one together. I told myself I'd stay until the village was settled and the people could defend themselves. I kept everyone at arm's-length distance, so no one would care too much when I eventually disappeared. I had no real relationships. I didn't tell anyone about myself or my past. I'd vanish for days at a time without telling a soul. That's how I got the nickname."

Kira nodded, listening to his story with a newfound understanding. Like her, Ghost struggled under the crushing weight of guilt for the mistakes he'd made. For years, he'd built homes for others but never allowed himself to truly belong.

A penance, of sorts, for abandoning Kira and her mother.

"Finally, I knew it was the right day," he said, shaking his head. "The anniversary had rolled around again. I woke up that morning, and I could feel it in my bones. I told the others I was going on a supply run. I thought about telling Brannigan over the radio—figured it would be rude to just disappear and never talk to him again—but he was dealing with enough problems. I just left, with no plans to return. I was going to follow the tracks back to the city, walk across the bridge with my shotgun hidden inside my jacket, and take out as many of your father's soldiers at the checkpoint as I could before they took me down."

Kira's breath caught in her throat as she listened. She could see it all so vividly in her mind—Ghost walking along the tracks, the cold steel of the shotgun pressing against his chest, the breeze carrying the scent of the river. "But you didn't do it. What stopped you?"

"I never made it to the city," he said, bringing his eyes to meet hers. "Instead, I walked into a dollar store in the middle of nowhere and found the girl I'd once prayed would be my daughter."

Ghost reached out and touched her shoulder, and for a moment, she saw the man he once was. The man without a disfiguring scar. The man who'd taken her on a ferry and bought her an ice cream cone.

The man who could've been her father.

Noah Hale.

Tears welled in her eyes, blurring her vision, as a torrent of emotions surged through her. Regret for the life they could have had. Sorrow for the years lost. A deep longing for the father she never knew she needed. She saw the pain in his eyes, and for the first time, she understood how much they had both lost.

Suddenly, classical music pierced the air, the song seeming to rise from the shadows themselves, its source impossible to pinpoint, and Noah's hand slipped from Kira's shoulder. The warmth that had briefly softened his features vanished, replaced by the cold, hard exterior she had grown accustomed to.

"Where's that music coming from?" she asked.

"There's only one place it could be coming from," Ghost said, reaching for the radio on his belt. "Vita Nova."

Chapter Forty-One

Ghost pulled the battered radio from his belt and adjusted the frequency knob with practiced ease. His scarred face betrayed no emotion as the music grew clearer, each note hanging in the air between the decaying buildings, as out of place in the dead town as the three of them.

Will appeared beside Kira. "What's going on? Where's that music coming from?"

As if on cue, the song finished playing, and a chorus of voices broke through the static.

Revere the Volunteer! Revere the Volunteer!

Kira's hand moved on its own, her index and middle fingers forming a V-shape and reaching for her heart. But she froze when her eyes met Will's. He was staring at her, his expression a mixture of horror and anger.

Her hand dropped to her side.

It's still a part of you. Even after everything that's happened, it still has a hold on you.

The broadcast continued, the cold, authoritative voice of Deputy Mayor Sienna Graves cutting through the static. *"Good evening, citizens of Vita Nova. Stay tuned for a special broadcast from Mayor Devlin tonight at seven o'clock."*

Another song began to play, but Kira was no longer listening. She glanced at her watch. Seven o'clock was only twenty-five minutes away.

Beside her, Ghost's hand tightened around the radio, his knuckles white against his tanned skin. He looked as though he wanted to hurl the radio against the nearest building. Or smash it to pieces on the ground.

"Turn it off," Will said, a storm brewing in his eyes. "Get rid of it. I'm not listening to him."

"No," Kira said, holding out her hand. "Give it to me."

Ghost hesitated, still looking as if he might ignore her and throw the radio into the river at any moment. But then, reluctantly, he handed it over to Kira.

Kira's fingers trembled as she fumbled with the volume knob on top, her movements sharp and agitated. At last, she managed to turn the radio off, silencing the music. She clipped the radio onto her belt, not trusting that either of the men would hesitate to destroy it if given the chance.

She had every intention of listening to the seven o'clock broadcast.

"Okay," she said, her voice more steady than she felt. "We need to find Aunt Reeva and anyone else still hiding in this town. They need to get out of here and link up with the others in Haven." She turned to Will. "Do you know who was still here when we left?"

"Yeah. There weren't many. Only three or four people, aside from Reeva."

"Do you remember where they were living?"

"I think so."

"Good. Go find them and tell them how to get to Haven. Tell them to avoid the railroad tracks and stick mainly to the woods." Before he could argue, she turned to Ghost. "There's a house a few blocks up on Ivy Street. Two stories, blue with white shutters, a broken swing on the front porch. That's Aunt Reeva's place. She usually stays in the basement in the evenings. Tell her that Will and Kira sent you, and don't startle her, or you're liable to get hurt."

The corner of Ghost's mouth ticked upward slightly. "This Aunt Reeva sounds like my kind of woman."

Kira blinked in surprise. "Was that a joke? I don't think I've ever heard you tell a joke before. Are you sure you're okay? Not lightheaded or anything?"

"I see you inherited your mother's sarcasm," he muttered, but there was a spark in his eyes that Kira hadn't seen before. "What about you? What are you going to do?"

"I'll check the church. It's the only other place Reeva might be. Let's meet back here at seven-thirty. That should give us enough time to find everyone. Then we'll regroup and figure out what to do about Teddy. Sound good?"

Ghost nodded. "Seven-thirty." His eyes lingered on Kira, as if he wanted to say something more, but then he seemed to decide against it. He gave her a brief nod and began to jog down the street, his black-clad figure merging with the shadows cast by the empty houses until he disappeared altogether.

When she turned back to him, Will was staring at her. "I don't think we should split up."

"We have to. It'll be dark soon, and this is the only way to cover more ground. Besides, I have this." She patted the pistol on her hip, trying to appear comfortable with the gun. "You taught me how to use it, remember?"

He shook his head. "This isn't right. I don't like this."

"I'll be fine." She forced a smile that she knew didn't quite reach her eyes. "The Patrols are gone. At least for now. They got what they wanted, but they'll be back. In the meantime, let's help as many people as we can. I'll be back here at seven-thirty with Aunt Reeva in tow. She'll be madder than a wet hen about leaving her flowers behind, but I'm going to tell her it was your idea."

He reached out and gently cupped her face, his thumb brushing away a damp strand of hair that had adhered itself to her cheek. Then he kissed her—and there was a new urgency in the way his lips lingered on hers, a desperation born from the fear of losing her. Things were different between them now, after they had both seen what happened to Avery and Nic. They knew how fragile life was and how quickly everything could be taken away.

"I love you, Kira," he whispered against her lips.

"I love you, too."

The kiss turned into an embrace, and Kira closed her eyes and clung to him, wishing she could stay in his arms forever. It was a comfort she didn't want to let go of, a sense of safety she hadn't known until Will entered her life.

"Will? Are we going to get him back?"

His arms tightened around her. "There are ways into the city. We'll find him."

He spoke with such conviction that Kira almost believed him. She took a half-step back and met his eyes, offering him a soft smile as she placed her hand on his chest.

"Thank you," she said, "for stepping into my office that day and turning my whole world upside down. Thank you for opening my eyes to the terrible things I was a part of."

"Your eyes were already open," he replied, covering her hand with his. "You just weren't ready to see it. But you knew. That's why I fell for you, Kira."

Her heart did a little flutter. "That's the reason?"

"Well, that and your looks. And the way you blushed every time you looked at me."

"I did not blush!" she protested.

"You did. I thought your face was going to catch fire."

She playfully punched him in the arm, and he clutched the spot with an exaggerated wince, their laughter echoing through the empty street.

A brief moment of lightness in a world gone dark.

"I guess I had that coming," he said.

"You absolutely did."

Their laughter faded as thunder grumbled in the distance.

There's a storm coming, Kira thought. *We're running out of time.*

She brushed her fingers against Will's one more time before pulling away. "We better get moving," she said. "I'll see you back here at seven-thirty."

Will nodded, his expression one of a man fighting an internal battle he knew he would lose. He tried and failed to mask it with a smile. "Seven-thirty."

In that moment, Kira took a mental photograph of Will, searing that beautiful lopsided-dimpled smile into her brain. The way he looked at her with a love she'd never thought she deserved. That image would be her motivation to complete her mission and return to his arms.

Without another word, she turned away from Will, forcing her tired body into a light jog.

She never looked back.

Chapter Forty-Two

Kira jogged toward the church, her senses heightened, on high alert for every sound and every flutter of movement. The sky above was a swirling mass of dark purple and black, lightning flashing within its depths. The static electricity in the air made her skin tingle.

"Citizens of Vita Nova, stay tuned for a special broadcast from Mayor Devlin tonight at seven o'clock."

Special broadcasts from her father never brought good news. A knot of anxiety tightened in her stomach as she wondered what had happened in Vita Nova since she'd left.

Without breaking her stride, she fumbled with her watch, setting an alarm for seven o'clock.

She couldn't afford to miss the broadcast, no matter how much she dreaded hearing it.

A few minutes later, the weathered metal cross atop the church came into view, standing tall against the backdrop of dilapidated buildings. It looked like a beacon, drawing her in and urging her to hurry.

Almost there.

She quickened her pace, her nerves on edge, driven by the need to get off the streets. She couldn't shake the feeling of being watched. There were too many houses. Too many empty windows from which someone could watch her, tracking her progress through the empty town.

A drop of rain struck her cheek where Will's hand had rested only minutes earlier. She wiped it away, ignoring the sharp pains in her ribs as she navigated around rusted vehicles, her legs tearing through the waist-high weeds.

Aunt Reeva won't be at the church, she reassured herself. *She would've gone home when she realized there was a storm coming. Ghost will find her there.*

As she reached the wrought-iron fence that encircled the church, a sharp crack of thunder split the air, and rain began to fall—heavy, icy drops that pulled her back to the present. Pushing through the gate, she hurried up the steps, eager to get inside before the rain soaked her.

The front doors of the church stood slightly ajar, swaying on their creaky hinges.

Kira hesitated, her hand hovering over the handle.

Something's wrong.

Aunt Reeva would never leave the doors open. The church was her home, the dahlias her children, and she protected them both with her life.

She's probably just inside, Kira reasoned. *Maybe she heard the storm coming, and she's getting ready to leave. She always waters her dahlias before heading home for the night.*

With a deep breath, she pushed the creaking doors open, stepping into the cool darkness of the vestibule. Sometimes, Aunt Reeva would prop open the double doors to the sanctuary to improve air circulation, but tonight, both were shut tight.

Kira leaned against the front door, still breathing heavily

from her jog across town, straining to hear any signs of life over the patter of rain on the roof. But there was nothing.

She quietly closed the doors behind her, sealing herself in the near-total darkness of the vestibule. It was darker than it should have been, the storm outside smothering what little light remained in the day, leaving only a faint sliver filtering through the narrow window above the door.

She reached for the side pocket on her rucksack where she'd stored her flashlight, but it was empty. Only then did she remember using it back in Haven to find her way around the cabin at night. She hadn't thought to retrieve it before she left.

With arms outstretched, Kira moved slowly through the vestibule toward the interior doors, counting each step. Anything to keep her mind occupied and distract herself from the awful thoughts that wanted to come.

Thoughts of what could be waiting behind those doors.

When her fingertips brushed against the wood, she didn't allow herself time to hesitate. She was too close to turning around and abandoning the church altogether. Too close to jogging back to the center of town and telling the others she'd searched it even though she hadn't.

She pushed through the doors.

The sanctuary wasn't much brighter than the hallway, despite the windows that lined the room. But there was enough light to see that it was empty.

She walked down the center aisle toward the metal lectern, navigating around the planters, her eyes scanning each pew as she passed. Shadows danced in the sanctuary, casting eerie shapes on the walls, making the room feel anything but empty.

The planters at the front of the church housed Aunt Reeva's prized possessions—vibrant purple blooms swirled with shades of yellow and azure. Without thinking, Kira stuck two fingers into the soil of the nearest planter, a habit formed from the many times she'd shadowed Aunt Reeva in the sanctuary. Her fingers brushed the surface, then pressed deeper, expecting the familiar coolness of damp earth.

But the dirt crumbled beneath her touch, dry as sand.

Frowning, she moved through the church, checking each of the planters. They all felt unnaturally dry, as if the soil had been forgotten for far too long.

Maybe the Patrols had passed through Emmitsburg, forcing Aunt Reeva to hunker down in her basement for a few days. Hopefully Ghost would find her there, madder than a hornet in a jar, but safe.

Rising to her feet, Kira scanned the room one final time.

There was still one place she hadn't checked.

Chapter Forty-Three

Kira headed back to the vestibule, weaving her way between the wilted dahlias in the aisle. A deep sense of unease settling inside her chest.

Was Render still down in the basement, unconscious, and tied to the hospital bed? What if the Patrols had come through town, forcing Aunt Reeva to flee and leave him behind?

If that happened, she reasoned, *the soldiers would have found him and taken him back to the city for medical care. He wouldn't still be here.*

But the sheer number of abandoned homes and buildings in Emmitsburg made her doubt whether they would have even found the basement, much less checked it.

What if they missed it?

What if Render was still down there, barely clinging to life?

Or worse—what if he was already dead, his body decomposing like the neglected dahlias?

"Stop it," she whispered to herself, her voice shaky. "Stop freaking out and just check the basement so you can get out of here."

The sound of her own voice brought a fleeting sense of calm, enough to spur her into action. She carefully lifted one of the wilting dahlias from its wooden stand and placed it on the floor. Then she picked up the stand and used it to prop open one of the doors leading into the vestibule.

She couldn't imagine going down into the basement with no light to guide her way. Hopefully, the dim light coming from the sanctuary would be enough.

Hesitating at the top of the stairs, Kira called out softly into the darkness, "Aunt Reeva?"

But the only response was another muffled rumble of thunder from outside. The rain pelted the roof, the sound reminding her of the last night she'd spent in the attic before leaving Emmitsburg. She hoped Will and Ghost had found shelter before the storm hit.

More than that, she prayed they'd found Aunt Reeva.

The temperature dropped as Kira descended the narrow stairwell, the cold air seeping through her damp jacket, chilling her. She ran her fingers over the rough stone walls as she made her way deeper into the darkness, where the meager light from the sanctuary could no longer reach. The sound of the storm faded, replaced by an unsettling silence.

At the bottom of the stairs, she turned into a narrow hallway. Just ahead, the door to the infirmary stood slightly ajar, the metal padlock hanging uselessly from its latch on the wall. A dim, flickering light spilled out from within, drawing her forward.

"Aunt Reeva?" she called out again, louder this time, her voice echoing off the stone walls.

No answer.

With one hand gripping the pistol on her hip, Kira moved around the open door and stepped into the infirmary. Her gaze swept over the rusted medical equipment cluttering the room before settling on the source of light: a battery-powered lantern positioned on a nightstand beside one of the old metal beds. The light cast bizarre, shifting patterns on the walls, making the shadows appear to dance in a macabre waltz.

"Aunt—?"

Kira's breath caught in her chest.

In the far corner of the infirmary, on the same hospital bed where Render had been restrained the last time she'd been here, a figure lay motionless, hidden beneath a white blanket.

The ropes that had once secured Render to the bed now hung loosely from the metal frame.

He's dead, she realized with sickening certainty. *Render is dead. Why else would he be untied?*

Kira's grip on the pistol tightened as she approached the bed, a whispered prayer escaping her lips. Even the quiet rustle of her clothes sounded deafening in the silence of the infirmary, but the form beneath the blanket did not move.

She could see no signs of movement, no rise and fall of breath where Render's chest should be.

But she had to be sure.

Her hand trembled as she reached for the edge of the blanket, her fingers curling around the rough fabric. Drawing in a deep, shaky breath, she slowly pulled it back, bracing herself for the awful state she feared his body might be in.

The dim light from the lantern revealed a shock of silver hair and familiar, weathered features.

Kira stared down at the face that had been hidden beneath the blanket, her mind refusing to accept what her eyes were seeing.

Aunt Reeva's eyes were closed, her expression serene, as if she'd simply crawled into the hospital bed to take a quick nap. But when Kira reached beneath the blanket and touched the old woman's arm, the skin was cold and lifeless beneath her fingers.

"Reeva?" she whispered, her voice cracking with grief.

But the old woman did not stir. Her eyelids did not flutter. Her expression did not change.

She wasn't sleeping.

The truth slammed into Kira like a physical blow, knocking the air from her lungs. The walls of the infirmary seemed to close in around her as she sank to her knees beside the bed, her hand still resting on Aunt Reeva's stiff arm. Tears streamed down her face, a small mercy that allowed her to no longer see the empty shell that had once been Aunt Reeva.

She squeezed her eyes shut, desperate to replace the image of Aunt Reeva's lifeless face with memories of a woman who had been so full of life.

Aunt Reeva in her bib overalls, a bucket of water in her hand, the grip of a handgun sticking out of her front pocket. A combination of frailty and grittiness that Kira had never seen before or since.

Aunt Reeva caring for Pastor Alwyn during his final moments—the love in her eyes, her tender movements.

Let him reach, honey.

Aunt Reeva hunched over a planter, teaching Kira about flowers, about life, about faith.

But the memories couldn't drown out the reality of what had happened. She opened her eyes, hoping against hope that the face beneath the blanket had somehow changed and that it wasn't Aunt Reeva lying there, cold and still.

But it was.

A boulder of grief crashed over her, threatening to crush her.

This isn't right.

This isn't how it's supposed to be.

Will would be devastated. So would Brack and Grace. Aunt Reeva was like a grandmother to them. A beacon of strength and wisdom in the chaos of their world. And now, like so much else, she was gone, ripped away from them far too soon.

How would Kira tell them?

With a trembling hand, Kira brushed a lock of silver hair away from Aunt Reeva's face. Then she pulled the blanket down farther, revealing the old woman's wrinkled hands, folded neatly on her chest as if in prayer.

A sharp cry tore from Kira's throat.

Between the faded chambray straps of Aunt Reeva's overalls, Kira saw them—a series of faint but unmistakable purplish bruises encircling the old woman's neck like a grotesque necklace. She traced the pattern of bruises with one finger, her mind racing to piece together what it all meant.

A tremor of revulsion ripped through her as the picture of what had happened to Aunt Reeva came together in her mind.

Render. He had done this.

She saw it clearly in her mind: Render on top of Aunt Reeva, his fingers tightening around her neck. Digging into her flesh. Strangling her.

Just as he'd tried to do to Kira.

Memories of that night in the kitchen flooded her mind. She could still feel the weight of Render's body pinning her against the kitchen floor, his hands tightening around her throat as he tried to squeeze the life out of her, his cold, merciless eyes staring into hers the entire time.

Was that the last thing Aunt Reeva had seen before she died—those same awful eyes?

Kira let out a sound that was somewhere between a wail and a sob, and she pulled the blanket over Aunt Reeva's face.

Even though Kira couldn't see the old woman's neck, the image of those bruises remained etched in her mind.

"I'm so sorry," she said, barely able to choke out the words. "I'm so sorry this happened to you."

Then a voice spoke up behind her.

"She's dead because of you."

Chapter Forty-Four

Kira's heart faltered as the low, gravelly voice slithered into the room like a serpent, wrapping itself around her chest and squeezing until she could no longer breathe.

It was a voice she knew all too well.

Slowly, she rose from the floor and turned to face the figure in the doorway of the infirmary.

Render leaned casually against the doorframe, his eyes colder and more calculating than she remembered. He appeared to be enjoying it, feeding off her pain like a vampire. His Patrol uniform shirt hung open, revealing a stained white t-shirt beneath, marked with sweat and dried blood. The gash on his left temple had healed nicely, a testament to Aunt Reeva's expert care.

"You're alive."

It was all she could think to say.

He pulled his right hand from behind his back, revealing Aunt Reeva's pistol, its barrel pointed at Kira's face.

This is how it ends, she thought numbly. *I'm going to die in this room, just like Reeva.*

"Take that Glock out of your pants and toss it away," Render ordered. "Same with the radio. Do it slow and easy. I'm not a marksman like your ex-boyfriend, Dayton, but at this range, I don't need to be."

Kira's mind raced, frantically trying to process what was happening. If she threw her Glock away, she would have no way of defending herself. But if she didn't obey, he would kill her without hesitation. She brought one hand to her hip, careful not to spook Render with any sudden movements. Slowly, she unsnapped the holster and removed Glock, her eyes never leaving Render's as she tossed it away. It slid across the floor and disappeared beneath a hospital bed. Then she unhooked the radio and dropped it at her feet.

"Good girl." Render's lips curled into a sardonic smile as he tucked Aunt Reeva's pistol into his waistband. "Surprised to see me, Kira? You shouldn't be. Didn't you know that Patrol soldiers can't be killed? We always finish our mission. We're immortal."

She almost believed him. There was something terrifyingly convincing about the way he spoke—the air of invincibility that surrounded him. It made her wonder, just for a moment, if there wasn't some truth to his words. After all, so many had died in the attack on Haven, yet every single Patrol soldier had escaped.

"What mission?" she whispered. "What do you want?"

Render chuckled, a low, mocking sound that made her skin crawl. "Always so direct. I want what I've always wanted—money. "There's still a bounty on your head, remember? I'm just here to collect what's mine." He pushed off the doorframe and inched closer, his movements slow and predatory. "You look different. Stronger. What happened to you out there?"

Memories from the past week flashed through her mind: the fear and uncertainty of leaving Emmitsburg, Teddy's laughter as he rode high on Brack's shoulders, her terror during the dollar store encounter, and the overwhelming relief of Ghost's rescue. She thought of the secrets she'd uncovered—Ghost's secrets concerning her mother—and the deeper love she'd found with Will. And, of course, the agony of the losses at Haven, still so fresh and raw.

So much had happened to her, more than she could ever explain. But she wouldn't share any of it with Render.

He didn't deserve to know how much she had lost or how much she had gained.

"What if I go first?" Render offered, his tone almost conversational. "I woke up two days ago, starving, with a mother of a headache. Felt like someone had taken a jackhammer to my skull. But I didn't let on that I was awake. Not right away. I needed to fully assess the situation first, so I pretended to be unconscious. It took a lot of self-control not to move when the old hag came around to change my bandages. The hardest part was when she undid my restraints to change the sheets. She was so close to me, but I had to know if there were others around or if she was the only one."

Kira's stomach turned as she imagined Aunt Reeva tending to Render, unaware that he was watching her and planning his next move.

"Last night, when she undid my restraints for the final time, she prayed for you." Render studied Kira's face, as if trying to gauge her reaction to his words. "That's the last thing she ever did. She said a prayer that you, Will, Brack, Grace, and Teddy were having a safe journey and that God would send you back to her. And in a way, her prayer was answered. You came back. But you were a few hours too late to help her."

The causal cruelty in his voice shatters something inside

Kira. Aunt Reeva had been praying for her. Praying until the moment Render tightened his hands around her neck and ended her life.

"Will. Brack. Grace." Render repeated, ticking off their names on his fingers. "I'll make sure to pass those names along to my leadership when I return to Vita Nova. It's always good to know who we're looking for. And what about the Easton brat? Where are you hiding him?"

Kira forced herself to stay calm, realizing that if Render didn't know that Teddy had been captured, he wasn't in contact with the soldiers who'd invaded Haven.

He was operating on his own.

That was good. It meant Will and Ghost might be safe.

Please God, she prayed. *Please keep them away from here.*

"Kira?" Render's voice broke into her thoughts. "I asked you a question. Where are you hiding the kid?"

So much had changed in the past week, but Render remained focused on one goal: finding Teddy and returning him to the city to be sacrificed. He would stop at nothing.

We always finish our mission. We're immortal.

"She was helping you," Kira said, trying to buy herself time to figure out what to do. "The woman you killed—her name was Reeva. She was a really good person. The only reason you're not dead right now is because she insisted on taking care of you."

"That wasn't very smart of her, was it?" Render smiled at Kira, his eyes gleaming, clearly relishing the pain he was inflicting. "Do you want to know how much she suffered?"

Kira swallowed the bile rising in her throat at the thought of Aunt Reeva's final moments. "Why didn't you leave?" she asked, forcing the words from between her teeth. "After you killed her, why didn't you go back to the city?"

Render's grin widened as he took another step closer to her.

"Because I thought there was a chance the old hag's prayer might work. If she thought you were coming back, maybe you were. I figured it was worth hanging around for a little while, just in case. And now here you are, and there's nothing stopping us from having a good time."

Those words. Render had said something similar a few weeks earlier, standing outside The Riverfront after their double date. The memory was jarring—the contrast between the handsome, cocky soldier from that night and the monster standing before her was almost too much to comprehend.

"So, what happens now?" she asked, slipping her hands into the pockets of her jacket. "Are you just going to strangle me, too? How many of us are there? How many women have you strangled to death out here?"

Render's smile faded, his upper lip twitching almost imperceptibly. Apparently, she'd hit a nerve.

"Yes, I'm going to strangle you, Kira. Then I'm going back to the city and coming back with an entire platoon of exterminators. That's what we are, you know. We're not soldiers—we're exterminators. We're going to march through this town, burn it to the ground, and kill anyone we find—except for the Easton brat. He's coming back with me. I'll return to Vita Nova as a hero. They might even throw us a parade."

Her fingertips brushed against something solid, hidden deep within the folds of her pocket—Will's knife. It had been there since that first day in Haven, when he'd passed it to her outside the cabin.

"You know what?" Render added. "I think I'll carry the Easton brat on my shoulders in the parade. We'll make it one of his Final Week activities. Brats love parades, and the city will love me."

Kira's anger smoldered, burning away the fear that had gripped her moments before. She imagined Teddy—that sweet, innocent little boy—forced to witness the parade that would march him to his death, and the fury inside her became almost unbearable.

As her fingers curled around the knife, she made a silent vow: she would not be a victim again, as she had been that night in the kitchen.

She would not die by Render's hands.

Tonight, she would be the one in control.

Chapter Forty-Five

The anger smoldering within Kira ignited, blazing hotter with each passing second until it coursed through her veins like fire, consuming her from the inside.

The words tumbled from her lips like boulders, heavy and destructive. "Do you know who attacked you the other night in the kitchen? Did you even see who it was?"

A flicker of uncertainty crossed his face. "I don't care who it was. Whoever it was, they were a coward for sneaking up on me."

"You don't care?" Kira laughed, her gaze briefly dropping to the gun tucked into the waistband of his pants. Did he even remember it was there? "Oh, I think you care. It was the woman you murdered last night. A tiny little thing, five-foot-nothing, and barely a hundred pounds soaking wet. But she still managed to get the best of you, didn't she? A little old lady with a bad back brought down the big, tough Patrol soldier."

Render's eyes darkened as he tried—and failed—to smile.

"But she didn't take me down, did she? I took *her* down. Want to hear how she begged for her life?"

Kira took a step closer, driven not by courage but by pure rage. She couldn't stop herself from taking one last jab at him. "You said you were immortal, right? Do immortals drool? Because when I left town, you were drooling like a baby. A pathetic, weak little—"

Before she could finish, Render lunged forward, arms extended, closing the distance between them before she could finish the sentence.

In one swift motion, she pulled the knife from her pocket, the blade snapping open with a sharp click. She swung the blade at his chest, slicing through his t-shirt and cutting a shallow line across his skin. He hissed in pain, his eyes narrowing in a mix of fury and surprise.

But the victory was short-lived.

With a snarl, Render swung his arm and knocked the knife from her hand. The blade clattered to the floor, skidding out of reach. Then he grabbed her by the shoulders, his grip like iron, and shoved her backward.

Kira stumbled, her back slamming against the wall, the impact knocking the wind out of her. Render's face twisted with rage as he leaned into her, his large hands closing around her neck, cutting off her air supply.

He was strangling her, just as he had in the kitchen. Just as he had done to Aunt Reeva. She clawed at his hands, struggling to pry them away, but he was too strong. Too determined.

The pressure on her neck was crushing, her vision blurring at the edges as darkness crept in. As the world around her dimmed, her mind drifted, and she was lifted out of the infirmary, out of the church, and into the stormy sky above the Unregulated Zone. She passed through the clouds, watching as the flashes of lightning sliced into the churning river below. She soared higher and higher until the bright lights of Vita Nova rose up to meet her.

I'm going home, she thought.

The vision shifted, and she was hovering over City Island, where thousands of people had gathered inside the Stadium. The entire field was covered with blue roses. The people in the seats stood, their fingers forming into v-shapes over their hearts as they chanted, "Revere the Volunteer!"

She exploded into color, filling the night sky with light.

A deafening sound echoed through the infirmary, snapping her back to the present.

Render's grip on her neck loosened.

She sucked in lungfuls of air and stumbled backward, breaking free from his grasp. Her heart pounded in her ears, drowning out all other sounds.

Why didn't he kill me?

She looked down at Render's chest, where a crimson rose bloomed on his white shirt.

Her eyes dropped lower, and she saw Aunt Reeva's pistol in her shaking hands, the metal still warm from Render's body heat.

Render's eyes locked onto hers, a mixture of shock and hatred swirling within their depths. He sputtered, his lips moving soundlessly as if trying to force out words that would never come. The color drained from his face, and he staggered backward, his hands clutching at the bullet wound on his chest. Blood seeped through his fingers as he put pressure on it, trying to mend something that even Aunt Reeva's skilled hands couldn't have healed.

And then he went down, his body hitting the floor with a sickening thud.

The gun slipped from Kira's grasp, clattering to the floor, but its weight still lingered in her hands.

Will spoke up in her mind: *When you take a life, even for survival, it changes something inside you. It's never easy to see something die, especially if you're the one responsible. No matter how many times you do it, no matter how much you tell yourself it was necessary, there's always a part of you that wishes it could've gone another way.*

Render was a murderer. A murderer who had taken Aunt Reeva's life and tried to take hers. But he wasn't a monster. He was a man twisted and broken by the same corrupt system her father had built.

A system that devoured souls.

Somewhere in Vita Nova, Render had a family. People who loved him. People who would mourn him.

Finally, his chest rose and fell for the last time, and then he was still.

Death is a horrible thing.

Chapter Forty-Six

A faint beeping pulled Kira out of her daze, jarring her back to the present.

Her watch.

The seven o'clock broadcast.

She fumbled to silence the alarm, then scanned the floor, her eyes landing on the handheld radio a few feet away, where she'd dropped it. She scrambled to retrieve it, her fingers closing around the cool metal. For a long moment, she only stared at the black dials on the top of the radio, her mind struggling to make sense of them. Which one was she supposed to turn? What if she chose the wrong one and lost the frequency for Vita Nova?

She grabbed the larger of the two dials and turned it. The radio crackled to life, the final notes of a song fading into silence.

Then a voice pierced through the static.

"Good evening, citizens of Vita Nova!"

Devlin usually spoke with a distant, commanding tone during broadcasts, but tonight he sounded almost cheerful.

It was unnerving.

As his words washed over her, a horrifying thought crept into her mind—what if, somehow, her father knew what she had just done? What if he was pleased that she'd finally become a killer, just like him?

"I greet you this evening with wonderful news," Devlin said. *"Thanks to the unwavering commitment and bravery of our Patrol soldiers, I'm pleased to announce that Theodore Easton, our youngest and most highly esteemed Volunteer, has been found and safely returned to the city!"*

Kira's fingers tightened around the radio, her breaths shallow as she tried to process Devlin's words. She had suspected Teddy had been taken during the attack on Haven, but hearing it confirmed by her father was a different kind of agony. Her mind flashed back to that day in Rolling Meadows when she'd found him in the game room, clinging to a stuffed panda bear. She'd tried so hard to rescue him from death. To give him a chance at life.

All of it was for nothing, she thought.

Devlin continued to speak, twisting the knife deeper with each word. *"The traitors who kidnapped him from his mother at Rolling Meadows took him into the Unregulated Zone and turned him over to the Lawless. I can only imagine what nefarious plans they had for the poor child. When our soldiers found him, he was dehydrated and near death. He clung to his rescuers as if his life depended on it and begged to be returned to Vita Nova. His home. Our home."*

"Liar," she whispered, her voice trembling with a mixture of fury and despair. "All you tell them are lies. They don't know the truth. They never will."

"I had the pleasure of speaking to Theodore Easton earlier this evening as he enjoyed a bounty of the city's best food in the Governor's Mansion with his lovely mother by his side. And do

you know what he asked me?" Devlin paused, as if the citizens gathered around their broadcast screens could answer him. *"He asked me how soon he could finish his Sacrifice. He said he still wants to be a superhero for the city."*

Kira's knees buckled, and she collapsed onto the worn linoleum floor. Even with miles of Unregulated Zone and the Susquehanna River separating her from Vita Nova, she could almost hear the gasps, breathless cries, and applause filling the city streets, drowning out any sense of reason or compassion.

"As a city, we are grateful to the Patrols for the safe return of our young Volunteer," Devlin said. *"In honor of Theodore's exceptional bravery, the likes of which we have never seen before, we are bestowing upon him the greatest honor that has ever been granted to a citizen of Vita Nova."*

Teddy.

"At tomorrow night's Reverence Ceremony, Theodore Easton will be the only Volunteer present."

They're going to kill him.

"Tomorrow, and in the days to follow, the city will honor him. After he has made his sacrifice, we shall revere him. His name will always be remembered. We will never forget him."

They're going to kill Teddy.

"Revere the Volunteer!"

Her father's voice faded from the radio, replaced by the opening strains of a classical piece that Kira recognized immediately: Beethoven's 3rd Symphony.

It was one of Victor Devlin's favorite compositions, a piece he often played during important city events, where he would stand before the citizens of Vita Nova, speaking of heroism and sacrifice, extolling them as the highest virtues. The music had always been a symbol of triumph, of the city's strength and unity, or so she had been told her entire life.

But it was all a lie.

The city that paraded itself as a beacon of hope and strength was nothing more than a tyrant, crushing the weak to maintain its power.

Kira remained on the floor, her hands resting on her knees, the room spinning around her. Vita Nova was going to murder Teddy *for the good of all.* In her attempt to save him, she had only prolonged his suffering and sealed his fate. Maybe if she had reasoned with her father instead of kidnapping Teddy, things could have been different. Maybe he would have found a way to spare Teddy's life while still saving face with the city.

Because of her actions, Aunt Reeva was dead, Avery was dead, and so many others had died in Haven.

In less than a week, Teddy would be dead, too.

Sacrifice was the only thing that mattered in Vita Nova.

As the music swelled, something inside of Kira hardened. Her father had chosen this piece for a reason. To him, it was a declaration of victory, a signal that everything was proceeding according to his grand design. But what he didn't understand was that Beethoven had composed this music for a hero— someone who fought against tyranny, not someone who enforced it.

She lifted her eyes to the other end of the room, where Aunt Reeva lay still on the hospital bed, her once-sharp mind now silenced forever.

The memory of their last conversation echoed in Kira's mind.

God is sending you into the wilderness for something far greater than me. I believe His plan is for you to face the tumult head-on.

Could God really have a plan for someone like her?

Aunt Reeva was the wisest person Kira had ever known, and she had thought so.

Still kneeling on the floor, Kira bowed her head, and in a

whispered voice choked with tears, she asked God for guidance, unsure if He was even listening. She asked Him to speak to her in whatever way He chose.

Even though she didn't deserve it.

Even though she'd made countless mistakes.

Even though she wasn't sure what she believed.

Still, she asked Him what to do.

And then, finally, a quiet voice whispered in the back of her mind, drowning out the music.

And she knew.

The symphony was her father's anthem, but Kira would make it the soundtrack to her rebellion.

Chapter 47

Epilogue

The Market Street Bridge stretched out before Kira, a monument of stone and concrete, its spans supported by thick piers that reached all the way to the riverbed below. It was a marvel of engineering, with its stone railings carved in intricate designs that seemed to tell a story. Each arch combined to create a corridor that bridged not just two shores but two worlds.

It was incredible, really. While the Unregulated Zone had fallen into ruin, the bridge remained pristine, withstanding the test of time when little else had.

During Kira's eight-mile jog from the church to the bridge, the storm had passed, and night had fallen on the city. The Governmental Sector buildings stood tall against the dark sky, their windows glowing with an ominous yellow light. The streets below were deserted in the wake of the evening's impromptu broadcast, lit by the occasional flickering of malfunctioning streetlights.

She gripped the railing, feeling the rough texture of the

weathered stone beneath her fingertips. The scent of rain and earth mingled with the fishy odor of the river.

At the center of the bridge, three Guards manned the checkpoint. Two men and a woman, their semi-automatic weapons slung over their shoulders, their dark gray uniforms blending seamlessly into the shadowed backdrop of Vita Nova's towering highrises.

They hadn't noticed her yet.

She released the railing and stepped forward.

Towering floodlights flanked the checkpoint, aimed at the Unregulated Zone, bathing the bridge in an unforgiving white light. She squinted against the glare, trying to keep her eyes on the Guards. She carried no weapon, no radio—nothing that could make her appear to be a threat. Nothing that could connect her to Ghost or the inhabitants of Haven.

She'd left everything behind in the infirmary, beside Render's body, along with a note for Ghost tucked into his shirt pocket. If anyone searched the dead Patrol soldier's body, it would be Ghost.

She hadn't been able to bring herself to write anything to Will. It hurt too much.

As she drew closer, the Guards finally noticed her, their expressions shifting from boredom to alertness. They straightened and unslung their weapons, the barrels aimed at Kira's chest.

"Halt!" one of them shouted.

She kept walking, her gaze fixed on the city behind them.

Vita Nova.

Home.

The Guards rushed toward her, their boots pounding against the concrete, shouting for her to get on the ground.

When they were just a dozen feet away, she dropped to her

knees, raising her hands in surrender. The two male Guards reached her first, grabbing her roughly by the shoulders and forcing her down onto the roadway. The cold, wet stones dug into her cheek as she lay on her stomach, her arms twisted painfully behind her back.

Will's voice echoed through her mind.

"I love you, Kira. Did I tell you that yet?"

"What are you doing here?" one of the Guards demanded, his knee digging into her back.

"My name is Kira Liebert."

The tallest of the three Guards, a man with a severe, angular face, stepped into Kira's line of sight. He was a sergeant, according to the rank on his uniform. "We know who you are, young lady," he said, his voice devoid of any hint of kindness. "You're famous." He turned to the female Guard. "Search her."

The weight on her back lessened slightly, and rough hands patted her down, searching every inch of her for hidden weapons or contraband. Finding nothing, the Guards hauled her to her feet, each keeping a firm grip on one of her arms.

The sergeant stepped closer, scrutinizing her with narrowed eyes. "You're the one who kidnapped the boy?" he asked, sounding almost surprised that someone like her could be capable of such a thing. "You trying to re-kidnap him or something?"

"Victor Devlin," she said. "I need to speak with Mayor Devlin."

"The mayor doesn't speak with defectors."

"Please," she begged. "Please, just tell him I'm here. He'll want to talk to me." She hesitated, the words lodging themselves in her throat until she forced them out. "He's...my father. I need to speak with my father."

"Your father?" the sergeant repeated, his voice tinged with disbelief. "You expect me to believe that Mayor Devlin is your father?"

"I don't care if you believe me. Just let him know I'm here. Trust me, he'll want to see me."

The sergeant stared at her for a long moment before pulling out his radio and walking a few paces away. Kira stared at his back, straining to hear, but the rushing river drowned out his words.

"Why did you come back?" the female Guard asked. "You must have known the whole city would be looking for you. Why on earth would you come back here?"

Kira took a deep breath, choosing her words carefully. "I had to come back," she said. "There are things Devlin needs to know. Things about the Unregulated Zone that could change everything for Vita Nova. For all of you."

"What things?"

Before Kira could answer, the sergeant returned, his expression grim. "Mayor Devlin says his daughter is home safe in her bed. He wants this defector brought to the Confines."

Kira's heart sank as she realized what that meant.

Devlin would rather have her thrown into the Confines than admit he was her father.

Before she could protest, the Guards began dragging her toward the checkpoint, the harsh glare of the floodlights making it hard to see anything. She glanced back at the Unregulated Zone one final time, its dark silhouette standing in stark contrast to the blinding lights of the checkpoint. She closed her eyes and said a silent prayer for God's protection over her friends, still out in the wilderness.

For the people of Haven.

For Grace, Brack, and their unborn child.

For Ghost, that he would abide by her wishes and protect Will, keeping him far away from the city, no matter what.

And she prayed that, someday, even if she never lived to see it, the walls that separated their two worlds would crumble.

Letter to Readers

I hope you enjoyed *Rebellion*! The last book, *Ransom*, is available now on Amazon or wherever you get your books. Click HERE to sign up for my newsletter and be the first to be notified when future books are released!

Or use this newsletter link: https://raenaroodbooks.ck.page/736c40c31a

Also, if you've enjoyed this book, please consider leaving a review on Amazon, Goodreads, BookBub, your book blog, or wherever you wish. Reviews are so important for indie authors as we try to compete in an increasingly crowded market space. I truly appreciate each and every review!

Acknowledgments

To my dear readers, friends, and family: Thank you for waiting so patiently for this book. This one was a true labor of love. On more than one occasion, I almost gave up on this story, which would've been such a disservice to Kira because I know she has important things to learn (and teach me). Whenever I thought about throwing in the towel, God would inevitably send one of you to encourage me through a supportive message, a positive review, or a simple, "Hey! When's the next book coming out? People keep asking me about it." Thank you all for holding my arms up when I was too weak to do it myself.

To Kimberly Murphree: Your friendship, editorial skills, and constant encouragement have been essential to my growth as a writer. I pray that one day God will allow me to bless you the way you've blessed me.

To my husband: Thank you for giving me the time and space to pursue this crazy little dream of mine. I wouldn't be able to write so honestly about love if I hadn't experienced it firsthand. I love you so much.

To my children: You three have inspired my writing in so many ways (mostly good!). I'm so proud of the young men you're becoming, and I'm forever grateful that God chose me to be your mother. Whatever you choose to do with your lives, always do it for the glory of God.

And above all else, thank you to my Lord and Savior, Jesus Christ. Thank You for giving up Your perfect and blameless life in the greatest Sacrifice that has ever been made *for the good of all.*

— Raena Rood

September 2024

About the Author

Raena lives with her husband and three children in rural Pennsylvania, where her hobbies include raising chickens, singing off-key while cleaning, and introducing her kids to cheesy 80's movies. When she's not writing, she spends way too much time thinking about buying more chickens. And possibly a goat.

Books by Raena Rood

The Subversive Trilogy

Subversive: Book 1 of The Subversive Trilogy

Sanctuary: Book 2 of The Subversive Trilogy

Salvation: Book 3 of The Subversive Trilogy

The Reverence Trilogy

Reverence: Book 1 of the Reverence Trilogy

Rebellion: Book 2 of the Reverence Trilogy

Ransom: Book 3 of the Reverence Trilogy